THE LORD'S CAPTIVE

BORDER SERIES BOOK TWO

CECELIA MECCA

To Billy and Jena. I love you both.

1

Northumbria, England, 1271

Sir Bryce Waryn wanted to rejoice, but the sight of his childhood home in partial ruins overshadowed his victory. The stench of battle hung in the air.

"What ails you, brother?"

Geoffrey, two years his senior, often treated him like a child.

Not today.

"This." He gestured to the carnage in front of them. "I fear it will never end."

They watched as a body was removed from the hall of Pele Tower, the center of activity at Bristol Manor.

"I wish I could disagree. Are you sure you want to inherit this mess?"

Bryce ignored Geoffrey's question. "Come with me." He had no destination in mind—only the urgent need to escape the smell. His brother nodded, and together they walked through the aftermath of a raid five years in the making.

The battle had started as the sun rose and ended before midmorn. Thanks to his brother's men, they'd overwhelmed the usurpers quickly, and they'd spent the better part of the day assessing the damages. Their losses could have been much worse.

Yes, he wanted to inherit Bristol Manor. Its proximity to the Scottish border guaranteed turmoil for years to come. But it was their home, and home meant something.

Although it should have been his brother's inheritance. As a feudal barony, the title was tied to the land. Now that Bristol was theirs once again, the title was his brother's by rights. But Geoffrey had already bequeathed the manor to him.

"I do," he said to Geoffrey. "Though it's an honor I don't deserve."

Geoffrey rolled his eyes. "We've been through this, Bryce. My home is with Sara, in Kenshire. Besides, I'm not doing you any favors here," he added, gesturing to the brutality all around them.

New grass attempted to peek through the dirty brown snow of the courtyard. It was a small bit of pleasantness, that bright green. Still, he could not deny the manor was very different from his memories.

"You do know we won the battle?" Sir Hugh Waryn, their uncle, walked toward them with purpose. His black hair was sprinkled with grey, but though he was past his prime, Hugh still towered over most of the other men scurrying around the courtyard to dispose of the dead.

Bryce let his more talkative brother answer.

"We wonder how soon the counterattack will come. You know as well as I do, peace is unlikely at Bristol."

Bryce handed his broadsword to his brother's squire, a young boy who had begged to take part in the battle. The squire doted on his brother, much as Bryce himself had done when they were children. Neither of the brothers had wished to see the boy hurt, but they'd reluctantly agreed to his request, and Reginald had held his own in the battle. They were both proud of the lad.

He turned his attention to Hugh. "Much needs to be done here. Uncle, I've no right to ask you this. You're newly wed. But—"

"My wife understands I'm needed at Bristol until it is fortified once again."

"I'll send word to Faye that you'll be staying with us," Geoffrey said.

"No," Bryce said. "Not us."

Both men turned and looked at him. Bryce's eyes narrowed.

"I promised your wife you'd return, unharmed, and by God, you'll do just that," he told his brother. "I've no wish to incur the wrath of Lady Sara. If not for your knights of Kenshire and the men Lord William sent, we would never have seen this day." For years they had lacked the manpower to take back Bristol. Now they had enough men to secure both the manor and the surrounding area.

"You'll need help to secure and restore Bristol," Geoffrey insisted.

"Aye, and I have help. Hugh will stay, and I plan to ask Thomas to take a permanent position here. You're needed at Kenshire." Bryce looked back and forth between two sets of eyes that matched his own, startling blue and unflinching. His brother had the uncanny and singular ability to make him break eye contact.

Yet he would not back down, both for the reasons he had given Geoffrey and for others he didn't wish to share.

"If you wish." Geoffrey gripped his arm. "I'm proud of you."

His chest constricted, but the feeling did not have time to take root. Geoffrey had already turned away to say something to their uncle.

Five years they'd sought their revenge. The Scots who'd invaded their home and killed their parents were finally defeated. Driven out. But now that the day of reckoning had arrived, Bryce felt unexpectedly devoid of emotion. He stared at the building in front of them, an old tower at the center of the manor. From the outside, it looked the same.

He'd balled his fists in anger when they went inside earlier.

The manor's decorative features were now distinctly Scottish. He would rectify that immediately.

"Excuse me, Uncle. Brother."

Walking through the courtyard, Bryce surveyed his land as he looked for his steward. Or the man he hoped would be his steward.

Built on river basin two days' ride from the border, Bristol Manor had started as nothing more than a single defense tower and an attached hall. Though it was still no grand castle like the one Geoffrey now occupied, it was a handsome stone structure that had been improved enough throughout the years to make it worth capturing. Surrounded by a curtain wall, an addition courtesy of Bryce's father, it was large enough to house the men who'd fought for them that day, but not many more. Bryce's father had also added the buildings he now passed, including the solar block, storerooms, and stable.

Finding his right-hand man in the courtyard was easy, for Thomas's long brown hair and beard made him appear as wild as the bears they had hunted as boys. Bryce, on the other hand, shaved nearly every day. It was a habit from his days as a squire, one of the many quirks he acquired at Huntington.

"Thomas."

Although they had height in common, their resemblance stopped there.

Thomas clapped him on the shoulder in greeting. "So grim for such a great victory. We lost just one man and Bristol is yours again."

"We'll celebrate once we've secured the area and stripped it of the Kerr stench. The hall reeks of Scots."

"We can be sure it's not you." Thomas leaned in as if to smell him. "I've yet to meet a maid that bathes as much."

Thomas didn't have a serious thought in his head. Bryce gave him a look that said as much.

"Very well." Thomas abruptly stopped smiling, drew his bushy eyebrows together, and gave him such a deliberately serious look it almost made him laugh.

Almost.

"Any news?" Before the raid ended that morning, he'd charged Thomas with scouting the area beyond Bristol in every direction.

"Aye," Thomas said, finally offering some useful information. "Most of the men have returned save those who were sent north. The village is secure, and there are no signs of Clan Kerr to the east or west."

Bryce frowned, and he watched as Thomas's easygoing grin transformed into a scowl that matched his own. He knew without asking that they were entertaining the same thought. In all likelihood, the usurpers had fled north, toward the holes from which they'd crawled in the first place. Which meant some ill fate might have befallen their men.

"The scouts should have returned by now," said Bryce.

"Most of that group are from Kenshire," Thomas offered. "Perhaps they're unused to the terrain?"

Both men looked in the direction the scouting party would have traveled. The lush, flat land where they stood gave way to rolling hills. From this distance, with spring finally upon them, the rising slopes appeared green and smooth. The terrain appeared ideally suited for an afternoon ride, but Bryce knew the reality of those mountains from experience. Only borderers could appreciate the stark contrast that was Northern England. One day's ride could offer wide-open fields, roaring rivers, and treacherous inclines which taxed all but the heartiest of steeds bred for such terrain.

"Thomas." Bryce put aside the thought of potential trouble to the north for a moment. Steeling himself for the possibility his friend would deny him, he said, "Will you stay on at Bristol Manor as its steward? I can offer continued raids, battles with our Scottish neighbors, and very likely retribution from Clan Kerr." He wished he were exaggerating.

The large knight gestured to the mostly muddy courtyard of the manor they had fought to reclaim.

"So tempting." His trademark grin returned. "It would be my honor. Mayhap I can even coax a smile from the Slayer as Bristol's new steward."

Thomas knew he despised that nickname, which was exactly why he'd used it. Unfortunately, it was not a comment on Bryce's battle prowess, as it sounded, but on his effect on women.

"Maybe not," Thomas said.

"When you're done joking, can you alert Geoffrey and Hugh? I'm going to find the search party." He sensed Thomas's displeasure but knew his new steward wouldn't attempt to dissuade him.

"You'll take men with you?" Thomas asked.

"Aye."

It appeared they may have started celebrating too soon.

SHE WAS GOING to have one hell of a headache. Father Simon and his penance be damned for using such a word. She hadn't said it out loud, after all.

Catrina Kerr had never felt a more intense pain in the twenty and two years she'd been alive. It shot from her head down through her back, which was currently prone on...

Where am I?

It hurt to open her eyes even though the sun was nowhere to be seen.

She heard the sound of trickling water moments before she registered the water penetrating her shoe. The river, then.

Toren! The raid.

It all came back at once. The bloodcurdling screams. Her brother's frantic yells for her to hurry.

One minute, she had been sitting on a low rock wall behind the manor watching the sun rise—just as she did nearly every morning. The next, shouts had come from every direction. Before the danger could sink in, her clansmen had pulled her from the wall and practically dragged her to the front of the manor house. How could she forget Toren's gut-wrenching screams as he called her name?

Where was her brother?

She had to get up.

Catrina tried to sit, but her head felt as if someone had taken a war hammer to it.

Where is everyone?

Dizzy and panicked, she lay back down and closed her eyes.

AFTER WASTING time in an argument with Geoffrey, who insisted on accompanying him, Bryce finally mounted his horse, ready to lead the small search party north as soon as his brother joined them. But before Geoffrey reappeared from the manor, a band of riders made their way toward them. Dust and mud kicked up everywhere. The thunderous sound of warhorses made further discussion impossible.

It would appear the impromptu rescue mission was unnecessary.

But something was wrong. Bryce was sure of it.

When the search party stopped in front of them, Bryce addressed the knight in the lead. His livery declared him a man of Lord William Thornhurst, vassal to Kenshire and seneschal of Camburg Castle. While Thornhurst himself had not been at liberty to join them, his men had added to their numbers, allowing Bristol Manor to be reclaimed with minimal damage or bloodshed. Bryce would forever be grateful to both his sister-in-law and her vassal for their support.

"Good timing, I was just preparing...what the devil?"

"Apologies, my lord, for our delay. As you can see, we ran into a bit of trouble."

As he spoke, the man dismounted and turned to help the rider next to him offload a bundle. Bryce approached the men, eager to see what they carried.

"Is that a—"

"Aye, my lord. It's a woman."

"Is she alive?"

The bundle didn't appear to be moving. Bryce moved closer, attempting to get a better look as they carried her toward the manor. He barely registered that Thomas had dismounted and followed them.

"Barely. She needs a healer, and quickly." The young knight rushed to explain. "We were crossing the river on our way back to Bristol when the girl was spotted lying face down on the bank. One of the men thought he saw her move, so we took a closer look."

Bryce's blood went cold as the implications filtered into his consciousness.

She was a Kerr.

"She hasn't woken but clearly breathes. After spending more time than necessary arguing about whether to leave her—" he shot his companion an unhappy glance, "—we decided an unarmed, nearly dead woman posed no threat."

"She's a Kerr." Bryce didn't hide his displeasure.

"Most likely," the other man replied. "But alone."

"You should have left her."

Everyone stopped at his words. Thomas, no longer grinning, had the sense to agree. "Who thought bringing the enemy back to Bristol was a good idea?"

The man carrying her turned, daring anyone, including the new lord of the manor, to refute him. "I did. We don't know for sure the woman is a Kerr. Also, she has red hair."

Bryce looked at the man as if he were daft. "And?"

"And my sister has red hair. We couldn't leave her there to die."

That news was enough to snap Bryce's normally well-controlled hold on the legendary Waryn temper.

"You're telling me—" he could hardly fathom the idea, "—we must now play nursemaid to a woman who is likely from the same clan that we just sent back to Scotland? The one responsible for the theft of my home and murder of my parents? Because your *sister* has red hair?"

"Bryce," Geoffrey cut in. Transported as he was by rage, Bryce had not noticed his brother's approach.

For the past five and a half years, Bryce had imagined countless variations of this day, and not one of them had included nursing a woman, a Kerr, back from the dead.

"Bring the woman to a clean bed in one of the private chambers," Geoffrey ordered.

AS THE MEN hurried to comply, Bryce and Geoffrey squared off in the center of the hall. Modest in size but appointed with plenty of trestle tables to feed their retainers, the hall also boasted a large fireplace against the wall with a flue that carried away the smoke. An arched timber ceiling spanned two floors high.

"We're not butchers of innocent woman, Bryce. Besides, we don't know for sure that she's one of them."

Bryce looked at the man who could be his twin. With the same jet-black hair and clear blue eyes, the only difference between them was a slight scar running down Geoffrey's cheek. And his brother's easy smile.

"Perhaps her clan should have taken better care of her. Abandoned to be captured by the enemy. Sounds like a Kerr to me."

A small crowd gathered to watch the two overly large men, both highly trained warriors, exhibit a rare discord.

"I agree," Geoffrey conceded, "but that doesn't mean we leave innocent women to die."

Bryce felt his pulse race at the quiet tone, recognizing his brother's subtle shift in tactics, as if he would ever be convinced any Kerr deserved to live. His brother, the finest warrior he'd ever known, had grown soft since meeting his lady wife. He'd thought it before, but now he was enraged enough to say it.

"You've grown soft."

The barb hit its mark. Geoffrey's blue eyes darkened as he stepped toward him, but Bryce held his ground.

"If you refer to my wife, I'll thank you to leave her out of this. Have the woman tossed back into the river, if you've the stomach for it. I'll not continue this argument with witnesses."

The reminder that they were not alone, far from it, invoked a curse from Bryce. In silent agreement, both men stared at the onlookers in question until they began to disperse, unnerved by the intimidating gaze of the Waryn brothers.

Geoffrey looked like he intended to say something else, but Bryce shook his head and walked away. They both knew he wouldn't hurt the girl, but the fact that a member of the Kerr household currently resided above stairs rankled. Injured… woman…it mattered naught.

No mercy.

It was the battle cry of the invaders who had taken Bristol from them. Although he and his siblings had not been present for the Kerrs' raid, the survivors all told the same tale of murder and bloodshed.

He'd repeated the phrase in his head since that day, silently promising to show the same courtesy to each and every Kerr who stood between Bristol and his family.

No mercy.

And yet he watched from the front window as horse and rider sped away to retrieve the village healer.

Forcing his mind to more important matters, Bryce concentrated for the remainder of the day on fortifying Bristol Manor, finding a cook and getting rid of every remnant of the occupiers.

Save one.

2

Catrina's head certainly wasn't feeling any better. Wanting to open her eyes but unable to do so, she concentrated instead on the muffled voices nearby. She could not understand what they were saying.

She felt as disoriented as she had by the river, only now there was a soft bed beneath her.

When she thought about the raid, her memories returned in scattered patches. Catrina remembered being pulled onto a mount. Remembered her brother riding alongside her, yelling orders the whole time.

But after that…nothing.

She was no longer wet, but she was most certainly injured. Suddenly, her stomach roiled. She sat up and heaved over the side of the bed into a well-placed chamber pot.

The effort made her head and body ache even more, if that were possible.

"Here."

The deep sound from behind her was so jarring, Catrina whipped her head around without thinking. God's bones, that hurt.

A cloth was thrust into her hands. She wiped her mouth with it without thinking and lay back onto the bed. Her eyes now open, she recognized her surroundings immediately.

Toren's bedchamber. But the man in front of her was most definitely not her brother.

A terrifyingly large English knight stood next to the bed, staring at her as if she were, well, Scottish.

He was going to kill her. She'd somehow survived the attack, and this man was here to finish the job. She had to get away!

"Whoa there. You're not going anywhere."

She wanted to disagree, but the pain prevented her from saying anything.

Catrina lay back down and tried to take it all in. She was in her brother's bedchamber, wounded, with a stranger standing next to the bed, presumably prepared to kill her. Was his metal hauberk for her benefit? A pity she wasn't armed.

Toren had often told her she was going to get herself killed one day. That it was reckless to have come to Bristol in the first place. That her unescorted rides would be the death of her.

Och, but her head hurt.

"So…you're going to kill me?"

He was in no rush to answer. She'd never seen such blue eyes before. They were unsettling—as if they could see right through her.

"Nay, but my brother Bryce might."

Catrina wasn't supposed to be scared. Toren had trained her as well as any boy in their clan. She'd been raised by brothers, lived amongst men. Prepared for the day the English would come to reclaim their land.

But truth be told, she struggled to breathe normally as the knight began pacing the room. His huge body seemed to suck up all the space.

Stay calm.

How the hell do you stay calm when you're about to die?

"The healer said you're lucky to be alive," he said.

Her eyes popped back open. She tried to turn her head, but the pain forced her eyes closed.

"Is Evelyn here?"

"Aye, she sent for me when you woke." Why had he sent for Evelyn if he was going to kill her?

With a final curious glance, the knight walked to the oak door and pulled on the cast iron handle she'd slammed more than once after an argument with her mule-headed brother.

Evelyn rushed inside, as quick a woman her age could walk. The healer sat on the edge of the large canopied bed and immediately placed her withered hand on her forehead.

Both women watched the Englishman leave.

Catrina's eyes filled with tears. "What happened?"

Evelyn, the village healer who terrified everyone other than Catrina, reached up to cup her cheek. The tender touch forced the release of the tears that had threatened to spill onto her cheeks since she'd awoken.

Catrina already knew the answer to her question.

"They've returned." Evelyn lifted the cotton blanket. She must be worried about a fever. Though a simple wimple covered her hair, white wisps threatened to escape. Rather than consider the words that marked the change of...*everything*, Catrina stared at Evelyn's royal blue head covering. The people of Bristol might be terrified of her, but servants and nobles alike treated the revered healer like a queen. Deservedly so.

"You look horrid." Evelyn took what looked like a sea sponge from her leather pouch, dipped it in a bowl of water sitting on a stool beside the bed, and wrung its contents into a cup. "Here, drink this."

Catrina lifted her head as best she could, sniffed the foul-smelling concoction, and drank it without question.

"Tell me." Catrina groaned as she lay back down, shifting the weight off her right shoulder. It stung worse than Hades' river of fire. "I need to know what happened."

"It's said they descended by the hundreds. Mounted knights and even bands of reivers. By the time word reached the village, most of your clan had already fled." Evelyn's voice softened. "I told your brother they would come back. I'm sorry."

What she left unsaid was that while Evelyn was sorry for the raid, she did not regret the return of the Englishmen.

Catrina refused to consider her brother may be injured. Or worse. "I don't remember anything about our escape. But I know my brother is alive." Catrina looked to Evelyn for a reaction. The old woman's wrinkled frown didn't tell her much.

"Judging by the size of the bump on your head, I'm not surprised you don't remember." Evelyn stood and leaned on the hand-carved cane she so cherished.

"Fourteen dead and more injured," Evelyn said.

Catrina had so many questions, but her strength was waning, and her resolve with it.

"The knight who was in here earlier?"

Evelyn's soft sigh told her all she needed to know. "Sir Geoffrey Waryn."

So they truly had returned. Her brother had prepared for this day, tried to shield her from it. Indeed, the possibility of this raid was the reason he'd urged her time and again to return to Brockburg Castle.

But she could be as stubborn as any of her brothers. She'd come here for a reason—to convince Toren to grant her permission to wed the man she loved—and she'd refused to leave without getting what she wanted.

"So that was the Lord of Bristol Manor."

"Nay, no longer. You've yet to meet the new lord. But more importantly, you need rest," Evelyn said.

No longer the lord? What did that mean? Evelyn's remark had

yielded even more questions, but Catrina couldn't resist closing her eyes. The healer had given her a sleeping draught...

Yawning, she vowed to get more answers after a wee rest.

BRYCE STOPPED PACING as Evelyn entered the hall.

"She is sleeping, Sir Bryce."

Geoffrey and Thomas sat across from him at the same ornate wooden table where he had played chess as a young man. It had been hand-carved by a man who'd died while he was away, training for knighthood. The skilled carpenter had etched the Waryn family crest into the center of the table. Bryce traced the mermaid with his fingers.

Everyone watched, apparently waiting for his reaction.

"He is no longer a sir." His brother clapped him on the back. "You're looking at the new Lord of Bristol Manor."

Bryce looked at his older brother, whose easy grin should have put him at ease. Under normal circumstances, it would have. He turned his attention to the healer.

"I mean to say, Lady Catrina is sleeping, my lord," Evelyn amended.

"As long as she's being guarded, the girl isn't my concern."

"Catrina is a woman, not a girl," the older woman snapped. " And a good one. Save your venom for the real enemy, boy."

From lord to boy. Only Evelyn could overstep her bounds without fear of reprisal. He couldn't understand his brother's affinity for the healer. She may have saved their hides from scrapes and broken bones when they were younger, but her disposition hadn't softened one bit.

He startled when she laid a hand on his shoulder. Ignoring the curious looks of his companions, she leaned closer to Bryce and whispered into his ear. "I know you're angry, and you have every reason to be. But if you harm that young woman in any way, you will be the one who needs a healer."

Evelyn's entire countenance changed when she moved her hand from his shoulder to his brother's. Her eyes nearly disappeared when she smiled at him.

He watched Geoffrey squeeze her hand back.

"I'm pleased to see you, Evie," Geoffrey said.

"Excuse me, gentlemen. I have injured men to look after. And I will check on the girl later this evening."

With that, Evelyn slowly made her way out of the hall.

"I thought you said she was a woman, not a girl, Evie?" Bryce called after her. The healer was undoubtedly high-handed, but Bryce loved her in spite of it.

"You will soon see for yourself, my lord."

Bryce turned back to his brother and received a stern glare for his efforts. No doubt Geoffrey had more to say on the subject of the *girl*. Well, he was in no mood to answer to his brother at the moment.

"It's not her fault she is Toren Kerr's sister," Geoffrey said.

"I don't give a shite whose fault it is. The girl is a Kerr."

Thomas, ever the diplomat, tried to mitigate the tension. "We can agree her presence is a problem. Aye?"

Both he and his brother replied at the same time. "Aye."

"And you clearly have two choices, Bryce. Keep her prisoner or send her north."

"Or kill her," Bryce said. He wasn't serious, but it was obvious they both took him at his word. "It's both of you who nag like old women, telling me to relax. I was only jesting."

"You don't jest," Thomas said.

The last thing he felt like doing was engaging in an argument about whether he possessed a sense of humor. "Need I remind you," he said, staring at his brother, "her bastard brother was responsible for killing our parents. For taking our home and your inheritance."

Though his comment was directed at Geoffrey, Thomas answered. "No one will be forgetting what her family did five years ago. Least of all Geoffrey."

Because of the reiving. After the Kerrs' raid of Bristol Manor, Geoffrey and Uncle Hugh had resorted to reiving, stealing cattle and goods along the border, in order to support the family and gather men for a counter-attack. He knew Geoffrey had resented thieving for a living, but his brother had always done what was necessary for their family's survival. Now, he'd married Sara, and that life was, thankfully, behind him.

"Then why the hell does it matter what happens to the sister?" Bryce clenched his fists and took a deep breath. Anger meant loss of control. But when it came to Clan Kerr, he had a difficult time remaining calm.

"Think, Bryce," Geoffrey leaned forward, putting his elbows on the table. "What will they do to keep the woman safe?"

It was difficult to understand those who were spawned from the devil. But he knew what his brother was getting at. "They'll come for her."

"Or at least try to bargain," said Thomas.

"So we keep her hostage in the meantime?" The thought repulsed him.

"Aye, it makes the most sense," Geoffrey said. "Send extra scouts north. We won't make the same mistake they did. If there's a Scot within two days' ride of Bristol, we'll know it."

"There's a Scot in my bedchamber, Geoffrey."

Thomas grabbed his beard, something he did whenever he was amused. "The Slayer, complaining that a woman lies in his bed. I'll be damned."

"Nay, not a woman." Bryce stood from the table. He needed to check on the men's progress in shoring up the defensive wall they themselves had breached. "A Kerr."

He scowled at Thomas's laugh and walked away before he said something he'd regret. There was much to do to secure the manor, and he hoped to pay a visit to the village before dark. When he walked through the covered, arched doorway into the courtyard, a darkened sky greeted him. This fuss about the girl had taken up far too much of his time.

As he continued on toward the hall, he took a bite of the hard bread that would serve as their dinner, the repast reminding him of their need to find a cook to replace the Scot that had been overseeing the kitchens. The aging woman who had served Bristol in his boyhood had died the year they lost the manor. Both the old cook and Evelyn had served Bristol before he was even born. Death was probably too terrified of Evelyn to claim her.

He approached the gaping hole at the western corner of the wall. Men who fought brilliantly against the Scots that morning had shed their armor, now hard at work repairing the very stones they damaged earlier. Lady Sara had sent an expert sapper to dig under the weakest section of the wall. A few nights of digging without notice, thanks to their knowledge of the land, had granted them easy access. But it needed to be repaired. Immediately.

He lay his sword on the ground and joined the others. Bryce complimented the men as he joined them in hauling stone toward the scaffold.

"You've done well in such a short time."

"'Tis necessary, my lord. They could be back anytime," one of the men handed him a rope.

My lord. He could hardly reconcile the use of that title on him.

"How many knots is that stone?" the man asked.

Bryce laid the rope on the rock and measured. "Two."

Handing back the rope, he continued to move between the hole in the wall and the fallen rock. With moonlight as their guide, the men worked into the night to repair the breach.

Hours of heavy labor were beginning to wear Bryce down. But until the wall was completed, the men would not rest—which meant he wouldn't either. Nothing mattered more than securing Bristol.

Bryce was startled out of his reverie. "Drink this." His uncle handed him a mug of ale. Hugh had been overseeing the wall's progress and spent the better part of the day here. He had evidentially taken a repast at the manor.

Bryce sent Thomas to the village to speak to the people and calm their worries. He knew most would celebrate their return. His family had ruled Bristol for three generations and treated the people well. Even so, they were likely worried after seeing their new lord routed and sent scurrying back to Scotland in one day's time.

"How goes progress at the manor?" Bryce asked.

"Quiet. The dead are buried. All of the wounded have been moved out and are being tended to by Evelyn. Most of the staff have made their way back. We're still lacking a head cook, alas."

"Good." Bryce handed back the mug. "The Scots will return."

"Aye, likely within six days."

Picking up a large rock, Bryce moved between his uncle and the repairs. "I doubt they'll care if they're within the law to counterattack. It could be any time. And don't forget, we have the girl."

When his uncle began to help, Bryce clapped a hand on his shoulder. "Go back to the manor, Hugh." Though large and well-built, Hugh was getting along in age. Bryce didn't want his uncle to injure himself.

"I'll thank you not to treat me as if I'm one step in the grave. I'm here to help."

Stubborn old ox.

"Have you seen Geoffrey?" Bryce asked.

"He's on patrol." Hugh stopped and stared behind him. "What's he doing here?"

Turning, Bryce watched a young servant from the kitchens

make his way toward them. Distinctly out of place, the boy looked nervously from side to side. "My lord, I'm sorry to disturb you, but the healer sent for you. Lady Catrina's condition is worsening."

What the hell did he care? One less Kerr in the world was a good thing.

"Why do you need me?" Every muscle in his back ached from lifting stone. Although the battle this morning had been quickly won, he'd hardly slept the night before due to anticipation. Bryce was exhausted and had no desire to attend to his enemy's bedside.

He was about to tell the messenger exactly that when Thomas walked up behind them.

"She asks for you. Go, I'll take your place at the wall."

"What does she want with me?"

His place was here.

"Bryce, go. Perhaps she has important information about her brother," Hugh said.

He stopped working and wiped his mud-soaked hand on the front of his tunic. What could she possibly have to say? Unless she wanted to help him kill her brother, he had no use for her. But with three expectant faces staring at him, he picked up his sword and followed the servant away from the damaged wall. He supposed he could use a break. It would be a long night.

"Hurry, my lord."

Although the boy carried a lantern, Bryce didn't need the light. Even after so many years away, he could navigate this courtyard in his sleep.

"She's not well. Evelyn said the bump on her head may be her undoing."

They walked through the entranceway and into the hall. The tapestries depicting Scottish battles that had hung on the stone walls were blessedly gone. Men slept on the floor, which, while not exactly clean, was at least free of dead or injured bodies.

His heart raced at the thought of meeting the sister of his

enemy. She may be a valuable prisoner, but he wanted nothing to do with her. The girl's clan stole his home, his brother's inheritance.

He stopped at the entrance.

Bryce walked into the bedchamber that was once his own and looked around the room. Although the hour was late, moonlight from a small window and candles throughout the room told him not much had changed. The large bed he approached was familiar to him. While the usurpers had attempted to make Bristol their own, remnants of his childhood were everywhere.

Was the carving he and Geoffrey had etched into the leg of the bed still there? A similar one graced his brother's bed as well courtesy of the wood carver's tutelage. Of course, the man did not intend for them to practice their skills on the furniture.

He navigated the room easily and caught his first glimpse of his enemy's sister when the candlelight flickered across her red hair. Nay, not red exactly. More like a shade between red and brown.

As he made his way closer, he realized he'd been deceived. Sitting up in bed and glaring at him, nursed very much back to health if his guess was accurate, was the most beautiful creature he'd ever laid eyes on. A perfectly shaped face and long, dark lashes as delicate-looking as her skin seemed at odds with an expression that was anything but dainty. Her lips, even pursed, were full and made to be ravished.

Ravished? Not bloody likely.

"I was told you were nearly dead."

"You're disappointed?" Her voice was like a splash of cold water. Why was he surprised this woman was so…feminine? She was a female, after all. A treacherous one. His enemy. But a female nonetheless.

"I don't like being lied to." And he didn't. Evelyn would answer for this deception.

"You would not have come otherwise."

It was a statement, not a question. And an accurate one.

"What do you want?"

"You can't give me what I want."

Oh, he was pretty sure he could.

He kept the ribald thought to himself. Dangerous, given her position. A cream robe covered enough of her chemise to avoid being scandalous, but not enough to hide the fact that she was quite well-endowed. Any man with eyes could see she was also a rare beauty.

"But since you're here," the woman continued, "I'd like to know what you plan to do with me."

"You were given access to our healer."

Her eyes narrowed even more, if that were possible. "*Your* healer?"

She trode on dangerous ground. "I believe we discuss your fate, not that of Bristol."

He couldn't reconcile the vision sitting propped up before him with the girl's hardened brother. Two years earlier, on a scouting mission close to Bristol, Bryce had seen the man for the first and only time. Toren Kerr of Brockburg and four of his clan members had ridden within calling distance of where Bryce was hidden on a path just two days' ride from Bristol. He had instantly known him for the clan's chief. The fierce-looking Scot bore little resemblance to the gently bred woman before him.

"What of my fate then, *my lord*?"

He would make her position very clear. "You are my hostage. And will remain as such until your filthy brother pays a king's ransom for your return."

Her face relaxed, the eyes that defied him moments earlier softening. He expected a retort, but instead the perplexing woman actually smiled.

Damn, she was lovely. A siren capable of making him temporarily forget about Bristol's defenses. About how angry he was that there was still a Kerr in his manor. He nearly asked what was so amusing but thought better of it. He cared not about the inner workings of his enemy's mind.

Without a word, he spun and left the room. Passing the guard stationed outside her door, Bryce reminded himself to send for a lady's maid. One who was a stranger to their hostage. And she clearly no longer needed a healer. He trusted Evelyn, but it was obvious she bore some tenderness for the girl. Better for Lady Catrina to remain in that chamber with only one person, a stranger, to bring her meals and tend to her needs. And with any luck, she would be the key to ensuring Bristol Manor remained in the Waryn family for many years to come.

3

He was alive. Catrina had hoped it with all her heart, but Bryce's words had confirmed it. Her brother was alive.

Evelyn must have known she had exaggerated her condition in order to get an audience with Sir Bryce. With any luck he wouldn't take his anger out on the poor old woman, though she had no doubt the healer could hold her own. But she'd needed answers.

In addition to the good news, he'd confirmed what she'd already feared. Her home, in one day's time, had become a prison.

She hadn't been sure what to expect from Sir Bryce, though she'd heard much about the great Waryn brothers over the years. Some, like Evelyn and the other villagers, thought the men were near-deities. Revered for their prowess in battle, the Englishmen's influence on Bristol was unmistakable. It had taken years for her brother and clan to gain acceptance.

Were we ever truly accepted?

Toren, on the other hand, accused the Waryn men of seeking favor from a weak and ineffectual king. He said the Englishmen had claimed land that rightfully belonged to her ancestors and to Scotland.

What Catrina had not expected was for her heart to race from the moment he entered the room. From fear? Nay, she knew herself better than that. She'd heard the rumors, of course. The village matrons spoke of the brothers in ways that would make Father Simon blush. Catrina had assumed the talk was exaggerated, but Sir Bryce was every rumor and whispered compliment combined. His brother was a handsome man, of course, but there was something about Sir Bryce that seduced the eye. Black hair to his shoulders in waves that any girl would envy, cheekbones that looked to be carved from stone, and wide shoulders that hinted at the muscle beneath. He wore tight-fitting breeches and a white linen shirt that hung loosely, displaying a fair amount of skin beneath. No cloak or tunic concealed his appealing physique.

She'd been told the man never smiled, so his mutinous expression had not surprised her. *What made him scowl so?* Her presence, most likely. To him, Catrina's family deserved everything that had happened that day.

She knew otherwise.

Closing her eyes for what felt like a moment but was likely much longer, Catrina startled to a hard knock at the door.

"Lady Catrina?"

A girl around her age whose dress and timid demeanor proclaimed her a servant entered the room. Catrina didn't recognize her.

"Is there anything else you require this evening?" The girl's voice was barely a whisper. A cap hid most of the servant's light brown hair.

Noticing her tightly clasped hands, Catrina tried to ease her mind. "Come in."

The girl took exactly two steps inside and stopped once again. Catrina sighed. This was going to be harder than she had hoped.

"What is your name?"

"Elise, my lady."

"Well, Elise, I'm pleased to meet you. You're from Bristol's village?"

Elise looked toward the door as if assessing her escape route.

"Never mind. But just so you know, Sir Bryce is wrong. I'm not planning to escape."

The girl's eyes widened.

She'd hit her mark. Sir Bryce had wisely chosen to send someone she didn't know, and it was obvious he'd warned her to be on guard.

"You have a wee bairn, am I right?"

If it were possible, Elise's eyes widened even more. The bump in the servant's plain brown kirtle revealed either a bairn or the recent delivery of one.

"I've always wanted one myself." Catrina shifted in the bed, grateful Evelyn's concoction seemed to have taken away the worst of her headache.

"'Tis wondrous, my lady." Timid, but at least she spoke.

"Is it a boy or a girl?"

Elise smiled, finally relaxing her hands. "A girl."

"Go and take care of...what's her name?"

"Mary, my lady."

"Attend to wee Mary. I don't need anything this eve." That much was true. Tomorrow would be soon enough to begin planning the escape she did indeed intend to make.

Elise bobbed a curtsy and left, the wooden door closing with a finality that made her shudder.

Congratulations, Sir Bryce. It would obviously take time to get Elise to trust her. But she would, eventually. And Catrina only needed one thing from the servant to leave this blasted bedchamber and make her way back to her brothers.

And then what?

Perhaps the re-taking of Bristol would be enough to convince her stubborn brother they needed more allies. His refusal to give Catrina and Graeme permission to wed was what had kept her at Bristol Manor these past years. Perhaps something good could come out of these horrors.

She yawned, the beginnings of a plan weaving together in her mind.

THREE DAYS after they took back Bristol from the Scots, Bryce embraced Geoffrey as he prepared to head southeast to his home in Kenshire.

They stood within shouting distance of Geoffrey's men. Hugh had said his goodbyes earlier, and Bryce was grateful to have at least one family member remain at Bristol.

"Take care, little brother," Geoffrey said.

"You're sure about this?"

His gaze was met and held by ice-blue eyes identical to his own. Geoffrey's normally affable expression turned serious.

"I would never have arranged it otherwise."

At first, Bryce had been opposed to his brother's plan to relinquish his inheritance to him. His brother had given up so much for their family. It was his title by right. They'd fought about it for days until his sister-in-law finally intervened. Geoffrey had argued that his place was at Kenshire, and Bristol needed a lord who could be present and protect it from inevitable border attacks. He reminded him of the twins—Emma and Neill. The youngest Waryn siblings, Geoffrey said, needed security after years of uncertainty. Emma remained at Kenshire while Neill trained with a friend and noble knight.

The Kerrs were not the only family, Scot or English, who claimed land in the disputed marches. Battles, raids, abductions. All were a part of life along a border only the kings recognized.

Years after the border was declared, battles for land and titles still occurred daily. But Bryce, determined to secure Bristol for his family and their future, clung to the possibility, however remote, of peace.

"Then I will secure Bristol and see that it remains in the Waryn family for generations to come."

Geoffrey cocked his head in a way that told Bryce he wouldn't like what his brother was about to say.

"I don't doubt it, Bryce. And you know if there's anything you need—"

Geoffrey's hand remained on his shoulder, squeezing it in a familiar farewell gesture. For a moment Bryce thought he was finished.

No such luck.

"But don't make the mistake I almost did. Revenge is a cold bed to keep company with at night."

Here it was again—another sign of how much his brother had changed since his marriage to Lady Sara. Bryce wasn't sure it was for the better. "Our parents' deaths will not go unavenged."

Geoffrey dropped his hand. "I support your decisions, Bryce —" though his expression said otherwise, "—and we'll give you as many men as you need. But know that there's more to life than duty. You should consider—"

"There's much to be done here. Repairs. The wool trade. New defenses—"

"At what expense? You aren't happy, brother."

He pushed too far. "I will be happy when Bristol is strong enough to withstand another attack." Bryce's voice was low, controlled. But firm.

"Will you?"

The remark startled him, and he stared again into his older brother's eyes. He respected this man, admired him above all others. Geoffrey deserved more than the lie that had nearly slipped from his tongue, so he gave the truth instead.

"I don't know."

"Tell me. What happened at Huntington?"

It wasn't the first time his brother had asked, but it was the first he seriously considered answering. His brother was convinced something happened in the place where he squired. And he was right.

The silence stretched.

"Go," Bryce said, refusing, once again, to lie to his brother. "Your men are waiting. Lady Sara is likely halfway to Bristol to fetch you by now."

Geoffrey didn't move. Bryce refused to back down. His brother eventually mounted the enormous black destrier that would take him back to his feisty wife. "Give Lady Sara my regards."

"I will. She adores you for some unholy reason and will be happy to know you're properly installed as the new Lord of Bristol Manor."

Bryce slapped the back side of his brother's mount. "Godspeed, Geoffrey."

Dust kicked up everywhere as the small retinue of men rode away. Most of the retainers his brother had brought from Kenshire remained to help Bristol rebuild. But as he watched Geoffrey and some of the men ride away, a sinking sensation forced him to turn toward the stables. He was intent on visiting the village when a voice from behind, so timid he could hardly hear her, called his name.

He turned to find the maid he'd assigned to Lady Catrina standing before him, wringing her hands.

The girl was clearly terrified of him. Perhaps the previous lord had been cruel—something he could easily imagine—or mayhap the girl was saddled with a heavy-handed father or husband. He would have Thomas inquire. He'd not have any woman under his care being abused.

"Yes, Elise?"

He must have surprised the maid by using her given name.

"Milord . . .well, the Lady Catrina . . ."

The Kerr girl.

"She wants to ride Davie," Elise blurted.

"Who the hell is Davie?" He hadn't intended to raise his voice, but for the briefest moment he'd imagined Lady Catrina naked, her long red-brown hair tumbling around her as she moved above a faceless man.

What is wrong with me?

When tears formed in the young girl's eyes, he was immediately contrite. Of course. Davie was Lady Catrina's horse.

"She will not be leaving that room, Elise, even to ride *Davie*."

The servant didn't move.

"Is there more?"

She swallowed hard. Bryce took pity on her and softened his tone. "What is it?"

"She said, my lord, if you said 'nay,' I should tell you that you can escort her yerself. It's just...she's worried about her horse."

The lady's horse would be exercised daily, but she must know that. This was more trickery.

"Two nights ago the woman claimed to be on her deathbed. And now she's intent on exercising her horse?"

Elise lowered her head and peered at him through thick lashes.

"Tell Lady Catrina's guard to escort her to the stables. Immediately."

Elise smiled and practically ran away from him.

That was a mistake. He had done it for the servant, *not* the woman.

Bryce turned back toward the stables. A familiar scent, a mixture of manure and hay, greeted him. He entered the wooden structure, which was larger than most in a manor this size thanks to his grandfather's affinity for horses.

The stable master was nowhere in sight.

"The palfrey, my lord?"

A young stable hand walked out of a stall, looking at Bryce

with the same trepidation he'd sensed from Elise. The boy was young, no more than ten. He'd be spending the better part of his days putting the servants at ease if this continued.

"Aye. And your name?"

The dusty, sandy-haired boy began to prepare his mount and muttered, "Arthur."

Bryce could understand the servants' unease. Those not old enough to remember his family wouldn't know they would be treated well. He had thought fortifying Bristol would be his most difficult job, but it seemed endearing himself to the people was going to be equally as challenging.

Not an easy task for someone like him.

"That's a fine-looking weapon, Arthur." He pointed to the dagger that hung from a worn leather belt around the lad's waist.

"A gift from . . ." The boy's smile faltered.

Bryce tried again. "Where is the groom?" Stable hands didn't typically tend to the horses beyond their feeding, but Arthur appeared to be alone. From the way he handled his horse, Bryce could tell it was a role the boy knew well.

"Killed in the battle, my lord."

How could he have forgotten? It was no wonder the lad was in a state.

"Was he a friend?"

Better get used to losing those close to you now. Life on the border will teach you heartbreak before long, if it hasn't already.

"Aye. Trained me when yer father beat my pa bloody for stealing cattle."

Bryce stared at him. That didn't sound like his father.

"He got caught when my ma turned him in. Pa beat her bloody too."

That made more sense. His father had never tolerated abuse toward women. Servant, serf...it mattered not. Though it was a man's right to beat his wife, his father had not allowed it to happen on his watch.

"I'm sorry for your loss, Arthur."

"I'm sure you are," a female voice called from the entrance. Nay, not a female. His enemy. And she'd best learn to curb that wicked tongue of hers. It wasn't the first time she had used that tone in his presence. But it would be the last.

4

He was sorry?

She shouldn't provoke the man who held her life in his hands, but Catrina, as usual, spoke before thinking.

In a few long strides, Sir Bryce was standing as close to her as possible without actually touching her. She had to tilt her head back to look him in the eyes. Which wasn't a very good idea.

"You *will* hold your tongue." His voice was low, stern, for her ears only. And then she did it again.

"How so, Sir Bryce?"

He grabbed her arm, his grasp easily penetrating the thick fabric of her sleeve. She hadn't dared ask for a riding gown, so there'd been no choice but to make do with one of the two gowns afforded to her on the second day of her captivity.

Tight but not overly so, his grip was actually less ominous than the way he looked at her. With his perfectly formed jaw locked into place, Sir Bryce's expression was one she'd seen on her brothers' faces many times.

He wanted to kill her.

But he wouldn't. If he could control his anger when she spoke with such open disrespect, he was unlikely to strike her. Or worse. Best she not tempt fate.

"My apologies."

His eyes narrowed. "I don't believe you're contrite."

Well, of course she wasn't, but he was a brute to point it out. Luckily Arthur interrupted, leading Davie to her. Lord knows what would have escaped her lips otherwise.

Sir Bryce released his grip, but apparently not his anger. He offered no assistance as he watched her mount the chestnut mare she'd brought from Brockburg. Which was just as well.

She didn't need it.

Mounted, she followed his lead away from the stables and through the small courtyard.

"People are staring." Catrina smiled, trying to appear calm and in control.

"Let them." Sir Bryce didn't bother to look at her but instead spoke as if she didn't exist.

"Where are we going?"

No answer.

She glanced at his profile and swallowed. His surcoat ended just below his waist. Emblazoned with the Waryn family crest, the deep blue and black garment made him appear nobler than he had that first night. At the time, she never would have guessed he was the second son of a baron. Not just because of his casual dress—he was also more braw than most Englishmen. Or at least the ones she'd seen.

They rode in silence, and after a time, Catrina realized they were heading toward the village. What would people think when they saw them together? The former lord's sister and the man who held her captive.

"I'd like to speak with you, Sir Bryce."

She could not force herself to use her brother's title. *He* was the rightful lord of Bristol Manor.

The man was proving stubborn, forcing her to change tactics.

If he truly intended to keep her locked away without any contact with the outside world, save Elise, then drastic action was necessary. Which meant she would have to get to know the enemy.

"Then speak."

This wasn't going to be easy. And before she could stop herself, her mouth was once again moving.

"Why don't you ever smile?"

He slowed his jet-black mount and turned to her, his lips pressed in a straight line, eyes expressionless.

"I ride alongside my enemy, Lady Catrina. The sister of the man who killed my parents."

"My brother did *not* kill your parents."

"His men, his hand. It matters naught."

Catrina's heart thudded in her chest. She wanted to defend her brother, her clan. But arguing a claim that had been debated for centuries would not help her cause. And both she and Toren were sorely sorry for the loss of his parents, but he would unlikely believe her if she said as much. She remained silent, concentrating instead on their surroundings. If not for the border separating their two countries, a less discerning eye wouldn't be able to tell them apart.

With spring upon them, the wide-open moorlands burgeoned with life. The locals called the area between the manor house and village "whitelands" and the heather-topped moorland to the east "blacklands." A visitor on this well-worn path would understand Bristol's appeal at once. To the north of the manor and still within sight lay the Cheviot Hills, their rising slopes breathtaking from this distance. Even they couldn't compete with Bristol Sprout, a rock-face waterfall just northwest of their current path.

A splash in the river that ran from north to south as far as the eye could see broke her reverie. She looked toward the water. Nothing seemed to be amiss. Except, of course, that she was the hostage of a brutish knight who rode stoically alongside her.

She wanted to rail against him, but to do so would be counterproductive to her goal. Get to know the man. Form a plan of escape.

"Why did you allow me on your ride?" Catrina chanced another glance at the Englishman. Her brothers were a fearsome lot, but none were as serious as this one.

He slowed his horse to a walk and finally looked at her. Lord have mercy, he could slay an army with that look.

"Your brother had the gall to issue a letter of slains this morning on behalf of his king. If anyone owes assythment, it's him." Sir Bryce turned away once again, staring fixedly ahead—just as he had since they'd left the manor.

"Did he make mention of me, perhaps?"

The most remarkable thing happened.

Was that a smile? Nay, it couldn't be. His lips curved ever so slightly, and so briefly, Catrina was sure she must have imagined it.

"Nay, he did not."

So he didn't know she was here. Or Sir Bryce was deliberately being coy. How did this information affect her plan?

"He likely thinks you dead."

Dead? Toren would be crushed. Which meant he might do something rash. If her brothers thought her dead, they would seek vengeance, not assythment. Unless Toren thought to lull Sir Bryce into believing the lives of his clansmen could be bought.

A voice inside her refused to quiet. One that reminded her the lives of the Englishmen, and of Sir Bryce's parents, had also been taken.

There was no doubt Toren was planning a counterattack. *Oh God, brother, don't do it!*

From what she could tell, the Englishmen wasted no time repairing the damage done when they had attacked. There were four times as many men guarding Bristol Manor than her brother kept. Without allies, and the Kerrs had precious few thanks to her brother's stubbornness and more than one blood feud, they would be defeated.

She must get back to him. She must convince him not to take such a foolish risk.

"It matters naught." She had to convince Sir Bryce that Toren wanted nothing more than compensation for his clansmen. Maybe then he would relax his guard enough for her to escape.

"Toren holds no special place in his heart for a sister who causes him nothing but trouble." At least the latter part of that statement was true, and her tone had sounded convincing enough to her own ears. "He cares more for his clan than for a woman, even his sister. He'd never put them at risk for me."

She peeked out of the corner of her eye. Was that skepticism she read on his face? His expression never changed, so it was hard to tell.

"I find that hard to believe."

Perhaps a dose of the truth might help her cause. "'Tis true. Our mother is English, you see."

There, she had said it.

"I remind him too much of the woman who abandoned us. Abandoned our family."

Finally, a reaction! He stopped his horse and turned to look at her. She stopped as well. Davie danced under her, impatient to move.

"Ask Evelyn if you don't believe me."

Evelyn could indeed support her story. She was the only person Catrina had told about her mother. But belatedly, Catrina realized Evelyn would disprove her tall tale about Toren's feelings toward her. That Catrina was coddled, revered by her older brothers, was not a secret. Even if Evelyn didn't tell him the truth, there were plenty of other people who would. Damn it to hell, why hadn't she thought of that sooner?

Catrina tried not to squirm under the intense scrutiny that was Sir Bryce's stare. She had nothing to lose by keeping up the pretense. "Did I ruin your plans? Toren isn't stupid. He must know I'm your prisoner. He just doesn't care. And now you're saddled with the *enemy's sister*, as you so kindly put it."

Before he could react, a loud crack in the sky made them both look up. The bright blue that had been dotted with clouds just moments earlier darkened before their eyes. A storm was coming, and they could not outrun it.

GODDAMMIT, they were about to get wet, or worse. Bryce might have welcomed the rain had he been alone. He'd never thought much of a good drenching until the day after he arrived at Huntington Castle. Proud to be serving such an important man—an arrangement his father had worked hard to facilitate—Bryce had found himself assisting the earl himself on a deer hunt. But a flash of lightning had found them without warning. Or had found one of Huntington's men, to be precise. The young man had died on the spot, and the incident had left Bryce uneasy about thunderstorms for years afterward. He would put himself at risk in this wide-open moorland, but he'd not endanger Lady Catrina.

She was too valuable, whatever ruse she thought to play.

"Follow me," he shouted and guided her to a nearby patch of trees as the sky opened above them. Bryce pointed to a rock formation which he knew enclosed a space large enough for them both. Lady Catrina dismounted, slipped from her mount, and nearly fell to the uneven ground below. Bryce reached out to steady her, but she caught herself. He took her horse's reins as she fled into the makeshift shelter.

He found a flat patch of land and tied their horses to two sturdy trees jutting high into the sky, too high to see the tops of their leaves. The sound of rain was drowned out by Bristol Sprout, a waterfall more than twenty feet high just steps from where he had sent Lady Catrina.

He and his siblings had spent many days in the pool beneath the waterfall half hidden by the surrounding heather and bracken. In all his travels, only the North Sea had offered as magnificent a sight as Bristol Sprout. After this rainfall, it would be an impressive sight indeed.

Almost as impressive as the woman who sat with her knees pulled up to her body, the bodice of her bright lavender dress, its neckline and sleeves lined in gold brocade, drenched and clinging to every inch of her body.

Bryce knew a beautiful woman when he saw one, and there was no doubt Catrina Kerr was extraordinarily pretty. As he watched, she pulled errant strands of hair to the side, braiding the long, wet locks. With just enough room for her to stand, the wet rocks offered shelter but was too small for him to avoid looking anywhere but at his companion.

Bryce laid down his sword and began to discard his wet leather boots. It was damned uncomfortable to undress without being able to fully stand.

With his belt and boots finally off, he grabbed the collar of his short overtunic and pulled it over his head. He only wore the garment because Hugh and Thomas had insisted he look the part of the new lord. He was proud of the Waryn crest inlay but despised unnecessary layers. During the five years of their forced exile, Bryce had become accustomed to the simpler garb worn by his extended family. Thomas nagged like an old woman about the dangers of traveling without more protection, but the only time he covered his loose linen shirt was in battle.

"You can't be serious?"

Bryce stopped, his hand on the hem of his tunic. He'd been about to lift it over his head when Lady Catrina finally broke her silence.

"You'll disrobe in front of a lady?"

"A lady? Where?" It wasn't like him to jest. But the expression on her face almost made him want to laugh.

Almost.

"No one will remove another garment."

She had gall, that much was evident.

"Or else?"

If she wasn't the sister of his enemy, Bryce would take pity on the sorry sight in front of him. With water dripping from the sleeves of her gown, her hair, darker now that it was wet, Lady Catrina was…breathtaking.

"You've gold specks in your eyes."

He said it without thinking.

"Aye, what of it?"

Bryce sat, resigned to remain in his wet clothes. Lucky for her, it was an unusually warm spring day, otherwise the lady's maidenly sensibilities would matter little. Had it been any colder, *both* of them would have needed to strip.

The silence stretched.

"I know this place," said Catrina. "'Tis lovely."

He was going to have a hard time ignoring her in such tight quarters. He could look out to watch the sheets of water fall from the high rock above, but his gaze kept returning to the Kerr girl.

The waterfall had indeed begun to roar, just as he'd known it would. When they were young, he and Geoffrey used to spend more time here than his father would have liked. A quick wash after training would turn into hours of tossing rocks into the pool of water below. He and his brothers used to talk about jumping the waterfall cliff, but it hadn't gone any further than talk. The jump would have seen them killed. They had little sense as boys, but enough to keep them alive.

Their sister had come here the least. She'd always been afraid to get "stuck" behind the curtain of water. They only persuaded her to swim a handful of times, always with one of them right by her side.

He found himself reaching into his pocket for Emma's ribbon. Without quite planning to, he said, "Five years ago, the day your brother attacked Bristol, my siblings and I were at a fair with my uncle. My sister, Emma, begged for a new ribbon. She tied one in her hair nearly every day. She was obsessed with their colors, the bold blues and bright reds that peddlers brought to the village." He paused, not planning to say any more. But something compelled him to do so. "The fair was my idea."

He rushed on, guilt consuming him as it did whenever he thought of that day. "When we received word the Scots had taken our home, killed my parents, Emma dropped the new yellow ribbon my uncle had bought her." He took out the small, ragged strand from his pocket and turned to the woman whose proximity was making the shelter distinctively uncomfortable.

Eyes wide, Lady Catrina looked almost innocent.

"I picked it up and carry it still. A reminder of what happened that day. As if I need one."

CATRINA LOOKED at the tattered strip of ribbon. *Was it really once yellow?* The hand beneath it was large and battle-worn. She looked up at the man who held the slip of decaying ribbon in his hand as gently as if it were a wee robin. She imagined herself reaching out to touch him. But that was ridiculous, of course. He neither grimaced nor smiled, but his eyes were still locked with hers. Did he expect a response?

No words came. They sat so close their legs were nearly touching, the waterfall so loud it almost drowned out his words.

How had she gotten here?

Hostage to a man who was her enemy. One who never smiled and wanted her and her brothers dead.

The most handsome man she'd ever laid eyes on.

"I'm sorry."

It took her a moment to realize the words had come from her

lips. The second apology in one day. Father Simon would be shocked. Of course, she hadn't meant it the first time.

"That your parents were killed, that is."

He closed his hand into a fist so tight it trembled ever so slightly. She couldn't look at him any longer. Toren had told her to always look a man in the eyes, but his were filled with such anger and sorrow that Catrina was afraid she'd say something she would regret. Lord knows she did that often enough.

"Not as sorry as I." Sir Bryce put the ribbon back into his pocket.

They sat in silence, watching the heavy rainfall. This was one thing her country had in common with its southern neighbor, a very wet spring. Then again, the land on the border somehow belonged to both of them.

"How long will we stay here?" She readjusted her wet skirts, attempting to get more comfortable.

He turned to her once again. His eyes were so blue, even more so than his brother's. This time she refused to look away. The anger and sadness were gone, replaced with...she wasn't sure. Indifference?

She licked her lips. Catrina desperately wanted to turn away but was too stubborn to do so. A trait that got her into trouble often enough. Like when the man she loved, Graeme deSowlis, had first asked Toren for her hand in marriage back in Brockburg. Her brother had refused, and Catrina had declined to eat for three days. She still got hungry thinking about it.

"Not a minute longer than necessary." His low, thick voice gave her the strangest sensation.

His animosity was understandable, but it was misguided of him to direct it at her.

She'd had enough.

"'Tis clear you hate me—" his expression didn't change, "—and you're certainly not my favorite person for obvious reasons."

She thought her brother Toren stoic at times. He was like a court jester compared to this Englishman.

"I was not present at the raid. And now, thanks to you, I'm the captive of my brother's enemy, unsure if my family lives, with a betrothed . . ."

That was plenty. No need to get into *that* mess. But at least she finally got a reaction.

"You're betrothed?"

With the rain coming down even harder now, Sir Bryce apparently decided to get comfortable. He shifted and leaned against the rock behind him, facing her with one elbow on his propped knee. If only his expression matched his demeanor. Catrina hated to admit it, but he made her nervous. She pretended to be as brave and strong as her brothers, but truth be told, she had to force her hands not to shake every time her captor was near.

"It's complicated."

"Actually it's quite a simple question. Are you betrothed? Yea or nay?"

"I'll answer if you promise me a question in return."

Since it didn't look like they'd be leaving soon, she took the lord's lead and inched backward to sit along the rock wall behind her.

"That depends on the question." While his demeanor was calm, she knew better than to think he was unaffected by her answer. Sir Bryce's high cheekbones and deep-set eyes remained motionless, but his lips flattened ever so slightly each time she annoyed him. Staring at the man's lips was not the worst way to pass time.

"What do you plan to do with me?"

"I meant what I said. I plan to ransom you and bankrupt your brother." His answer was automatic, far too direct to be a lie. And Toren would do it, too. If her brothers failed to take Bristol by force, they would give anything to have her back. The man that sat so casually across from her wanted to ruin her clan...destroy her family.

Nothing she could say would dissuade him. She had to escape. And to do that, she needed more freedom.

"No, I'm not betrothed."

"Then why did you say you were?"

"I'd prefer not to discuss it."

"Tell me." His insistence didn't surprise Catrina. She knew a thing or two about pig-headed men. Sir Bryce was not going to let this go. Nevertheless, she would try.

"You bargained for one answer, sir, and I gave one."

Her heart raced as the man who'd just admitted to his plan to ruin her clan sat calmly across from her. Staring. Waiting.

"Fine, but I'll have another question," she said finally.

His slight nod was nearly imperceptible.

"My feet are wet." She was mostly dry save for her hair, sleeves, and shoes. To delay the awkward conversation, and perhaps throw Sir Bryce a bit off-balance, she pulled her sopping leather boots out from under her skirts and removed them. They really were uncomfortable. Of course, her hose was also wet, but she wasn't *that* bold.

She did feel a bit better. Placing the boots beside her, Catrina repositioned herself, squeezing a bit of excess water from her long braid onto the muddy, rocky ground. So much for this gown.

"Your betrothed?"

She thought perhaps he may have forgotten.

"Very well. His name is Graeme deSowlis of Clan Scott. We grew up neighbors and were promised to each other, though never formally. When Graeme's man accidentally killed my cousin in the Battle of Brockenridge, Toren refused to consider him for my husband. You can imagine their relationship now."

"Do you want to marry him?"

It was an intimate question, but she had nothing to lose by answering. "Aye, I do. I've imagined myself as his wife for most of my life." And she wanted that more than anything in the world. A husband, bairns, her own family.

Stability. Acceptance.

"But the chief of Clan Kerr doesn't care what his sister wants, I take it."

He made Toren sound awful. She sat up straight. "Toren only wants what's best for me, he—"

Damn, damn, damn. The blasted Englishman preyed on her greatest weakness: her inability to stop talking.

And then the most amazing thing happened. He actually smiled. A real smile. For the first time in their short, fraught acquaintance, the blasted man's lips curved up, his eyes dancing as he leaned forward with silent mirth, telling her with his facial expression what she already knew. She had unwittingly revealed the truth of her relationship with her brother.

He was clearly pleased with himself.

"My men found you unconscious, a nasty gash on your head, nearly drowned in a stream. How did you come to be there?"

She couldn't have answered if she wanted. Catrina's last memory was being pulled away from the manor by her clansmen, and her feeling of dread having to leave Davie.

"Oh no, it's my turn for a question. Perhaps I'll bargain for a third."

While he was no longer smiling, his harsh grimace was gone. Catrina was glad for it. Her next question was a serious one.

"Why does your family claim Bristol as theirs when it was once a Scottish holding? Toren was acting on orders from our king to reclaim it."

"You expect me to believe your sovereign, in a time of peace, sanctioned a raid on a small English manor? To what end?" His tone reflected the change in topic. It was measured. Angry. "One held by the Waryns for three generations? *After* the border was established?"

She hesitated. Even her brothers debated the politics of that very question. While the land was, indeed, south of the Solway-Tweed line, which made it an English holding, it was also true the manor and its small village had once been considered part of Scotland. But it wasn't for her, or her family, to question orders from their king. The chief of Clan Kerr had been asked to claim and hold Bristol, and he had.

Until now.

"Aye. That's exactly what I expect. I've no reason to lie to you, Sir Bryce."

"You mean, you've no reason to lie again. I already caught you in one untruth today." They both looked outside to see the rain had slowed to a steady drizzle. "Come."

Gladly.

She struggled to put on her wet boots and then scrambled out of the shelter. Although the rain had slowed, it was still falling, but the worst of the storm seemed to have passed.

Catrina shook out her gown and watched Sir Bryce reattach his belt, sliding his sword back into place. Try as she might, she couldn't pull her eyes away as he eased the fine overtunic over his head.

He looked up and caught her staring. Sir Bryce closed the space between them in two strides. Not for the first time that day, they were close enough to be touching. A tingle ran through her for this time, his intentions were quite clear.

5

Bryce felt an overwhelming desire to kiss her. Which was absurd. He despised Lady Catrina...and her family. But he'd hardened to the point of discomfort when she lifted her skirts to remove her boots. He'd seen his share of shapely legs before, but his traitorous body didn't seem to understand that this particular woman was off-limits.

His muscles had tensed at the mention of her betrothed, though he assured himself it was only because the information was relevant to her ransom. What she did after he released her back to Toren Kerr was none of his concern. It was simple curiosity that had made him question her further.

And then she licked her lips.

Despite himself, he could no longer deny that he wanted her. Enemy or nay, he responded to Lady Catrina for what she was, a beautiful woman who didn't yet know her own appeal.

He would not kiss a Kerr.

Turning from temptation, he instead untied their horses. "We'll head back to the manor for you to change."

"You still want to visit the village today? With me?"

Bryce helped the lady mount and turned to his own steed.

"Aye, I need to speak to the blacksmith. You're welcome to stay at the manor, however."

"To be locked up again? Nay! I'll accompany you."

"Then let's go." He was used to issuing orders but found himself shorter with her than most. Understandable, given her surname.

Neither spoke on the ride back to Bristol Manor. The cursed rain that had forced them to take shelter finally stopped. Having given strict orders for her escort, Bryce waited for Lady Catrina, passing the time by inspecting the manor's progress.

After less than a week, the courtyard already looked much like it had before the raid. Although not overly large, the manor itself was a sound building capable of defending itself. He planned to build on that and also expand the gatehouse to include a guardroom. Camaraderie between members of the garrison was as important as their training.

Luckily, Bristol's wool trade didn't appear to have suffered during their absence. The lucrative trade allowed their tenants to hunt without paying fees, an admittedly unusual arrangement. His father had always taught them that unhappy tenants or servants reflected on the lord who ruled them.

A hefty ransom would allow them to start building sooner.

"Now there's a sight. The Slayer, daydreamin'."

Bryce grunted in response. If Thomas expected a response, then he could use his given name.

"Back already?"

"Not exactly," answered Bryce.

A brood of hens squawked nearby.

"Coming back to life," said Thomas.

Indeed. The manor was almost fully staffed. Servants' children once again played alongside meandering livestock. The only evidence of their raid was the lack of a head cook. But Bryce would not rest until their defenses were strong enough to protect them from Clan Kerr.

"So did you make it to the—"

Thomas froze as the large, iron-studded oak doors opened. Lady Catrina walked through the entrance of Bristol Manor as if she were its lady. The only evidence to the contrary was an armed guard at her side.

Her sodden, mud-stained dress had been replaced with a modest royal-blue riding gown with an attached hood. More noble-looking than the wood nymph he had sat with at Bristol Sprout, Lady Catrina turned every head in the courtyard.

Although she didn't seem to notice people staring. Instead, she looked straight ahead.

At him.

He couldn't take his eyes from her.

"My lord…Sir Thomas," she greeted them properly.

Thomas's bushy eyebrows drew together as he assisted Lady Catrina onto her palfrey. No doubt Bryce would answer for this outing with a litany of questions later. He'd intended to keep their captive confined to her room, and now he was going on an outing with her.

Mounted, Bryce angled back toward his steward. "So you agree it would be wise to move the blacksmith's forge from the village closer to the manor?" he asked, hoping to distract him—and convey that their outing had a legitimate purpose.

"Aye, my lord. The old buttery has interior walls and would be a good location, I think. You're planning to speak to the blacksmith?"

"Aye." Turning toward his captive, he motioned for her to follow, leaving his friend staring after them.

If Thomas was confused, Bryce was even more so. Not only had Lady Catrina called him "my lord" for the first time, but she also sat atop her beloved Davie with a smile serene enough to make an abbess jealous.

She was up to something.

He set the pace deliberately slow to allow for discussion.

"Tell me." His tone was harsh, but he'd spent the better part of his day deciphering the motives of this woman.

"I'm not sure what you mean, Sir Bryce."

"Precisely. Why was I 'my lord' earlier and am 'Sir Bryce' now?"

The silence was punctuated only by the sound of the horses as they rode through wide open fields of marshland grass still glistening from the storm.

"I would not shame you in front of your men."

"Why not?"

It made no sense. *She* made no sense.

"It would not help my cause."

That much was true.

"From your lips, my title sounds like a condemnation. My given name will do," Bryce said.

That managed to surprise Lady Catrina Kerr, and he found he liked keeping her off balance.

"Very well, *Bryce*. I'll ask for the same courtesy."

She was asking for acceptance. *That* he could never give her, no matter how beautiful she was. But to follow her own logic, angering her would only make his life more difficult. He needed the lady in one piece to ransom her back to her brother.

"Very well, Catrina."

Although it was just a name, using it felt too intimate somehow. As it should. Such informality was typically reserved for family and close friends.

It had been a mistake.

Spurring his horse forward, Bryce forced Catrina to do the same as they made their way toward Bristol's village.

CATRINA WATCHED as vast moorlands gave way to fertile fields being plowed as they rode past. With Lady Day well behind them, work had begun weeks earlier to prepare the pastures for the sowing of spring crops. The land here was virtually indistinguishable from Brockburg. The plough teams pulled by oxen could just as easily be across the border in Scotland. Why must men make enemies of each other when they were so much alike?

Sir Bryce rode alongside her, never once glancing her way. Even so, there was no way she'd escape him, and she wasn't stupid enough to think she could survive the ride back to Brockburg alone.

But there was one person who could help.

After their impromptu visit to Bristol Sprout, Catrina had assumed Sir Bryce would rescind his invitation to accompany him to the village. He'd wondered at her good mood earlier, she knew, but it had been impossible to contain herself. Although Catrina couldn't get much information from Elise, the maid had revealed that her countryman still remained in the village.

Fergus.

With his help, she could get back to Toren before her brother did something rash.

Large for a manor the size of Bristol, this village was Catrina's favorite thing about England. Idyllic. That was the first word that had come to mind when she'd arrived three years earlier, and she still thought it described the place perfectly.

Of course, it was a border town, which meant it was never truly safe.

Sir Bryce led them to the stables, where a groom took both their mounts. Catrina had to hurry to catch up to the brutish knight who was back to being surly.

"Where are we going?"

He didn't even bother to acknowledge her question.

"Bryce."

His name felt strange on her tongue, but at least it got his attention. He turned as she caught up to him.

"Catrina?"

Lord, his eyes were blue.

"You're fairly running."

No answer.

Father Simon always said, despite her sinful mouth—as if it were her fault she'd been raised by brothers—she had the patience of a saint. If he ever witnessed her dealings with Sir Bryce, the priest may form a different opinion.

"Mayhap you didn't hear me." She couldn't keep the sarcasm from her voice. "Where are we going?" She *must* see Fergus.

Bryce took a long breath as if *he* were the one short on patience. She had done nothing but ask a simple question.

"Listening clearly isn't one of your strengths."

He walked away.

Catrina noticed the strange looks, but she'd expected them. Most of these people knew her, and they likely understood her plight. Which was why she decided now was as good a time as any to stand her ground.

She didn't move.

He passed two thatch-roofed houses before realizing she wasn't following. When he stalked back in front of her, his expression was no longer stoic.

"What…is the problem?"

"*You.*"

And now he was going to kill her. She'd managed to stay alive until this moment, but the look in his eyes—blue fire—told her she'd pushed too far.

So be it.

"Catrina." He ground out her name as if it pained him. "Perhaps you would enjoy the loss of your freedom?"

If only she could close her mouth long enough to think through her actions. If she wanted to find Fergus, angering the Englishman was not the way to do it.

"Nay, my lord. Continue." She gestured for him to resume his ungodly fast pace, but he refused to budge.

"I will know the cause of your ire."

She had certainly never thought it possible, but Bryce was actually more high-handed than all of her brothers combined.

"If you must know..." She chose to ignore the fact that he rolled his eyes. "I don't like being ignored."

He stared at her as if she were a simpleton.

"Well?"

"You are my prisoner, Catrina."

She was well aware of that fact.

"People are staring. We will continue this conversation at a later time," he said.

And they were. A few people had been watching them before, but they were quickly becoming the center of attention.

Bryce turned toward the forge without another word. Lifting her skirts, Catrina was left with no choice but to follow along like a biddable miss. As they approached the blacksmith's shop, the sounds of clanging metal became louder. The black anvil on the wooden sign hanging above the entranceway was hardly necessary. Catrina watched as the sign swayed back and forth in the wind. A sudden wind chilled the air, prompting her to raise her hood once again.

"Bryce?"

Just before entering the forge, he turned. Why was he looking at her so strangely?

"I'd like to speak to the alewife." And before he could refuse, she hurried to add, "She's just right there—" she pointed to a house not far from where they stood, "—and I promise to stay there until you're finished with your business."

She really didn't think he'd let her go alone, but he conceded.

"Go. But Catrina—" he lowered his voice and leaned toward her, "—don't do anything foolish."

She wouldn't, today.

"If you do," apparently, he wasn't satisfied with her nod, "I will hunt you down. And when I find you, there'll be no mistaking you are my prisoner and not a guest of Bristol Manor. Do you understand?"

"Aye, I understand."

She hurried away before he could change his mind, slipping into the brewhouse across the way. Please, by the grace of God, let Fergus be inside. He was the alewife's assistant, and had been for these many years.

"My lady!"

The alewife, Mary, nearly dropped her large copper pot in her haste to get to Catrina. The large woman engulfed her in a hug, and the smell of mashed malt filled her nostrils. Toren had often accused Catrina of spending more time in the alewife's house than at the manor.

It reminded her of home. Unlike Brockburg Castle, Bristol Manor did not have its own brewhouse. And Mary reminded her of Brockburg's brewer, the closest person she had to a mother.

"Are ye alone, my lady?"

All that time spent working with Fergus had left a mark on the Englishwoman's speech. Fergus, a Highlander, had found his way to Brockburg at the tender age of four and ten. The son of a freeman, a peasant farmer, he'd formed a quick friendship with Toren and had accompanied him to Bristol.

Toren had spent the better part of three years, since the day Catrina had arrived, urging her to return home. He'd always known the Waryn men would attempt to reclaim Bristol. It was only a matter of when. They'd established long ago that Fergus would remain, at least for a time, in the event of an attack.

"The new lord is at the forge." She wrinkled her nose at the thought.

Mary wiped her hands on an apron that must have been white at some point.

"Come sit, a new batch is soaking."

She'd love to reacquaint with her friend, but there was no

time. Bryce could be along any moment. Catrina grasped Mary's hands and implored her to understand.

"Mary, I need to speak to Fergus. Please tell me—"

"He's helpin' in the fields again today, mi'lady. Since the raid, they be shorthanded. They need crops even more than ale these days. The supply grows thin."

Damnation to hell.

"I'll get 'em a message."

She couldn't tell Mary she needed his help to escape Bristol. While the alewife likely suspected as much, she would not endanger Mary by sharing her plan.

"Nay, I'll speak to him another time." But when? Every day she stayed here placed her family in more danger.

"Sit."

She knew arguing with the woman was pointless. When Mary wanted her way, she got it. Catrina sat at the simple wooden table and accepted a mug of ale. Putting down her hood, she took a hearty sip of the best brew in Bristol. There were other brew-houses, but Mary supplied the manor and was a master of her craft.

"The lord be treatin' you well?" Mary sat across from her, the welcoming smile on her plump face a relief from Bryce's surliness.

"Aye. Well enough."

"I told ye, my lady. I've known the Waryn boys since they—"

"I know, since they were babes suckling at their mother's teat." She added in a whisper, "Apologies, Father Simon."

"Beggin' yer pardon for saying so, but yer always begging that stodgy Father Simon's pardon. If I've ever a mind to travel to Scotland, it will be to box the man's ears."

Catrina laughed. "Box the ears of a priest?"

A movement in the window caught her eye. "Speaking of men without mirth."

Catrina had suspected he wouldn't trust her for long, but his conversation with Bristol's blacksmith must have been an especially short one. She'd only been in here for a moment.

As usual, Bryce did not look particularly happy.

THE BLACKSMITH MUST THINK him mad. Bryce didn't know what he had been thinking to allow Catrina to visit Mary unescorted. He'd changed his mind almost immediately. After making short work of informing the man the forge would be moved to the manor, he'd immediately excused himself to the alewife's house.

Blessedly, he could see through the small window as he approached. It was irrational to think she'd have gone far, which was why he'd agreed to her request before taking the time to consider it. But as he stood in the entranceway, he let out a deep breath and watched Catrina's interaction with Mary.

She was his captive. His enemy. She should be afraid for her life. Instead, she smiled easily and laughed with the alewife, acting again as if she were the lady of Bristol Manor.

He entered without knocking, ducking into the entranceway. "It's time to leave."

The women looked at him, both of their smiles disappearing.

"Good day, my lord." Mary scrambled to her feet and curtsied.

"Good day, Mary. It's nice to see you." And it was. He'd always liked the alewife. Both she and Evelyn had been widowed in the same raid many years ago, a bloody battle that had prompted the building of the wall that now surrounded Bristol Manor.

"And you, my lord."

In the last two days, he had visited every home in the village, getting reacquainted with Bristol's people. With the exception of a handful of Scots whom Thomas had spoken to more than once, all of the villagers were Bristol natives, born and raised. Although he and his family had always been well liked, it was only after speaking with them that he felt comfortable in his new position.

Oddly, it seemed his people had acclimated to Clan Kerr fairly easily. Including Catrina. That they welcomed their rightful lord was a relief.

"Lady Catrina," he said.

The curious woman drank the remainder of her ale before following him out. He'd never met anyone quite like her. She had the manners of a lady but acted, at times, like a man. It intrigued him.

He wanted to comment on her relationship with Mary or her preference for ale, but he said nothing. She was a Kerr, and he'd do well to remember it.

Unfortunately, she had no such qualms about speaking to him. "Did your meeting go well?"

He walked ahead so he wouldn't have to look at her. His traitorous body stirred nearly every time he glanced her way.

"So we're back to that?"

Aye, we are. Bryce had planned on a longer visit. He would do well to check with the miller about the discrepancies Thomas had found in the amount of banalities they were owed. But he needed to get away from Catrina. He didn't like the familiarity that was growing between them. Or maybe it was the fact that he *did* like it that worried him.

"We're leaving so soon?"

He grunted in response and helped the stable hand prepare their horses. He had no intention of interacting with her for the remainder of the day.

They rode back in silence, Catrina obviously realizing she would not get a response from him. By the time they returned, the sun had dipped below the horizon. Bryce took no chances—he escorted her to the manor and then walked her above stairs himself.

"See that she is fed," he said to the guard who followed them.

He turned toward the stairs.

"Wait! My lord, please."

He knew he should walk away, but his body didn't heed his mind. It turned toward her instead.

"Can I take supper in the hall?"

"Leave us," Bryce said to the guard.

The armored knight walked away as promptly as he had appeared. The moment they were left alone, Bryce knew this was another mistake.

"I don't trust you, Catrina. You have every reason to attempt escape and none to remain here as my prisoner."

She swallowed hard. He could sense her nervousness.

"Please, Bryce."

Every damn time she said his name, his cock stirred. She was so beautiful. And obviously an innocent. He had never expected his enemy to have a body made to be touched. Skin so smooth he ached to feel it under his hands.

Aye, being alone with her was a terrible idea.

"For supper. And only when I'm in attendance. Otherwise, you will remain in your chamber."

She blinked, her dark lashes a bold contrast to the creamy white skin of her cheeks.

"Do you understand?"

She was so close he could reach out and touch her.

"Aye."

And then she smiled. Perfect white teeth, a mouth so sensual she'd no doubt instinctively know how to use it.

Unless she's already practiced with her betrothed?

"Have you kissed a man before, Catrina?"

She was clearly puzzled by his question. As was he. He hadn't intended to speak the words out loud.

"Aye."

Aye?

"Your betrothed?"

"Nay, never."

He wasn't thinking straight. His loins ached, and his hands

itched to grab her around the waist and pull her toward him so she could compare his kiss to that of this unnamed man and find it superior.

But he wasn't some untried lad who couldn't control his impulses. He was lord of Bristol Manor, a man whose sole purpose was to keep his brother's...his...inheritance safe. From *her* family.

He walked away and called back to her. "Don't be late."

A SHORT TIME LATER, Bryce entered the hall, which smelled of roasted duck. A full staff, or as close to one as could be expected, prepared for the evening meal. Rich tapestries now hung on the walls, telling tales of English military battles and hunts. They had arrived yesterday in a wagonload of supplies courtesy of Lady Sara. The roaring fire in the massive hearth at the southernmost corner of the hall made the interior of Bristol Manor more intimate than the one at Kenshire, but just as inviting.

And now it was his home again. This time for good.

"Kind of you to change for supper, my lord." His new steward approached, freshly washed. A rarity. And he wore a new surcoat.

He had not bothered changing for the meal. "Who am I to impress. You?"

"Your people, my lord."

Bryce rolled his eyes. "You know my name. Use it."

"Lady Sara would not approve of your attire."

"Another reason not to take a wife." He changed the topic. "Have your eye on a maid then, Thomas?"

The steward immediately glanced at a serving girl placing mugs and iron spoons on each of the trestle tables.

"Not sure what you mean, ol' man," he said. His grin told another story.

"Good for you, Thomas. After the hell I've put you through, you deserve a bit of fun."

"And what about you, Bryce? Don't you deserve the same?"

Without thinking, he looked toward the stairs, and damned if she didn't materialize before his eyes.

Catrina wore the same gown as earlier, but her hair was unbound. It was neither braided nor covered and cascaded over her shoulders in waves of reddish brown.

Lady Catrina Kerr, the sister of a man he would either ruin or kill. Maybe both. He had lied to her about the contents of her brother's message. Her family knew she was safe at Bristol and the answer he'd sent back had included a ransom note. There was a good chance Toren Kerr would pay to see his sister returned, but an even better one he'd choose to fight instead.

Bryce welcomed either.

"What is she doing, Bryce?"

A fair question. "Dining in the hall."

Thomas stroked his beard, clearly wanting to say more but keeping his mouth closed. His forbearance was a welcome surprise. Bryce couldn't understand his own reasons for inviting her, which meant he certainly couldn't explain them to Thomas.

"Good eve, my lord. Sir Thomas."

Her smooth, velvety voice greeted them so prettily. But in the day they'd spent together, Bryce had learned one thing about the lady. She was clever. She had an ulterior motive for every word, and giving her any freedom was likely a mistake. And yet here she was, in his hall, greeting his steward as politely as a gentle-bred Englishwoman. Something about Catrina made him act much more impulsively.

"I shall seat myself at— "

"The lord's table," Thomas finished.

Bryce gave him a sharp glance. He may have invited her to dine in the hall, but she was still his captive.

Thomas frowned at him until he finally nodded to Catrina. She glided toward the head table.

"What the hell were you—"

"Me? You question *my* motives?" Thomas answered him in an undertone. "Bryce, you can scowl at me all you like. But you invited her to dine with us. And while she may be a Kerr, she's also a lady. You can see for yourself, the woman is respected. Admired. It serves no purpose to publicly humiliate her."

"Thomas, she's a goddamn prisoner."

"Aye, and one who likely gave the orders in this very hall just a few days past. You asked her here, not I."

His friend was insolent, but as usual, he was also right.

"Fine, she dines with us. But her privileges end there."

"Whatever you say, my lord."

"You can wipe that grin from your face, Thomas."

"As you command, my lord. But she dines with you, not us. I've an errand to run with Hugh, if you'll remember. That is, after I arrange a late night meeting with a certain serving wench."

He watched Thomas walk away and glanced toward the dais. Catrina looked very comfortable in the seat next to his. She obviously did command respect despite the fact that she was Scottish. And an outsider.

He should never have allowed a visit with Mary.

So why did you? And why is she drinking ale at the lord's table and not locked away, alone?

The only answer he could summon was appalling.

6

She did it!

Thank you, St. Clare. If not for the storm this morning, she and Bryce would never have been forced to sit alone together for so long. They would not have been forced to talk, and she'd likely be sitting in her room right now.

Wait...was it wrong to thank the saint for *bad* weather? Catrina's tutor at Brockburg, a monk who'd educated an entire generation of Kerrs, had a long-standing argument with Father Simon about the notion of praying to a saint for personal gain. Nevertheless, their priest made it a common practice. When the Feast of St. Martin arrived each year, he fervently prayed to St. Clare for good weather.

Who would have thought she'd miss the man so much?

God, please help me get back home. I'll do my best to think before I talk and curb my "wee foul tongue," as your servant Father Simon is fond of saying.

"Thank you," she said to the servant who filled her mug.

She may have convinced Bryce to give her some freedom, but if the look he gave her as he approached the dais was any indication, she may have celebrated too soon.

"You'll ask permission to speak to anyone but me."

"The hell I will!"

That was not well said.

Bryce's eyes widened. Clearly he wasn't used to being spoken to in such a way. Why did she insist on angering him when she should be endearing him to her instead?

She may despise him. Hate everything about him. His arrogance especially. But unless this man began to trust her, she could count this day as the first and last she'd be allowed outside her chamber.

"What I mean to say, my lord, is that your request seems rather extreme."

Bryce didn't bother to answer. Although he sat next to her, he faced the crowd of knights and retainers in front of them.

Typical.

"Where would I go?" She accepted a linen towel from a male servant whom she didn't recognize and wiped her hands. "Shall I try to walk back home and wait for your men to recapture me? Or perhaps I'll ask the groom very sweetly to borrow Davie for a quick jaunt back to Scotland? Or maybe request assistance from the brigands I'm sure to meet along the way—"

"That's enough."

If any of her brothers ever spoke to her with that tone, she'd have more than a few choice words for them. But if she wanted get back home to actually *see* her brothers, Catrina would need to hold her tongue.

It was the hardest thing she'd ever done in her life.

Well, with the exception of traveling to Bristol to beg her stubborn brother to allow her to marry Graeme. Toren had been spitting mad, but she'd made it clear she intended to hold her ground. And she was still here.

A trencher of roasted duck and quince pie was placed before them. She was expected to share with him?

"Is your steward joining us?"

"Nay. He and my uncle Hugh left for..." His voice trailed off.

Of course. He didn't trust her with any information. She didn't blame him.

Bryce nodded for her to eat.

Catrina broke off a piece of choice meat and placed it in her mouth. She tried to be delicate but was ravenous. It was only when she realized Bryce was watching her rather than eating himself that she paused.

"I'm hungry."

"I can see that."

And there it was again. The faintest of smiles.

A shiver started in her gut and made its way down to her core. It was the strangest sensation. She swallowed, in awe of Bryce's transformation.

The smile had relaxed the hard lines of his jawbone and softened his blue eyes. Though he was still fierce-looking, the slight smile made him seem more approachable somehow. She suddenly had the strangest desire to touch him. To see if he was indeed human.

The smile slipped away, but it wasn't replaced with his usual scowl. He looked as if he wanted to devour her as readily as she had the duck.

"Your hair is as black as the earl of Hell's waistcoat," Catrina said.

Bryce threw his head back and laughed. Honest to God, the man actually laughed.

Catrina wasn't the only one surprised by such a sound. Nearly every head turned toward them, some gaping openly at the deep sound of their lord's pleasure.

She couldn't help but smile as well.

"Where did you acquire such an expression?"

He wouldn't like the answer. Instead, she silently asked forgiveness and promptly lied. "Father Simon. Brockburg's priest."

It was near enough to the truth. Toren and Father Simon were extremely close, after all.

"He must be an unconventional man, this Father Simon, to speak thusly?"

Bryce finally began to eat as Catrina took a healthy swig of ale.

"You could say that. He tries his best to "tame" us."

"Us?"

"My brothers and I. Father Simon says he took up permanent residence at Brockburg to save our souls."

That much was true.

Movement in the back of the hall caught their attention. Two men stood and faced each other, poised to fight.

Bryce stood.

"Never—" Every person in the hall turned toward his raised voice. Though loud enough for all to hear, it wasn't quite a shout. "—raise a hand in my hall. Violence has no place here. Either sit, take your quarrel outside, or remove yourself permanently from Bristol Manor."

From their dress, Catrina could tell the men were both knights. Big men whose sword arms would likely be missed if they chose to leave. But there was no mistaking Bryce's tone. His threat was not an idle one.

They sat. One of the men moved to another table.

Bryce sat slowly, still watching the men.

They both reached for the trencher at the same time.

Their fingers touched.

Bryce was looking at her the way he had before she blurted out her ridiculous comment about his hair. And, Lord help her, she didn't want to look away. He was so serious. And so incredibly handsome.

He was also strictly off-limits.

Bryce pulled his hand back and reached for his mug instead. They ate the rest of the meal in silence.

"A refill, my lady?" asked a serving maid.

She was loath to go back to her bedchamber prison, but he clearly wanted her to leave. The way he'd pulled away from her hand told her as much.

Instead, she readily agreed to more ale.

"Why are you here?" Bryce asked. He pushed his large wooden chair back slightly, turning toward her. Her gaze fell on the tanned chest that peeked out from an opening at the front of his loose shirt. Did the man ever wear a surcoat? Or armor for that matter? He dressed more like a peasant than a noble.

She blinked. *What was his question?*

"Your brother was ordered, as you say, to take and hold Bristol Manor, but why are *you* here?"

Oh, that.

"Toren refused to relent on the issue of my betrothal. I thought perhaps he would be more agreeable in person."

"And so you traveled to England, to an unsafe holding in the Borderlands, to convince him otherwise?"

"We're in Scotland, not England. Aye, it seemed to be the only way to convince him."

"Did it work?"

"Not exactly."

Bryce's blue eyes narrowed. "Not exactly?"

"Not yet."

"How long have you been at Bristol?"

"Three years."

The new lord of Bristol choked on his ale.

"Three years? The man is likely married already by now."

"That hardly matters, does it, *my lord*? I can assure you leaving Bristol with my life has become more of a priority than getting married."

"Catrina." His voice was so deep, her name on his lips mesmerizing. Catrina shifted in her seat, unnerved by his intensity. "You will not be harmed. I'm sure you know that."

She did. It was her brother she was worried about. Wisely, she held her tongue. That was not a topic that would endear her to her captor.

"Graeme is not yet married." He had written to her brother just the month before, asking to visit Bristol. To visit her.

Bryce leaned forward with one elbow on each knee. "I will not harm you. But understand this. Your brothers' actions saw my home taken. Nay, don't argue that fact. It's been in my family for three generations. Bristol is *my* home. Not yours."

Catrina was prepared to dispute that particular point, but somehow she knew it was a good time to stay silent.

He leaned toward her and reached under the table. *What was he about?*

"Here," he said.

He reached back up and took her hand. She drew a sharp breath. The warmth and strength of his grip as he splayed it atop her own sent a shiver down her core.

Bryce guided her hand under the wooden table directly in front of her until she felt the faint carving.

"What is it?" she asked.

"A mark my brother and I left behind. And not without repercussion."

He pulled his hand from hers as abruptly as he took it.

Catrina drew a deep, steadying breath.

"Your brother will pay handsomely for your return. When he does, your prospects for marriage will be limited. This Graeme deSowlis of Clan Scott may be the only choice you have for a husband."

God's bones, what utter nonsense! "Is that supposed to comfort me? The prospect of seeing my clan in ruins?"

He sat back in his chair. "You want to marry a man you think you love. Raise the family you never had. You should be pleased."

What an insufferable, arrogant...Englishman. "Do you think so little of your own family that such a prospect would please you? What of *your* brother? *Your* sister?"

So much for not angering him.

"What do you know of my sister?"

"Only that you have one. You forget I lived here for the past three years. I know more about you than you think."

"A fact that would be hard to forget as my sister lived modestly those years with my aunt and uncle, not having any other home to speak of."

A fact she was sorry for but didn't say so aloud.

"And yet you're unafraid of me. Why?"

Indeed. Why? From everything she knew of the Waryn brothers, she had every right to be terrified. Both had reputations as fierce warriors and excellent swordsmen and were reputed to be undefeated in a tournament. But she also knew from Evelyn, among others, that they were neither cruel nor quick-tempered.

"You would never harm the person who could make you rich enough to fortify Bristol Manor."

She managed to surprise him.

"How did you know—"

"Because it's what Toren would do. You aren't very different, you and my brother."

It was true. After her mother's abandonment, she had harbored ill feelings toward everything English for a time. But that had been nothing more than ignorance. Her countrymen and the Northumbrians were virtually indistinguishable.

"I don't kill innocent women." His expression had not changed, but both of Bryce's hands were balled into fists.

He was furious.

"I'm sorry, Bryce. My brother is sorry. My clan is sorry. The man who killed your mother was—"

"Enough!" He stood and, without a backward glance, walked away.

Halfway across the hall, without even bothering to turn around, he called out, rather unkindly, "You are in England, not Scotland."

Catrina watched him speak to her guard at the entrance of the hall. What had started as a promising day was ending in disaster. If the possibility of her escape meant curbing her tongue and feigning deference, by Christ's toes, that's what she would do.

Starting tomorrow.

HER CHANCE NEVER CAME. On the next day or the one after it. She sat on a wooden stool in her new quarters—a bedchamber reserved for guests. The entire room would take up only a quarter of the lord's chambers. At least a small window afforded a view of the manor's courtyard. She spent most of her time watching Bristol Manor come back to life.

Bryce had been smart to move her here. She would never harm Elise, but putting a knife to the chambermaid's throat might convince her to switch places with her. If only she had access to the weapon which lay in a chest in her own bedchamber just down the hall. Or what used to be her bedchamber.

She'd never admit it to him, but Toren was right. She should have gone home long ago. When it became clear her brother would not relent—the new bitterness he felt for Clan deSowlis ran too deep—she should have returned to Brockburg. And yet... Bristol had come to feel like home. Oddly, she was judged less here for being Scottish than she was back home for being half English. Of course, much of the turmoil following the initial attack on Bristol had settled before she arrived. The people here lived too close to the border to harbor resentment. Accepting a new lord was easier when there were no other options.

This morning, Evelyn had been given leave to visit, to check on her head. But she'd given her no news or information. Worse, she'd had nothing but praise for the new lord.

With each passing hour, Catrina worried more about her brothers' safety. She knew they had to be planning a rescue, but the manor was too well-fortified for an outright attack—now more so than ever. Which meant one of them, likely Toren, would risk his own neck to sneak inside.

She could not allow it. Unfortunately, she wasn't in a position to prevent the fool's errand at the moment.

Much to her dismay, if she wasn't dreaming up ways to escape, her thoughts kept returning to a certain blue-eyed lord. The heated way he'd looked at her during their last meal gave her chills even now. She despised the man, of course. He was everything she imagined him to be.

And more.

When the door opened, she wasn't surprised to see Elise there. But when two male servants entered behind her, Catrina bounded from her seat and hugged the maid.

"A bath! Oh, thank you, Elise. Thank you."

They placed the wooden tub in the only area large enough to accommodate it and were followed by a stream of servants carrying copper pots of water. Once the bath was filled and the men were gone, Catrina wasted no time stripping down with Elise's assistance. When she sank into the tub of steaming hot water, her cheeks tingled with unshed tears of joy.

She closed her eyes. "Thank you, Elise."

"Only followin' orders, my lady. Knock when you're finished, and they'll remove the tub." The maid handed her lavender-scented soap and laid two drying cloths on the bed.

Why would Bryce order a bath for her? It took a small army to fill the tub with hot water from the kitchens. After their ill-fated meal, he'd refused to see her, refused to allow her to sup in the hall. Why offer this kindness?

She distracted herself from thoughts of the Englishman by scrubbing every inch of her body with the sweet-smelling soap. When finished, she dried and dressed in the simple cotton chemise Elise had left behind. She must have fetched it from her chamber.

Thank you, Elise!

She knocked on the door, which was answered by her ever-present guard. Unlike the new lord, this man always wore armor, his chainmail tunic and ominous sword a constant reminder, as if she needed one, that she was indeed a prisoner.

After the tub was removed, Catrina sat on a bench near the small fireplace that warmed the room and tried to concentrate on her escape plans.

The door creaked opened behind her.

"They removed the tub, Elise—"

"Did you enjoy your bath?" She whipped her head around at the deep male voice, certainly not Elise.

"My lord! What are you doing—"

"I asked you a question, Catrina."

Remembering her vow, even in the face of his high-handed tone, Catrina walked toward Bryce and answered simply, "Aye, very much."

She should be embarrassed by her state of dress. Should chastise him for being here alone, and while she was in her chemise. It was indecent. Scandalous.

Instead, she said nothing.

"I want to apologize." His expression was a familiar one. Indifferent. Fierce. Certainly not apologetic. Freshly washed himself, his hair still damp, Bryce looked every inch the warrior.

"Apologize?" For someone often accused of talking too much, she was unable to formulate a thought. Her pulse raced as he walked toward her.

"I made a vow, promised to allow you supper in the hall. A Waryn does not break his word." He was mere inches from her now.

"And I'm sorry for speaking of your mother. I—"

"No more."

What did he want her to say?

"We won't speak of the skirmish. Either one of us. There's

been no word from your brother, so I'm unsure how long you'll be here. But for this to work, there can be no discussion of rights or raids. Is that understood?"

Oh, she understood fine. Only one person was allowed an opinion, and it wasn't her. God, he was insufferable. Taking a deep breath, she prayed to St. Clare for patience and agreed.

"Aye, that's—"

He moved so quickly, she didn't have time to think. Before she knew what he was about, Bryce pulled her toward him.

His hands grasped her face, and he placed his lips on hers.

When she put her hands on his chest, it was to steady herself, not to push him away. Because she wanted this. Had dreamed of it.

"Open your lips, Catrina."

Open her lips? A potential suitor had stolen a kiss from her once, but it had been so fleeting she hardly remembered it. But she'd certainly never opened her lips. *That* she'd remember.

She looked into his eyes. They pleaded with her, pulsing with the same desire she'd seen there before their argument at supper.

And, Lord help her, she was going to do it.

7

What the hell was he doing?

As he stared into her eyes, Bryce knew without a doubt it was wrong. He'd done a good job of avoiding her for these past two days, which was easy with her being locked away. She was his captive. The sister of a man he planned to destroy.

But he *had* promised to allow her meals in the hall.

The Scot bewitched everyone around her. Evelyn, Thomas, even her guard. All begged him to allow her some freedom. She could not possibly escape, they argued. Alone. Unguarded.

And much to his dismay, he couldn't stop thinking of her. The most comely servant at Bristol Manor had invited him to her bed the evening before, and Thomas had gaped in disbelief when he overheard him declining her offer. The girl paled in comparison to the vixen who stood before him now, trying to decide if he were mad.

He knew this was a mistake when he told the guard to inform him when her bath was finished. He knew it when he told Elise to retire for the evening. And he knew it now, standing before her, the sweet smell of lavender invading his senses. But after spending two sleepless nights assaulted by visions of Catrina's full lips and expressive eyes, he'd decided it was the only way to clear his mind.

One kiss.

The muscles in his chest tightened under her hands as her lips parted ever so slightly. He knew she desired him but didn't know if she would admit it. To herself or to him.

Bryce needed no further invitation. He lowered his head and gently coaxed her mouth wider with his tongue. Catrina's eyes flew open. He stroked his thumb on her cheek to calm her and then moved his hand to the back of her head, pulling her closer and fitting his mouth fully on hers. His cock strained as she responded by opening for him. She may have kissed a man before, but never like this. Bryce showed her with his tongue what he expected, and Catrina didn't disappoint.

Fully understanding, she touched her tongue to his. More firmly, he moved his mouth against her, shaking in his need to bring her even closer. She moved her lips across his with abandon, and the deep kiss quickly spun out of control.

He moaned, the pleasure so intense from a simple kiss. He couldn't get enough. Pressing her against him, he was sure she could feel his need. Only a thin chemise and his trousers separated them. She would not understand, and it wasn't for him to show her.

Bryce had bargained for a kiss. Not for this unchecked passion which threatened to overcome them both.

He pulled away.

Her chest rose and fell, her lips still wet with his kiss. Hair unbound once again, she looked like the same nymph who had stared at him with a full measure of bravado and wide-eyed innocence in their shelter from the rain.

"That, my lady, was a kiss."

"Why?"

Indeed, why?

"I wanted it. You wanted it."

"I did not." She stepped back, as if to avoid his touch. He wanted nothing more than to reach out and pull her back, proving otherwise. But nothing good would come of it.

"Oh aye, you did."

And he wanted to do it again. But one mistake did not mean a second was inevitable. He had achieved his purpose. Now he could concentrate on what was important.

"Have no fear, my lady. It won't happen again."

He didn't want to see her face before he turned to leave. But he did. She was confused. Rightly so, he supposed. It hardly made sense to him either.

"I will see you tomorrow at supper, Catrina."

Without a backward glance, he walked away.

By St. Thomas's blood and all that was holy, what was that?

Catrina could have stopped him at any time. But she hadn't. He was right, of course. She closed her eyes at night, hating herself for imagining his lips on hers. Hating herself for the way her heart had nearly beaten out of her chest when she realized what Bryce was about.

Lord help her, she desired her captor. The man who'd run her family from their home. Granted, it was a home they'd never wanted. Their family may have had a claim to Bristol from generations ago, back when the area was firmly in Scottish hands. But if Toren hadn't been ordered to take it, he would not have spread his clan so thin by venturing this far south.

She lay for what must have been hours before finally falling asleep. When the sun rose, Catrina was startled to find Elise at her bedside with a light repast. It wasn't like her to sleep so late.

"A fresh shift and gown, my lady."

"Thank you, Elise. But I'm hardly in need of it for a day spent—"

"You're to be given freedom of the manor, my lady."

Catrina stared at Elise, whose smile told her it was true.

"For meals, you mean?"

Catrina allowed Elise to assist her in getting dressed. She slipped on her soft brown leather shoes. Her brothers teased her mercilessly about them. But when her gown was long enough and none could see her feet, why did it matter they were as old as she? They continued to serve her well.

"I'm not sure. My lord awaits your presence in the hall."

Bryce. She hadn't expected to see him again so soon.

"My hair, Elise. Leave it down."

"Aye, my lady."

They finished quickly, Catrina nearly running down the spiraling stairs which led to the hall in her haste to confirm it was true.

But when she entered the hall, Bryce was nowhere to be seen. The trestle tables were stacked against the sides of the walls. It was later than she had realized.

The new steward, Sir Thomas, approached and offered his arm.

"A walk, Lady Catrina?"

She took the Englishman's arm, and he led her past the buttery. They stepped out a door leading to the manor's gardens.

When she arrived at Bristol, the garden had lacked a woman's touch. While bountiful in food to supply the kitchen—cabbages, onions, leeks, and medicinal herbs for the healer's use—it had contained no flowers for pleasure. With her brothers' blessing, they'd added azaleas and primula. Lattices strewn with roses now adorned the plain stone wall and hedging surrounding the area. It was her favorite part of the manor. A retreat she needed now more than ever.

Catrina had spent many hours in their garden back home when she was young, escaping the jeers of mean-spirited children who had reveled in taunting her for her mother's absence and heritage.

"I understand you're responsible for this."

The burly man by her side reminded her of their clan's tacksman back home. A warrior, to be sure, but with a certain amount of gentleness out of place among his peers.

"I've taken some responsibility, aye. But the garden existed before I arrived, and will continue to do so long after I leave."

Sir Thomas stroked his beard, looking at her with a mixture of confusion and, mayhap, admiration?

"Bryce is in the training yard. He asked for me to stay behind until you awoke. You're not an early riser, my lady."

Typically she was. But thoughts of a certain kiss had kept her awake long into the night.

"Why am I here rather than locked up in—"

"You have free rein of Bristol Manor, including its gardens. But all else is off limits. You're not to venture outside the walls, and you'll be guarded at all times. You're also not to speak to anyone except your guard, Elise, and myself."

Despite his harsh tone and the harsher restrictions, Catrina was elated. It was more than she could have hoped for.

"Is that all?" She attempted to hide the excitement bubbling inside her. It wouldn't do for Bryce's man to think her too happy about the altered arrangements.

"Aye. And my lady." Sir Thomas gave her a harsh stare—a warning stare—but she wanted to hug the man who'd just given her freedom. "Do not try anything foolish. It will only get you locked back up for good."

She bowed her head, imitating the simpering ladies who visited Brockburg in the hopes of claiming Toren's hand in marriage.

Sir Thomas seemed satisfied. He returned to the manor, and a guard appeared at the entrance. He stared straight ahead as if he didn't see her, but Catrina sensed the faintest of smiles on the knight's face.

She was free!

Wasting no time, Catrina braided her hair and tied the end with a ribbon she kept in an inside fold sewn into her gown. The garden needed tending, and she needed a new plan. She'd learned from Elise her old bedchamber was occupied by the steward, so retrieving her knife was not a possibility. And it seemed unlikely she'd be able to get word to Fergus anytime soon.

There was no help for it.

She would have to find an opportunity to leave, alone. With God's own luck, she'd make the three days' ride to Brockburg without encountering any of the reivers and brigands that roamed the Borderlands. It was a risky plan. Mayhap a foolish one. But it was the only one she had.

8

"That's enough."

Thomas helped the young knight to his feet, giving Bryce a look that clearly conveyed his displeasure. His old friend was the only non-relative who could talk to him that way and live to tell the tale.

Men trained all around them—experienced knights and young lads—some with bows and others honing their skill with the broadsword. The activity reminded Bryce of the many days he and his brother spent here.

Bryce knew he pushed the men hard. Mayhap too hard. But he firmly believed the training yard was not a place to relax your guard. As much as he had hated leaving Bristol to become a squire, his father had been right to force the issue. It was an honor to train under a man whose reputation as a fighter was unrivaled. Lord Huntington was so fond of fighting, he'd commissioned a list to be constructed near Huntington Castle with berfrois so grand they could accommodate as many spectators as the spectacle attracted.

As a leader, the lord was disciplined, if not rigid, and expected much of his men. He often said, "Every battle is real." Whether in training, in a tournament, or on the battlefield, Lord Huntington demanded the same. No quarter was given on account of it being "practice."

Bryce sheathed his sword, took off his helm, and handed it to his young squire. Though Bryce was sorry Reginald returned with Geoffrey, this lad had nearly as much promise.

"Come with me."

He handed a cloth back to the squire after wiping his face. Thomas fell in step with him as they left the clanging of swords and shouts of men behind. They walked in silence toward the newly repaired wall, which enclosed the entire courtyard. Here, where the men had so recently hammered and split stone to fix the gaping hole, it was now eerily silent. Only distant shouts from the training yard and the occasional song of the curlew above them broke the quiet.

"What do you see, Thomas?"

His friend looked in every direction.

"I see mighty fine repairs on a wall that was very recently vulnerable to attack. I see your future. My future."

Bryce remained silent.

"Knowing you, I also see a vulnerability."

"Where?"

Beyond the jests and burly build, the man who could be his brother was also intelligent. Bryce had no doubt he would understand his concern.

"Everywhere," Thomas said. He walked closer to the wall and laid his hand on a grey stone, knocking at it as if it were a door.

Bryce agreed. "What was vulnerable for the Kerrs will not be any more secure for us. Sara and Geoffrey's men give us the kind of strength not seen in a manor this size, but we need more men of our own and a second wall built around this one."

"A second wall?"

"Do you remember the Welshman you met at Bristol?"

Thomas nodded. "I do. A friend of Geoffrey's—"

"Aye. And he told Geoffrey and I about a new design at Beaumaris in Wales. An ingenious plan actually."

Bryce began to pace. "An outer wall, lower than the inner, to give the watch a clear view of—and a clearer shot at—the enemy."

They'd never seen such a construction, but a second line of defense could mean the difference between victory and defeat.

"I've been looking at the books," Thomas said doubtfully. "The wool trade is still lucrative, but—"

"We have to make it work," Bryce insisted.

His pulse raced, as it did every time he thought of his mother and father, lying dead among strangers. They had died alone. They had died because of him.

"What happened in the raid will never happen again here, Thomas."

"Perhaps if the girl's ransom—"

"He'll never agree."

"You don't know that. It's said Toren Kerr—"

"Is a strong leader and fair man," Bryce finished. "From what I've heard, I'm not surprised at how quickly Bristol's people acclimated to such a man."

"Bryce, you're making my head spin."

He stopped and turned toward the manor.

"If what we hear is true, we can expect a surprise attack or an attempt at treachery. I do not believe he'll be funding our new wall."

"We have his sister."

"Aye, which is why I want no visitors while Catrina resides at Bristol."

"But you said— "

"I know what I said. Things have changed."

"You mean Catrina now has the run of the manor."

Thomas was one of the people who'd begged him to allow the lady out of her room for God's sake. "You agreed it was the right thing to do."

"Bryce, listen to me." Thomas was rarely so serious. "I think you were right to allow her more freedom. And it makes sense for everyone to be vigilant. But we can't just sit around and wait for her brother to attack."

"What do you suggest?"

Bryce knew what was coming. His uncle had suggested the same. While taking Toren Kerr's sister hostage had seemed like a good idea at the outset, as more time passed, it only made them a target. Hugh had argued that re-building Bristol should be the new lord's priority. That a ransom was a much-needed, but unlikely, boon.

"Let her go. I know your brother—"

"No."

"The manor is fully staffed, the wool trade booming. Repairs are complete. You're talking about building another wall. Bristol is in a position—"

"To be attacked again." He was losing patience.

"To prosper. Are there vulnerabilities? Yes. But holding Catrina Kerr hostage is not helping anyone. Send her back."

"*Thomas.*"

Thomas's voice rose in a rare display of temper. "Your desire for revenge will kill you, Bryce. And only you, if you're lucky."

"If you were any other man—"

"But I'm not. I'm the one you met at Huntington on the very first day you arrived as a squire. The one who watched you learn to fight and slay ladies' hearts as fiercely as you did opponents on the battlefield. Who saw what that Huntington bitch did to you. The one who knows that, despite what you think, you're as deserving to be lord of Bristol Manor as your brother."

Bryce's hands shook.

"And I'm the man who saw what happened to you after your parents' death. The one who knows you somehow think it was your fault."

What Bryce could see of Thomas's face behind that bushy

beard was red. It was the angriest he'd seen his friend off the battlefield.

"So yes, I know how much you want revenge. I also know you talk of peace, but with that girl here, with your need to destroy her family, there will never be peace at Bristol."

He didn't know what to say.

"I know you want to strike me, but you won't. That's the problem with you." Thomas abruptly turned and walked away.

Bryce took a deep breath, attempting to calm himself. He began walking the length of the curtain wall, trying with every step to get his mind off Thomas's words.

There weren't enough turrets for the lookouts to keep watch in every direction, which had allowed them to make their clandestine attack. That, and so many other fortifications, needed immediate attention. More men would arrive any day from Kenshire to begin some of the work, but they needed to sustain themselves without the help of Kenshire's men or income.

He couldn't get his friend's words out of his head. Thomas was right, of course. But that didn't mean he'd send the girl back. He knew the Kerr chief would have received his answer by now, which meant they could fully expect some kind of attack. To avoid any mistakes, watches were added where no lookouts existed. It was a temporary solution to the permanent problem of living so close to the border.

Then there was Catrina. He'd thought kissing her would solve that problem. He hated what she was. Who she was. But when he closed his eyes at night, it was her face he saw. It had likely been yet another mistake to allow her freedom of the manor. Or perhaps he gave her too much credit?

No, she had a determination, even ruthlessness, not typical of a female in her station. Raised by men—*Kerr* men—she was anything but typical, and he had to admit that her unconventional thinking was part of her appeal. Hell, who was he kidding? Nearly everything about her appealed to him, except her surname.

Could he do as Geoffrey and Thomas suggested? Just let Catrina go? Allow their parents to go unavenged?

Never.

He had watched his brother change since meeting Sara. But *he* would not go soft. He'd been trained at Huntington to defeat any man in battle, and no one had bested him in a fight since. He would not start turning tail now.

Catrina would remain at Bristol to root out her clansmen.

And then he would destroy them.

"I ASSURE YOU, there is nowhere for me to go down here."

Catrina rolled her eyes at the guard who had started to follow her into Bristol's buttery. It wasn't much of a plan, but it was the best one she had at the moment. She knew from Mary they'd been low on ale before the attack. If they needed more, perhaps she could convince Bryce to allow her a visit. She really did not want to try riding to Brockburg alone, but time was running out.

For a moment, she thought her guard would follow her into the cramped space. Catrina walked by dozens of wooden wine barrels and hundreds of candles toward the steps at the back of the small storage room. Her oil lamp gave just enough light to help her navigate the staircase that led to the beer cellar below. The cold room was so much smaller than the one in Brockburg. She was actually scared the first few times coming down here. Dark and cold, it was a room built purely for function, not comfort.

But in a manor the size of Bristol, everyone had multiple roles to play, including her.

Back home, at Brockburg, her brother Alex told everyone who would listen that she could master any craft after the first attempt.

Alex.

She missed her brothers so much. They must be frantic with worry.

She lifted the lamp to count the wooden barrels. Just as she'd suspected.

What was that?

Muffled voices, she realized, just above her. Catrina turned toward the entrance as the voices gave way to a pinpoint of light. Someone was coming. Her guard? Catrina's heart raced. There was a reason she hated it down here.

"Catrina?"

Bryce. He ducked through the entrance, and soon the face she hadn't been able to exorcise from her mind was staring back at her. The candle he held cast a soft glow on him that made him appear less fierce, almost human.

"What the hell are you doing?"

Until he opened his mouth.

"Well, being that I—"

"A straight answer, please." The ceiling of the small beer cellar just inches above his head made Bryce appear even larger. And he didn't sound happy.

"I'm counting beer barrels. We need a new supply. Perhaps I should—"

"We have people to take care of our ale supply." His eyes narrowed. "What are you planning?"

Had the cellar smelled damp, like moss, just moments before? Because now it had the distinct smell of sweat. And sandalwood.

Nay, that was Bryce's smell.

Lord help her, she needed to get out of here.

"Excuse me, I—"

"What...are you planning?"

He stood at the entranceway, blocking her exit. He must have come from the training yard.

"Were you training to kill my brothers?" she snapped.

His grimace deepened. "Aye. And every other Kerr who dares step foot at Bristol."

"I am a Kerr. Do you plan to kill me? If Toren doesn't pay the ransom?"

She knew the answer. Or thought she did. But why tempt fate by asking?

She tried to remember to breathe. His eyes were so light, they looked almost translucent.

"What shall I do with you, Catrina?"

She did not want him to kiss her. Bryce Waryn was her captor. Not her suitor, for God's sake. She did *not* want him to kiss her.

"Answer me."

"You are the most arrogant, insufferable—"

He grabbed her arm and pulled her close to him.

"Watch your tongue, wench. Remember who you are."

She was forced to look up. "Oh, I know *exactly* who I am."

A slight movement in his jaw was the only indication he heard her.

"I would appreciate if you could decide between locking me back in my chamber or allowing me freedom. Your suspicions are tedious."

"And warranted."

That much may be true, but she certainly couldn't say so. If she gave him any indication she planned to escape, Catrina had no doubt she would be locked up quicker than a wee fairy spotted by a human.

She backed up. It was too hard to think when standing this close to him.

"I know you think I plan to escape. But I'm no fool. Even if I could manage to smuggle Davie from Bristol unnoticed, I'd never make it alone without being set upon by reivers. Or worse."

Bryce switched the candle he held from one hand to the other and cocked his head. "What's worse than a reiver?"

He didn't smile exactly, but his face softened. Was he teasing her?

"Do you tease me?" Catrina was surprised to feel herself grinning from ear to ear, but then *she* had no apprehension about showing pleasure.

"I don't tease."

"Why are you always so serious?"

"I'm not having this conversation in a beer cellar."

"Ah, but you are." She lifted her lamp to reveal the wooden barrels sitting on the shelves as quiet witnesses to their conversation.

This time she was sure a hint of a smile revealed itself.

"Because I find conversations with my captive, the sibling to our family's greatest enemy, somewhat...difficult."

"Rubbish. You are the same around everyone. As if you're preparing to chop off someone's head at any moment." Lord help her, she actually enjoyed teasing him. It was so easy. And to her utter surprise, he actually answered her question.

"It is my role. To be the serious one."

She assumed he meant among his siblings. Comparing himself to his older brother appeared to be one of Bryce's favorite pastimes.

"But why?"

He actually seemed to consider her question.

"As a child, I'm not sure. Geoffrey was raised and knighted at Bristol. I was the first son my father could afford to have fostered. The wool trade business did well, and as my father's influence continued to grow, I was sent to Huntington."

"What happened at Huntington to make you so suspicious?"

"Why do you ask so many questions?"

Catrina wasn't sure. She'd tell her brothers it was to find a weakness she could exploit. But she was afraid that wasn't the real reason—or at least not the only one.

"Tell me, why does the lady of the manor assist the alewife?

Advise the gardener and assist the healer in a home that isn't even hers?"

Evelyn always did talk too much.

"My brother's home is my own. And I already told you—"

"Aye, I know what you told me."

They stared at each other, not moving. Barely breathing.

"Come."

The spell was broken. Bryce turned and began to climb the stairs.

Catrina followed him through the storage room and buttery and finally into the great hall. Preparations for supper were already underway. She stopped. She had thought he was going to kiss her down there. Was she actually disappointed? It was good that he had not. Certainly she hadn't wanted a kiss.

Of course she hadn't.

Bryce stopped, said something to her guard, and left the hall.

He was too suspicious to allow her a visit with the alewife. That plan had failed, and it was clear Fergus's help was lost to her. There was no way she could reach him undetected.

But Bryce had given her another idea. If she had to cross the border alone, so be it. But she could not do it on foot. And there was only one way he'd allow her to ride Davie.

She would be leaving Bristol Manor tomorrow. And Lord help her because she needed Bryce's assistance to make her plan work.

9

Bryce paced at the entrance to the manor. He didn't know if he was angrier at himself or Catrina. She goaded him at every turn, but he sought her out.

What did he care if she counted barrels of beer? Never mind that a lady should prefer wine. Or should be ignorant of the needs of the manor's stores. Had Kerr's household been so short-staffed?

She was limited to the manor and under guard, but for some reason he had felt compelled to assure himself of her whereabouts because she was so valuable.

Nay, because he wanted her. That blasted kiss had done nothing to temper his desire.

He turned when a retinue of men rode through the gate. Horses' hooves kicked up dirt and mud as they approached.

They stopped in the bailey, not far from where Bryce stood. The new captain of his guard dismounted and took off his helm as Bryce joined him. Thomas came up from behind as the courtyard erupted in chaos. All of the soldiers spoke at once, and Bryce had to strain to hear what was being said.

"The captain only," he shouted above the noise.

"My lord, a band of reivers attacked the village. The damages are being assessed—"

"How do you know they're reivers?"

Helm in hand, the captain walked toward him. "They stole at least six head of cattle before they were noticed. One of the locals said it was the Riley brothers."

Bryce smiled. It was good to be home.

"They did no damage, I assume?"

The fierce, unmarried knight from Kenshire who had elected to remain at Bristol with Sara's consent was not yet acclimated to the true border region. He appeared understandably confused.

"No, my lord, but how did you—"

He was cut off by another group of riders. Thomas answered the man's question.

"The Riley brothers, and their ancestors before them, have been raiding Bristol for centuries. Am I correct, my lord?"

This would be as much enjoyment as he'd had since...he refused to think about her now.

"Aye, Sir Thomas. For centuries."

Bryce addressed the group of men, some from Kenshire and others who had committed their swords while he and his brothers were on the run. Only a handful of knights remained from before the Kerrs' attack—those who had refused to serve the new lord.

Most of them appeared confused.

"Get back on your horses, men. Thomas, get the hound." He looked for his squire and found the boy who had followed him from Kenshire. "Light armor. Quickly."

Preparations for the counter-raid were organized in minutes. Those foreign to Bristol continued to look uneasy. They would understand soon enough.

"Gentleman," he called to the group of twenty or so riders. "We search with hound and horn for the thieves who dared disturb the peace of Bristol. We recover our cattle and take any man along the way to assist with our search or be named as a reiver. But above all, no one is to be harmed."

He looked to the manor and watched the group of men and women peering out through its doors. Catrina was not among them, but he ordered Thomas to stay behind just in case this proved to be a ruse, though he doubted that was the case. More likely his long-time rivals and uneasy friends had finally decided to welcome him home.

With a nod to his steward, who looked none too happy about the arrangement, Bryce led the mounted men through the courtyard and out into the open moorland. With any luck, they would return before the first course of supper was served.

WHEN BRYCE and his raiding party did not return, Catrina asked for the meal in her room. She needed time to think. But Sir Thomas had convinced her to take supper in the hall, and now she sat beside him on the dais, struggling to concentrate on their conversation.

"My lady?"

"I'm sorry, Sir Thomas. You were saying?"

The steward eyed her warily. She must pay more attention.

"You seem distracted this evening."

With good reason. "Aye, sir. I've much to think about with my home overrun by Englishmen and—"

Damn! She'd never learn.

"And?"

He didn't seem to take offense.

"You're very unlike your lord."

"I hope that's true, my lady." Sir Thomas shoved a morsel of spiced meat into his mouth.

"You don't wish to be compared to Bryce?"

Barely finished chewing, Thomas shook his head. "There is no comparison to that man."

The pride in his voice reminded Catrina that he spoke not just as the steward but as Bryce's best friend.

"How did you meet?" She was genuinely curious to know how two men, so obviously opposites, had become so close.

"At Huntington. We both squired there. It didn't take a scholar to know Bryce was destined for greatness. I may be the fourth son of a baron with no prospects of my own inheritance, but my father is well-connected. He sent me there because Huntington only fostered the best. Even among the brightest and strongest knights, Bryce stood out."

"Mayhap that is true. But he is always so stern."

"He came to Huntington a serious young man. And after the incident with—"

Sir Thomas must have realized he'd said too much. His brows furrowed and he gave more attention to his food and drink than finishing his thought. Every attempt to pull the story from him was met with a grunt or a shrug.

"Shouldn't they be back by now? I thought you said the raiders were more friends than enemies?"

A hot trod, or counter-raid, was both legal and expected. When only minor goods were involved, some raids even led to celebrations when the beasts were re-captured. While the mood had never been so light here at Bristol with her brother in charge, she understood the difference between a dangerous raid and one that was meant as a nuisance or for sport. They had similar *relationships* with border clans back home.

Home.

According to their king, this was her family's home, the land theirs by right. And even though she'd spent only three years here to the twenty she'd spent in Brockburg, her heart tugged a little at the thought of leaving.

The sound of doors slamming open was replaced with shouts

as a group of wet and muddy men entered the hall. The rain must have returned, along with the raiding party.

And Bryce.

She spotted him easily. The tallest among the knights who made their way inside, he was also the only one not smiling. The raid must have gone well if the others' mood was any indication.

Once all eyes were on their leader, Bryce put a fist in the air, and the entire hall erupted in cheers. Mugs slammed on the tables. Shouts quieted down only when Bryce lowered his fist. It seemed the somber mood that had followed the exchange of hands back to the Waryns was finally lifted. The only remnant of the last five years was her presence.

It was sobering, that.

Reminding herself of her new plan, Catrina set her mind on how best to proceed. Bryce was cunning. Even if she got him to agree to a ride the next day, she still needed to find a way to administer the sleeping draught to him. Evelyn had left just enough to put him down for a few hours.

It had been left for Catrina to use, of course, but she'd saved it, knowing it may come in handy.

Steeling herself for a long evening, she straightened her back and waited for Bryce to approach. After many slaps on the back and a whispered word to Thomas, he sat down beside her.

Her shoulder sank as she realized it would be the last formal meal they shared. Tomorrow would either bring her release from this English prison or have her locked back in the bedchamber.

Or worse.

"I take it the raid was successful?"

"Aye." Not even a glance in her direction.

Concentrating on his meal, Bryce ate slowly. Everything he did was so deliberate. She couldn't help comparing him to Toren. Fierce and frightening to their enemies, both men constantly took measure of everything around them. It was a trait she admired, but one she had never embodied.

Normally, she would ignore Bryce's reticence. But not tonight. "Does that mean it's safe at the moment?"

His sharp glance told her it was the wrong thing to ask.

"It's never safe this close to the border. You of all people should know that."

His sharp tone was not warranted. She itched to tell him exactly that, but goading him into an argument would not do. "I do, but this confinement—"

"You're my prisoner, Catrina. Not an honored guest to be entertained."

Thomas looked up. The steward had shifted to Bryce's right and, until now, seemed fairly intent on his own meal. He gave Bryce a puzzled look.

Lord, this might just kill her. "I apologize for angering you." If her brothers were here, they would have choked on their ale at this display of submissiveness. "But surely if you accompany me on a short ride—"

He cut her off once again. "No."

No? That's it? She tried to slow her racing heartbeat. It could not be as simple as that. He could not say no! Her escape depended on it.

"Take her, Bryce. I will see to the training."

Thomas. Bless the man.

"You can shut your mouth anytime, Thomas."

The steward laughed easily, slapping Bryce on the back. "And why would I do that? 'Tis much more fun goading you." Ignoring them both, he grabbed a fistful of bread and ate like a man who hadn't seen a meal in months.

Bryce closed his eyes and locked his jaw. Was a ride with her so abhorrent to him? Was there so much to be done he couldn't spare a few hours?

"Very well."

Thank you, Thomas!

Trying not to appear elated, she calmly took a sip of wine.

Though she preferred ale, their best stores had been opened to celebrate the successful raid, and even she wasn't immune to fine French wine.

"Splendid. I will pack a mid-day meal." And before he could argue, she added, "Thank you. It will be a wonderful afternoon."

He looked at her, eyebrows raised. Had she gone too far?

She met his gaze. He was angry at her, although she wasn't sure why. But all that mattered was that he had agreed, thanks to Thomas. Tomorrow she would be free.

10

Today she would go home. Catrina didn't have any delusions the ride would be an easy one. If she made it to Brockburg, her brothers might well kill her straight away for having attempted such a foolish thing. But there was no doubt her clan was mounting a counter-attack, one that would see more of her people, perhaps even some of her family, killed. And she didn't wish for the people here to endure another raid.

Catrina didn't have a choice.

Packing a small bag with the sleeping draught, she debated fetching her dagger for the hundredth time. On the one hand, if she were caught in Thomas's room, her plan would be foiled. Bryce would have no doubt she was up to something. On the other, it would be madness to attempt to cross the border alone without a weapon.

Who was she kidding? It was madness even with one.

Davie was well-equipped for the mountainous terrain, and she had no fear of navigating the trickier sections. She was fairly certain she knew the path, having taken deliberate notice of the landmarks on her journey to Bristol. While it was some time ago, Catrina's memory never failed her. She would find the way.

Which left the brigands. Knights looking for sport, border reivers without good names to uphold... She was a fool to attempt such a thing.

But she had a plan.

There was one thing men on both sides of the border feared.

Witchcraft.

Father Simon was oddly fascinated by the healing arts and had made them a study of sorts. Like his contemporaries, he believed in both white and black witches, but he did not agree that magic was an act of the devil or a crime against God. He believed it was nothing more than a heightened form of healing, though one that could be twisted for nefarious use or personal gain. And without any other defense, she would use that knowledge against any potential attackers. It was terrifying to think about being punished as a witch, but such a fate would be preferable to the possibility of rape. Or worse.

Dressed in a thin linen chemise and hose which stopped at her knees, Catrina waited for Elise to assist her. The tight-fitting kirtle she planned to wear for the ride could not be managed without the maid's help.

As if on cue, a quick knock was followed by a creak as the door to her bedchamber opened.

"I'm sorry, my lady. The babe refused to eat this morn. 'Tis the second day now."

Elise rushed into the chamber, worry etched onto her young face.

As Catrina stepped into the kirtle Elise extended to her, she thought about the cook at Brockburg. Her first babe had become quite ill after refusing to eat. No wet nurses had been available, so she had searched for information on the babe's condition. Finding nothing, she'd finally taken a cue from the stable master.

"Soak a rag in milk and feed the bairn that way. Bread will work too, but not as well."

Elise stopped lacing her sleeves and stared at her.

"If she refuses to eat, she'll die. Either find a wet nurse, or do as I tell you." Though her words were harsh, her tone was gentle. The girl needed to understand the importance of following her instructions without questioning how she knew such a thing.

"A rag, my lady?"

"Aye, a rag. I may be Scottish, but I am not a fool."

Elise continued to help her dress. Though she looked skeptical, Catrina thought it likely she would follow her directions. Sometimes a tone of confidence was all it took to sway people.

Finally prepared for her fateful ride—Bryce had told her to be ready after the morning meal, which she had skipped in anticipation—Catrina gathered a few belongings, but not enough to cause notice.

"Go home, Elise. I can manage myself. Feed your bairn."

"Thank you, my lady. The meal you asked for is packed."

Her stomach lurched. Bryce might think it odd that she'd insisted on packing a meal, but he *couldn't* suspect anything. Too much was at stake.

"Thank you. Now go!" She wanted to say more, thank the girl for assisting her these past weeks. But saying goodbye to the wrong person the wrong way could raise suspicions.

With a bob and curtsy, the maid left her chamber. Catrina smiled, remembering how reticent Elise had been on her first visit. They'd come far together.

Catrina walked into the corridor and met the guard at the top of the stairs. With a nod, she walked past him, moving down the stairs and into the hall. Bryce stood there, watching her. Catrina could feel his gaze as soon as she turned the corner. Whether it was because she planned to escape that day or for some other reason, she wasn't sure. But there was no doubt Bryce affected her in a way that no one man had before him.

Even Graeme. The man she'd always planned to marry. Before their families' falling out, she and Graeme had practically grown up together. All of the other girls had begun to notice him as a man before she had. To her, he was still the boy who used to pull leaves from her hair. She wasn't sure exactly when she had decided to marry him, but he was everything a girl could want for a husband.

Graeme deSowlis was handsome. Honorable. And now a chief. And he accepted her wayward ways and wanted to have a family of his own too. But there was no denying he had never once made her feel warm all over the way she did in this moment.

In typical fashion, Bryce wore no chainmail or surcoat, just a simple, unadorned tunic and hose. His boots were higher than normal, perfect for riding. With a start, Catrina was mortified to realize she'd been staring.

He didn't smile, exactly, but Bryce's slightly upturned lips meant she had, indeed, been caught.

"I'm ready for our ride," he said.

His double meaning was obvious. As she moved closer, the subtle changes in his face told her what she'd begun to suspect. Or what his kiss confirmed.

Bryce desired her.

She had spent her whole life around men, so she knew full and well what his look meant. But, if she were being honest, she'd never felt it for herself. Never quite understood what all the fuss was about. Of course she'd known handsome men, like Graeme. But this overwhelming feeling inside her gut, the sensations that assaulted her every time the English knight was in her presence, they were new for her.

"I can see that." By God's bones, that was certainly not the right thing to say!

"I'd return the compliment, but telling a Kerr she looks lovely would be akin to asking the King of Scotland to dine with me."

Was he teasing her? If there was one thing her brothers had taught her, it was how to verbally spar.

"No need for a compliment. You misunderstand me. I spoke only of your servants' apparent readiness. Not yours."

His confusion quickly gave way to comprehension, which was her cue to exit the hall.

She could feel his presence behind her. They entered the courtyard, their horses already saddled and waiting for them. Once mounted, they left the bustling manor behind. Catrina realized with a lurch that this was likely the last she'd see of it—and she hadn't said so much as a goodbye to the people she'd grown to love over the past three years. Though she'd been tempted earlier to seek out the healer, Catrina had decided against it. If anyone sensed the finality in her parting and put Bryce on alert, her escape would fail.

Without wanting to draw attention to herself, Catrina allowed Bryce to set the course and pace. She would have preferred to head due north, of course, but any destination would have to do.

They rode in surprisingly companionable silence, and she soon realized where they were headed. Bristol Sprout. Her mind raced as she calculated the distance between the waterfall and the river which would lead her toward home. Although the border between their countries had been established years earlier, no one recognized it. Both sides' shared urge to push boundaries was why they found themselves in this current predicament. Only an abbey and a few miles of hilly countryside separated Brockburg from the supposed border between England and Scotland. Her goal was to get to the abbey and send word to her brothers from there. She knew she could travel faster this time, without any retainers to slow her down, than on the single other occasion she'd made the trip. The only question was, once she managed to get away from Bryce, could she reach the abbey by nightfall?

"Look familiar?" Bryce slowed to a stop, dismounting.

As the rush of water pounded in her ears, Catrina thought back to the day they were trapped here, the rain forcing a companionship she could no longer deny.

She should hate him. Instead, her heart raced in anticipation every time he was near.

"Aye." She handed her reins to Bryce, whose expression was as soft as she'd ever seen it. He was beginning to trust her, she realized. Now, when the moment she intended to break that trust loomed. The sooner she escaped, the better. The thought of sleeping under the stars with nothing but wolves and brigands as company terrified her.

Catrina would have asked him to spread their meal and join her already if she hadn't feared it would raise suspicion. It was too soon. Better to bide her time.

As they approached the waterfall, Bryce pulled off his tunic and laid it on a rock.

"What are you doing?" She had a bad feeling she already knew the answer.

Rather than respond, Bryce tugged off his linen shirt and tossed it atop the tunic.

She could not breathe. His back to her, Catrina could only stare at the display in front of her. Every inch of his torso looked as if it were sculpted from rock. And then he turned.

His broad, tanned chest was that of a warrior who trained with the broadsword often. She'd seen a muscled chest before. Three brothers who did nothing but hone their battle skills for most of the day should have prepared her for this, but it had not. It was so very different to see *him* this way.

She tried so hard not to notice the path of muscle that seemed to pull her eyes lower, toward the opening of his…no he was not!

"You can't be serious?"

The lout chose this moment to reveal a wicked smile. A small, sensual smile that told her how much he enjoyed her discomfort. He began to unbutton his breeches, and Catrina suddenly knew what it meant to be weak in the knees.

"If you're offended, look away."

He was taunting her. Of course she was offended. He knew that. What kind of gentleman undressed in front of a lady?

She spun around just in time. Catrina couldn't hear his movements over the roar of the waterfall, but Lord help her, she could imagine what the rest of his body looked like.

Bryce Waryn was magnificent in every sense of the word.

And a cad for subjecting her to such a thing.

When she heard the splash of water, Catrina finally turned to see him in the pool beneath the sprout. Sunlight glinted on his dark, wet locks as she moved closer to the bank of the small plunge pool.

She briefly considered making a run for it, but even though he was submerged at the moment, she knew she wouldn't get far. Bryce never took his eyes off her.

"Join me for a swim, Catrina."

Though his tone told her it wasn't a serious request, at least not much, Catrina imagined herself stripping bare and jumping into the water, sliding her hands over his taut muscles and allowing him to pull her against him.

What is wrong with you?

She should be concentrating on the powder that was hidden inside a pocket in her kirtle. Evelyn had told her it was enough for one good night's sleep, so she didn't worry about the dose. It was getting it in his drink she fretted over.

"Are you getting hungry?" she asked.

He swam to the edge of the water, where she sat on a rock high above him. She had to shout over the sound of the water that spilled into the pool with spectacular force.

"I am."

The look he gave her was unmistakable. She shivered, and the core of her womanhood tightened as his stare lingered. What an odd sensation. She'd never felt anything like it. But truly she had also never seen anything quite like him.

His gaze held hers for a moment longer until he slipped under the water, disappearing from view. The seconds ticked by. *Where was he?* She stood and looked closer for telltale signs of his presence under the water.

Finally, he came to the surface as she circled the area. One look at her face and he actually began laughing. *Laughing!* My God, when he wasn't so serious, the man had an absolute knack for making her lightheaded. The deep sound, so rare and genuine, almost made her feel guilty for what she was about to do. Which was absurd. He was her captor. She had nothing to feel guilty about.

"Perhaps you should turn your back."

She whirled about quickly and marveled at the immediate snicker behind her. This was so unlike the Bryce she'd come to know.

Walking to Davie, she began to unpack the bags at his sides. Eventually Bryce joined her and did the same with his own mount.

Without speaking, they moved to a flat, grassy area in the glade that made a perfect spot for a meal. Laying out a blanket and taking out the cook's finely packed meal, Catrina had a hard time concentrating on the task at hand. It was a perfect, sunny day. They were surrounded by green, mossy rocks and blooming flowers that marked the season. It was lovely. Perfect even.

But she couldn't forget her purpose.

When it came time to pour the wine from the flask, Catrina felt the air whoosh out of her. This was by far the most dangerous part of her plan. Somehow she had to turn his attention elsewhere.

Fortunately, she had planned for this.

"It seems I forgot the sack of bread and cheese," she managed to say. "Can you get it, please?"

It worked. Without flinching, Bryce stood and walked to where the horses were tied. Her hands shook as she reached for the vial, popped it open with one hand, as she had practiced a hundred times, and sprinkled the contents into his glass. There was even time to circle it around a few times before he returned.

Catrina let out a breath.

She had done it. Surely he would drink the wine. The draught was virtually undetectable.

She could see Brockburg in her mind, imagined her brothers' reactions when she strode through the gates. And her family would finally be safe.

BRYCE'S entire body felt heavy as he walked back to their makeshift meal. A goddamn picnic. It was his first, and last.

He'd suspected something was amiss from the moment she asked for this outing. The best way to reveal her plan, he had decided, was to play along with it. He'd been alert for some form of trickery, and his suspicions were confirmed when he watched her slip something into his drink. A sleeping potion? *That* he had not expected, but it made sense.

Evelyn.

The healer had asked his permission to administer the sleeping concoction to Catrina. The cunning woman had saved it instead, and now she planned to use it on him.

He'd actually begun to enjoy himself. Knowing she was already jittery, Bryce had decided to throw her even more off balance. The idea of disrobing in front of her had taken hold during their ride. But the look on her face had almost been enough for him to put an immediate halt to the 'game.'

She'd stared as if she'd never seen a man's bare chest before, which he knew could not be true. Not for a woman raised by men.

By the time he jumped into the water, he was so hard the cold barely affected him.

Aye, the kiss meant to dampen his desire had instead inflamed it. He kept imagining those full lips on his, her breasts cupped under his hands. Thinking of how it would feel to touch them, tease them. Make her nipple harden beneath his fingertips. It seemed he could think of little else.

Taking a deep breath, he closed his eyes and prepared himself to forget how she made him feel. Forget everything save the fact that she was his captive and she was trying to escape.

"Found it." He tossed the sack onto their makeshift table and took the goblet she offered but did not sit down. He would need to dispense of its contents without giving away her ploy.

"Did you hear something?" He carried the offending wine with him to "explore." A safe distance away, he tossed the tainted contents and returned, pretending to drink heavily.

"'Twas nothing but a squirrel," he said. Tilting the goblet toward him so she would not see it emptied, Bryce reached for a slice of cheese and popped it into his mouth.

"Tell me, Catrina, what makes you suddenly so pliable?"

If he hadn't been watching for a reaction, he would have missed the flash of uncertainty. As it was, he saw it quite clearly.

"I'm not sure what you mean."

Oh yes, you are.

"The picnic lunch and agreeable nature that you've yet to display since my scouting party found you unconscious on the river bank."

She was actually close to death that day. If they had not found her—

"I'm usually very agreeable. Being held captive tends to bring out the worst in a person."

Since coming back to Bristol, he'd inquired around the village and learned as much as possible about the lovely Catrina Kerr. "Demure" was one word he had never heard used to describe her.

"Ahh, so you traveling across the border and putting yourself in danger to challenge your Toren's authority in person qualifies as agreeable?"

There it was. The slightly furrowed brows and hard set line of her lips that told him he was in for an earful. It was precisely the reaction he had hoped for.

"How kind of you to remind me of my broken betrothal. So much for your English knightly code of conduct. My *lord.*"

He took another sip of his empty goblet. Bryce didn't have much experience with a sleeping draught but knew their conversation would have to come to an end. Soon. He looked forward to watching her plan unfold.

"My pleasure." And he meant it. Conversing with Catrina was easy. Enjoyable. He could almost forget how much he hated her brother. Under different circumstances, he wasn't sure how he'd feel about the shapely woman sitting so prettily across from him. Likely the same way he felt about most noble-born women. They were off limits, enjoyable to look at, but not to touch. The last thing he needed to distract him from his mission to secure Bristol once and for all was a woman to make him soft. He mistrusted them, and with good reason. Now for a piece of acting…

"Och, you're impossible."

"So I've been told."

He was going to enjoy this. Bryce let his eyes drift shut and then opened them, watching her reaction. Hopeful. Afraid.

He lay down and closed his eyes once again, imagining all the while what it would be like to share this story with Thomas and his siblings.

The sound of the waterfall drowned out her movement, but he could sense Catrina was no longer sitting across from him. He waited another moment and opened his eyes, watching her untie and mount Davie.

And then she was gone. The madwoman truly thought to escape back to Scotland, alone. If she didn't manage to get herself killed, he was going to do it himself.

11

Her heart still pounding furiously, Catrina wasted no time making her escape. The draught had worked more quickly than expected. One minute, Bryce was talking. The next, he was sleeping. The dose was meant for her, and she had no idea how his extra weight would alter the effects. She had at least a few hours, though, and could ride through the open moorland as quickly as anyone.

But could she reach Jedburg Abbey by nightfall? Catrina sped along the river, knowing she risked exposure. If she left the river, getting lost was also a risk, so she decided it was the preferable path. The other option, hiding herself among the trees to the east, would force her to use the tracking skills her brother Alex had taught her. And while he was an expert tracker, she was only passably good at understanding clues left behind by those less observant, and the trees could hide any number of ill-intentioned men. Besides, this was the flattest route home and she needed to be fast. Thank the saints, the highest peaks, Cheviot Hills, were far enough to the west to avoid, but there was at least one incline that would test Davie's skills.

No signs of reivers. Other than the abbey, there was nothing other than a few farmhouses and abandoned pele towers between Brockburg and Bristol. Of course, that only accounted for anyone traveling between north and south.

Better to think of something other than brigands. But not Bryce. If only her traitorous mind would obey. She could hardly reconcile his easy manner earlier.

And those muscles. Dear lord, what a body. She should have been quite scandalized but had instead stared unabashedly. It hurt to think about him waking up alone by Bristol Sprout. He'd hate her, no doubt. Just as she'd begun to break down his walls, she'd ruined it by betraying his trust. But what was a promise made to a person who held you captive?

She would never see him again.

As the open terrain gave way to a thicket of trees, Catrina was forced to slow. Looking constantly in every direction, her heart sank when she spied three riders on her left.

She had two options. Run or stay. On open terrain, she'd put Davie's speed and stamina against the best.

They spotted her.

One of the men pointed and all three sped up. She'd hesitated too long and had no other options now.

Maybe they would greet her and move along?

Maybe Davie will sprout wings and fly to Brockburg.

She stopped when all three riders circled her. Reivers. The hobblers they rode were bred for navigating difficult terrain and their sleeveless leather jacks clearly marked them as thieves of the north. Scottish or English, she couldn't be sure, but their leader carried a flag with the designation of each country on either side. Traitors with an allegiance only to themselves.

"Greetings, my lady."

Maybe they would be nice reivers.

"Are ye lost?"

Scots. Not that it mattered.

"Nay, kind sirs. I'm a visitor to Jedburg and just returning from a ride."

It was an absurd claim, and everyone knew it. They all moved closer. These men would not be letting her go anytime soon. At least, not without some sport first.

"Ye must be tired then. It's a long way from Jedburg." The man with the flag, the tallest one of the group, dismounted and rammed the flag into the earth.

"Stop!" He didn't move toward her. Not yet. But she knew her reprieve wouldn't last for long. Catrina's hands slipped on her reins. A wave of dizziness gripped her. She'd known fear before. At Bristol when she awoke from her injury. When she first met Bryce. But never like this. Somehow she'd known the Waryn men would never hurt her. These reivers, however, were not knights. They were thieves who preyed on both sides of the border, taking what they wanted and giving nothing in return. No clan. No crown. No honor.

"I am a witch." Somehow her voice didn't waver, even when the other two dismounted and walked toward her.

She was trapped.

"Will you put a spell on us?" The leader laughed. He didn't appear at all intimidated.

"Aye. Take one more step, and I will do just that."

The conviction in her voice gave them pause. It was going to work. She knew the superstition of her people.

They glanced at one another, close enough that their stench nearly made her gag. Every instinct told her to flee, to use the advantage of being mounted and get away. But if she were caught, Catrina had no other defense but this one. It *had* to work.

Before she could elaborate, the tall man grabbed her by the leg and pulled hard. Catrina fell into his arms as all three groped her at once. She kicked and clawed at them. "Unhand me!" They were immune to her screams.

A lady, alone, was apparently too tempting to resist.

Suddenly one of the men, whose hand was wrapped around her arm, was thrown backward so forcefully, he nearly took her with him.

"What the hell?" He sounded as surprised as she was.

The others released her and Catrina fell into the ground.

She pushed herself up in the mud, the smell of the wet ground replacing the horrid stench of the men. *What was happening?*

"Stay down!"

It couldn't be. But that voice was unmistakable. She could only see the back of one of the reivers and another lying on the ground. He was bleeding from his shoulder. She shuddered, watching as Bryce kicked one man in the gut and, at the exact same time, thrust his broadsword at the one who'd pulled her from Davie. She couldn't see exactly where Bryce's sword found its mark, but apparently it did. The man's scream was a testament to his injury. Now two of the men lay on the ground. The third apparently thought better of engaging Bryce and ran toward his horse. Sheathing his sword, Bryce watched him go, walking toward her.

What just happened? How did he get here so quickly?

Perhaps she was safer with the reivers. Bryce was enraged, his anger made more ferocious by the sweat and blood mixed on his face. He pulled her up and, without a single word, placed her on his horse. Mounting in front of her, Bryce forced her arms around him and signaled for Davie to follow.

And thus they began a long, slow ride back to Bristol.

She had failed and was very nearly raped. Mayhap would have been killed. She kept her hands from shaking by grasping Bryce's tunic, now stained with the blood of the reivers. Were they dead? She wanted to ask but was afraid to talk.

They rode for what seemed like hours. In stony silence, Bryce expertly navigated the lush green landscape. Border country was dangerous. Tumultuous. But no one could argue the beauty of this untamed land. Instead, with a mounting sense of dread, she watched as the increasingly familiar Bristol Sprout came into view.

Bryce dismounted and fairly flung her off his horse. Gallantry was never his strong suit, but this...she'd never seen him so raw. Bryce's well-controlled emotions were legendary, but his mask of indifference had fled like the third reiver. Without so much as a backward glance at her, he tied both horses and walked away.

She watched as he began to disrobe for the second time that day. Just a few hours earlier, she had marveled at the sensuous sight before her. Now, as the sun began to dip in the sky, casting a warm glow over every part of the glen, she turned from his quick, angry movements. She wanted to wash as well. Although not quite as muddy, and certainly not as bloody, Catrina felt dirty.

And confused.

The same questions kept whirling around in her mind. *How is he even awake? Are the reivers dead? Why do I feel so badly about drugging him? Why do I even care if he's angry?*

Because he had saved her, again. She shuddered again at the thought of what would have happened if he hadn't intervened.

Shoved back into reality by the hand that spun her around, Catrina prepared to defend herself.

BRYCE SHOULD HAVE STOPPED her much sooner, but curiosity had gotten the better of him. Did the woman actually think to ride across the border alone?

As soon as he saw those men, he rode as fast as the terrain would allow. By the time he reached them, Catrina had already been pulled from her horse. Rage unlike anything he'd ever experienced engulfed him. The kind of anger that surfaced every time he thought of the day of the Kerrs' raid.

He would kill each of the men who'd dared lay a finger on Catrina.

Bryce was not usually quick to judge. His uncle and brother, after all, had stooped to reiving to support their family. But the way these reivers had handled Catrina told him all he needed to know about their character.

By the time Catrina was safe and the two men who'd touched her lay dead by the river, the haze of fury that had gripped him began to recede. He regained enough presence of mind to allow the third man to escape with his life.

Although the men he'd cut down had deserved to die, the intensity of his rage was more than a little unsettling. For the first time in his life, Bryce was actually afraid. Not the jittering of nerves that came before a fight or the fear that was natural before a battle. This was a fear that gripped him so deeply, he knew the carefully constructed walls he'd erected since Huntington were slowly being torn down.

By a Kerr.

He couldn't even speak to her on the ride back. He was furious with her. For drugging him. For putting her own life at risk. But he couldn't focus on that; all he could see was the vision of her being surrounded by thieves.

He would not return to Bristol Manor like this. His people needed reassurance that he could keep calm and collected in the face of danger, and he knew he looked like a savage brute. So instead of bringing her home, he rode back to the sprout.

After washing away the blood, dirt, and sweat from his body, Bryce prepared to tell Catrina exactly what he thought of her escape attempt.

But rather than giving her the tongue lashing she deserved, he grabbed her arm and pulled her toward him. Her face was streaked with mud, her hair a tangled mess.

She was beautiful.

Bryce pulled her against his bare chest and brought his mouth down.

"What are you—" She gasped when she realized his intent. But rather than push away, she allowed him the access he desperately needed. His mouth moved over hers, his tongue wasting no time exploring the sweetness within. He groaned as her hands gripped the bare flesh of his back as if he supported her weight to stand.

They felt so small, so soft.

Bryce kissed her, deeply, for as long as he dared. No longer hesitant, she touched her tongue to his. He gladly claimed it. His cock pulsed, begging for release.

When he finally pulled back, it wasn't because he wanted to stop. Just the opposite. If this continued much longer, he would dishonor himself, his family, and the woman in his arms by taking her, consequences be damned.

He didn't, however, let her go.

"What in the hell were you thinking, Catrina?"

Still wrapped in his arms, her face inches away from his, Catrina blinked, one lonely tear forming in the corner of eye.

"I...I wasn't, apparently."

He wiped away the tear, his thumb moving slowly across her face. He kissed the smooth skin where the tear had been. He kissed her cheek, her neck. She leaned her head back, giving him access to the soft, perfect flesh that led...he would not think of it.

"Bryce, how—"

"Nay, not now."

As much as he wanted to understand fully what she planned—he was still incredulous at her audacity—he decided their discussion could wait.

He would not dishonor them both, but he was no monk.

More gently, now assured she was indeed alive and uninjured, he trailed his lips down her neck, over the top of her chest. He kissed as low as her riding gown would allow. And when he reached the offending barrier, layers of clothing inhibiting his progress, he turned his attention back to her lips. He moved his hands under her breasts, cupping them and squeezing gently.

She moaned against his lips and pressed herself against him.

He circled his hips and allowed her to feel his need, even though she wouldn't understand.

He wanted to be inside her. Wanted her more than he ever wanted anything in his life. And that was nearly as terrifying as watching her be manhandled by a marauding gang of border reivers.

"Turn around." His voice was hardly recognizable to his own ears. Thick with desire. Not the typical desire he felt with a willing woman in his hands. This was less controlled, more powerful.

That she did so without question almost stilled his hands. This woman had been through so much. She'd survived her injuries, only to be captured by Toren's enemy. She'd done something incredibly stupid and brave by attempting to escape alone, and now here she was, a captive once again. She had as much right to hate him as he did her. The thought startled him. Bryce had been so focused on how much he despised Toren Kerr that he'd never once considered the fact that she, too, had been wronged.

Now was not the time for such revelations.

He made quick work of the ties at her back. He helped her step out of the gown that was already ruined and tossed it aside. Spinning her back toward him, he crushed her to him, frantically running his hands over every inch of her kirtle. He kissed her deeply, lowering his hands to her buttocks.

Bryce pulled her so close that, if it weren't for his hose and the thin layer of cloth between them, they could be joined. It was heaven…and torture. Her tongue met his every thrust, and as their bodies pressed together, she gave herself over to him completely.

He wasn't so sure he could stop.

THIS COULD NOT CONTINUE. But did one willingly forgo pleasure this intense? It was nothing like their first kiss. This one held the promise of more. And though she knew it was wrong, hated him for making her feel this way, Catrina tilted her head to allow for even greater access.

The muscles she had appreciated from afar earlier that day were now beneath her fingertips. Catrina had understood his intent the moment he told her to turn around. And yet she'd done it without question. The feeling of his strong fingers removing her stays sent surges of pleasure throughout her body, pooling in her core, and her knees almost buckled as he pulled their bodies together. Her head spinning and knees weak, Catrina decided it was futile to deny what was obvious. She wanted him to kiss her.

She was curious.

You've never been this curious about Graeme.

Oh God, her betrothed. Or the man she thought to marry, at least. What was she thinking? This was not right.

Pulling away from Bryce was one of the hardest things she'd ever done.

"Bryce, stop."

And just like that, it was over. He stepped away from her, looking down as the haze of desire lifted for them both.

She stared at his tan, muscled chest. The one that had wielded a sword so expertly against the reivers. She itched to touch him again. She wanted to apologize for the foolish words that had made him stop.

Instead, she reached for her gown. She stepped into it wordlessly and allowed the Englishman to re-tie her laces.

"Have you had much practice at being a lady's maid then?"

She immediately regretted her words. They were meant as a jest, but it sounded more like an accusation.

"Aye, I have."

The lout wasn't even joking. He had taken her seriously and answered in kind. Now she was genuinely curious. "I wouldn't think a knight on the run would have much opportunity for such sport."

She couldn't see his face, but mirth was evident in his voice. "You'd be surprised."

He finished and spun her around once again. And sure enough, Bryce was actually smiling.

"You are much more handsome when you smile." Good Lord, had she really just said that out loud? Instead of taking offense, he raised his eyebrows and smiled wider.

"Alas, another compliment I've heard many times before."

"You are a beast!" Though she tried to look stern, his smile was contagious.

"So you do have a sense of humor? I hadn't thought it possible."

Bryce sighed, his smile fading.

"I keep it well-hidden." And though the words were said lightly, she sensed a deeper meaning. So he did work at being the stone-faced, humorless man she first met. *Why?*

"Did you honestly think to escape back home, alone?"

"Do you honestly think I feel the need to explain myself…to my captor?"

And just like that, they were back to being enemies.

"Suit yourself. But know this. You'll not have the run of Bristol Manor any longer. You can't be trusted."

It was nothing less than she'd expected. And feared.

"Pardon me, my lord, if I don't sit docilely by as you attempt to lure my brother back to Bristol to be slaughtered. Don't bother looking surprised. You're after revenge, and you'll be just as satisfied, maybe more, if he doesn't pay the ransom. It doesn't take a master tactician to understand your motives. But know this. It will not work. Toren will never allow himself to be killed by coming to the aid of a sister who managed to get herself captured by the enemy."

Whether he believed her or not, it didn't matter. Convincing

Bryce that she was nothing more than a drain on his resources was the only plan she had left because there was no way he'd allow himself to be duped a second time.

Which reminded her…

"How are you even awake?"

"That, my dear Catrina, is a good question. One you're welcome to ponder as you sit alone in your chamber waiting for the errant brother you insist will not come."

With that, he spun away from her.

Damn the man to hell.

Because Toren would come. Soon. And it would be the death of him.

12

A week had passed since her failed escape. True to his word, Bryce had locked Catrina back in the small bedchamber with no other company than her maid. Nearly mad with worry, she tried more than once to appeal to Bryce, through Elise, for information.

Nothing. It didn't help that the maid was peeved at her for attempting to leave without so much as a goodbye.

When she wasn't worrying about her family, Catrina's thoughts returned to the very man who imprisoned her. She pictured his muscled arms wrapped around her. His lips on hers.

Would Graeme make her feel that way?

He was nearly as large, a warrior in every sense. The clan chief was handsome and infinitely honorable, insisting he would honor the vow he'd made when they were young children.

Someday, she would be his wife despite their clans' feud. The argument that had turned the Kerr and deSowlis clans from friend to foe mattered little to her. Thinking of herself wed to Graeme at least took her thoughts away from ones that were much more dangerous.

A knock at the door interrupted her thoughts. The normally

quiet Elise burst into the room in a flurry of activity. She had apparently forgiven Catrina for her escape attempt. That her daughter was eating well likely had something to do with the girl's cheery temperament.

"Hurry, milady. You need to be changing for the midday meal." Without waiting for a response, she began looking through the carved chest at the foot of the bed. Pulling out a serviceable dark blue gown, one of Catrina's favorites as she had assisted in dyeing the color herself, Elise descended on her.

"I'm not sure I understand," Catrina thought aloud. Was she really being let out of her chamber? Why?

"The lord requested your presence. And sent me to fetch you. 'Quickly now.' Those were his exact words."

Though she allowed Elise to assist her, Catrina absolutely refused to do it "quickly." She closed her eyes as the maid ran a brush through her long, sometimes unwieldy hair. The air was damp, even more so than usual for spring. A natural wave to her hair that seemed to be worse this time of year made poor Elise's task more difficult.

"Shall I add a veil, my lady?"

Because she was unmarried, Catrina could wear her hair unbound. Most ladies covered at least part of their heads, but she was reluctant to do so. She wasn't sure why, but it just seemed…excessive.

"Nay, and slow down, Elise. There's no hurry."

"No hurry?" Elise bit her lip, looking so worried Catrina laughed and put her hand over the other girl's slender fingers. "Listen to me, Elise. There will always, always, be someone more powerful than you telling you what to do. Take small victories when you can and do it with conviction."

She could tell Elise wasn't convinced. Who could blame her? Catrina rued the freedom her brothers were given that she was not, but Elise had even less than she did.

"Aye, milady."

"I can see you're worried. Come."

She stood, adjusted the gold-braided hip belt, and lifted her gown so that Elise could slip on her favorite soft brown leather shoes.

Passing the guard who hadn't spoken to her since her attempted escape, Catrina made her way down the winding staircase. The first course was already being served. She walked up to the slightly raised dais and, for the first time since entering the hall, looked at Bryce.

Glowering at her as fiercely as he had upon their first meeting, he nodded to the seat next to him. She sat and accepted a mug of ale.

"Your brother received my reply and sent his own. It seems we're at an impasse."

So that's why she was here. To discuss terms. Catrina carefully avoided touching him while reaching for a piece of roasted duck from their shared trencher. Unfortunately, their separation didn't seem to have quelled the tension between them. It was as if invisible spider webs bound them together.

"He refused to pay the ransom," she ventured.

"Not exactly."

That did surprise her. A quick glance at his profile confirmed he was telling the truth.

"He offered to meet to discuss the terms of your release."

Ha! Toren would discuss serving Bryce's head for dinner, but not much else. She could sense he was still looking at her, watching her for a reaction, so Catrina concentrated on her meal instead. What did he expect her to say?

"Look at me, Catrina."

No. She would not be ordered about by him any longer.

"Catrina, I said look at me." His low voice had an edge she'd heard before, on the day of her botched escape. She looked and wish she hadn't. Bryce's jaw was locked, his clear eyes narrowed. He looked distinctly...dangerous.

"Toren is gathering an army."

Somehow she managed to appear calm. Disinterested. An army? Of whose men? How did he know that?

"Oh?" She calmly took a sip of ale. "That's nice."

"It appears his allies have answered the call on account of your captivity."

"Splendid." She took another bite of duck. The cook had done a fine job of spicing a meat she typically disliked.

"We anticipated as much. With one exception."

She refused to give him a reaction. "I imagine you did."

Catrina would *not* look at him.

"A clan large enough to necessitate reinforcements from Kenshire."

Why was he telling her this? She was, after all, his prisoner, something of which she needed no reminder after this last week. Then again, Catrina supposed she had no one to relay the information to. She lifted the mug once again to her lips.

"Clan deSowlis."

She swallowed the ale so quickly it threw her into a coughing fit. She was lucky not to have spilled the contents on herself. deSowlis? Impossible. They hated each other.

She finally met Bryce's intense gaze.

"That can't be." Kerr and deSowlis? Working together? Had Toren asked Graeme for help? Graeme would have requested a betrothal first. Did that mean...

"Am I betrothed?" He, of course, wouldn't know the answer. "And why do you look like you want to murder me?" She certainly hadn't done anything wrong. But it was true. Bryce looked as angry as she'd ever seen him. "And how do you know all of this?"

"You're surprised?" he asked in response.

"Surprised? Were you listening to me when I told you about Graeme? Of course I'm surprised. It makes no sense."

And then it dawned on her.

"You don't believe me? You think what I told you of Graeme was a decoy to keep you from the truth?"

He answered with a frown.

"It wasn't a lie, Bryce. Ask anyone. Our clans have been enemies since an incident in battle."

"I'm asking you. And aye, it occurred to me you may have lied. Lord knows you don't have a propensity for the truth."

Her shock turned to anger. "I don't remember making an oath to the man who captured me. I owe you nothing, Bryce."

"Except your life."

Well, maybe that. What an awful feeling, not having a retort.

"It hardly matters. We're prepared, or will be, for any attack your brother may launch. But this isn't what I expected."

"Oh? How had you hoped my captivity to end? With Bristol's coffers overflowing? My brother dead? How, Bryce? Pray tell me." She didn't care that she'd raised her voice enough that people were staring. She was tired of playing the part of the docile prisoner hoping for any bit of kindness.

"Lower your voice, Catrina."

"Nay, I will not. Tell me, my *lord*. Is this not how a captive should act? Please instruct me on how best to behave. How exactly shall I speak to the man holding me hostage?'"

If he didn't throttle her now, he never would.

Bryce did grab her arm with the pretense of escorting her from the table. Instead, he fairly dragged her from the hall. Most of the retainers they passed were unfamiliar to her, but a few had served at Bristol when Toren was lord. Catrina shrugged her shoulders at one man who looked at her as she "walked" away. Was that concern etched on his face?

Perhaps she had finally pushed him too far. Deliberately goading the man who held her life in his hands was, even for her, a tad dangerous.

Bryce shoved her into the solar. Well, maybe not shoved, but he certainly didn't give her much room to navigate. He slammed the door closed behind them.

"I'll tell you exactly how I want your captivity to end, Catrina."

He was not happy.

"With you alive. I didn't ask to be burdened with Toren Kerr's sister in my home, but here you are. And, by God, I will see you safely through this ordeal, despite your best intentions."

He sat down on an overly large, cushioned chair. Catrina watched as the man who hardly ever showed emotion—well, maybe he did get angry more often than not around her—put his head in his hands.

She was stunned. Had she found a crack in the lord's armor at last? Could it truly be... *her*?

"Then let me go." Her voice was barely a whisper. She believed him, but his logic made no sense.

"I can't." He lifted his head. His usually clean-shaven face had more than a day's growth of whiskers. It made him look wilder than usual, less in control, especially since he was dressed in his casual outfit of hose and a linen shirt.

"Why?"

Bryce didn't answer. Catrina walked to the wooden chair adjacent to him. Of all the rooms in Bristol Manor, this one reminded her most of Brockburg. Vibrant tapestries sent from Kenshire hung on every wall, and decorative woodwork made it the most ornate room in the manor. The stone fireplace was a perfect, smaller replica of the one in the hall.

Catrina listened to the wood crackle. Sounds of Bristol's midday meal were quieted by the solar's thick walls. The silence of this quiet corner of an otherwise bustling manor was strangely calming.

"You're not going to answer," she asked. Not that it mattered. She already knew his response. He wanted revenge. It was why she kept risking her life to get away.

"We're leaving on the morrow."

"Leaving? We?"

Bryce leaned back in the chair, more at ease. His controlled, emotionless expression was firmly back in place.

"Aye. You and I. And a small retinue of men."

"Where? Why?" If she sounded panicked, it was with good cause. Unless they were leaving for Scotland, this did not bode well.

"If the rumors are true, and my sources assure me they are, your clan's departure from Scotland is imminent. When they arrive here, I'll give them no cause to attack Bristol."

He watched her carefully. Was it a lie? A trick?

"Where will we go?"

"To Kenshire."

"To your brother?"

"As I said, I will avoid another attack at all costs. I've no doubt Bristol Manor is well fortified and would not fall, but..."

She couldn't help making a face. His eyes narrowed.

"You'll abandon Bristol?" Perhaps it made sense for her to leave, but for him to come with her?

She sensed he objected to the word "abandon."

"I will. I trust Thomas to keep it safe. I'll take no chances with your care."

"Bloody hell. Just say it, Bryce. What you mean is that you'll take no chances letting the lure escape." She stood and began to pace.

She could not leave. Kenshire was on the eastern coast, farther south and definitely more difficult to navigate alone. If she had the chance, of course. Which she wouldn't. Because *he* would be watching her every move.

As he was now.

Catrina stopped and looked him straight in the eye. Bryce's earlier anger seemed to have completely disappeared. For a man who was usually so measured, his mood was unpredictable this afternoon. She had to say something. Do something.

Or did she?

More than anything, she wanted her brothers to be safe. Would they attack Bristol if she wasn't in residence?

Bryce was correct. They likely would not.

But they would come for her. She knew enough about Kenshire Castle not to be disillusioned about a victory there. Once the seat of Northumbrian kings, it was impregnable.

So what happens next?

Toren would be forced to capitulate.

Bryce stared at her, his expression inscrutable.

Dear lord, why must he be so handsome? She hated herself for thinking about him in any way other than as her captor. But when he looked at her like that, she thought of the kisses they had shared. The feel of him underneath her fingertips.

Catrina thought of the few times he let her see the real Bryce. He was no uncaring, unforgiving monster. She'd felt the caress of an honorable man. A man of deep feeling.

She would have to talk him out of it. Toren, too.

HER BROTHER BELIEVED the truth of his claim. Bristol had once, long ago, belonged to her people. And while her brother would never disregard his sovereign's wishes, perhaps she could convince him of what she'd come to realize—the Waryns' claim was at least equally strong, and Bristol Manor was their home. Besides, backed by the Countess of Kenshire, they were unlikely to be defeated. If she could talk sense into both Bryce and her brothers…

SHE KNEW it wasn't likely. But damned if she wouldn't try.

Catrina met his gaze.

"You are remarkable," he said.

Her heart lurched. That was not at all what she had imagined he would say. And, by God's bones, she wished it were otherwise, but she wanted him to kiss her again.

She nearly said, "So are you," but stopped herself. He was not a suitor or a friend. He was the man who refused to give her freedom. She turned away. Lord, it was so hard. Catrina stood instead in front of the fire, listening to the crackles and hisses, trying to pretend she didn't feel the weight of a presence behind her.

"Come here, Catrina."

BRYCE HAD SPENT a week trying to convince himself to stay away from her. To focus on making Bristol stronger. But then the news about Clan Kerr's army had arrived.

Clan Kerr would be coming to Bristol to end their feud once and for all. That Toren had recruited Clans Scott and deSowlis was unexpected, especially if Catrina had told him the truth about her broken "betrothal."

But it didn't matter. Bristol had more men, thanks to Kenshire. The wall had been repaired, and with a recent sale of wool thanks to Thomas's negotiation skills, work on a second curtain wall would start as soon as new workers arrived. It would not be completed, of course, for a battle with the Scots, but Bryce was happy with the progress they'd made in such a short time.

But then there was the girl.

Or woman, as Evelyn had so kindly pointed out on that first day. Though he had tried like hell, Bryce could not get her out of his mind. In the wake of his fading anger over her failed escape attempt, there was a respect for the indomitable will of a woman desperate to return home. The cunning she had displayed by saving the sleeping draught to use at just the right moment. The bravery it had taken to actually ride across the border alone, however misguided. And damned if Catrina didn't know, well, just about everything. She picked up skills the way a hawk picked up its prey. Surely and swiftly.

She really was remarkable.

But then, he reminded himself, she was also the sister of the man who had killed his parents. Taken his brother's birthright and forced them all to live, for five years, with relatives who could barely support their own family. Forced his brother and uncle to become reivers in order for them to survive.

He couldn't separate Catrina and her brothers.

"Thank you."

She said it with her back to him, responding to his earlier compliment but ignoring his request. He stared at her back and the waves of hair that looked more brown than red indoors but just the opposite in the sunlight.

Being this close to her was torture. Perhaps she was right. Did he really need to travel with her? Thomas was pleased that Bryce was entrusting Bristol to his care, but wouldn't Catrina be just as safe on the three to four-day journey to Kenshire without him?

No. Catrina was right. She was the lure, and he would not lose her.

"Catrina, would you please come over here?"

Geoffrey and Thomas would be on their knees with laughter if they could hear him now. But this woman was beyond stubborn, and she did not take well to commands. Even—no, especially—from her captor.

She turned.

He had told her once there were gold specks in her eyes. He couldn't see them from this distance, but that didn't stop his memory from summoning them up. Little windows to her soul. Tiny reminders that Catrina was always ready to smile at any moment.

He envied that about her.

"I know this has been hard for you, and I'm sorry for it." He almost wished she had not turned around. "Catrina, leave the scowling to me. You're much more beautiful when you smile."

Shite. The second compliment that day.

"What I mean to say is that my earlier anger was not directed at you."

Her laugh was unexpected.

"I appreciate the sentiment," she said, "but that was hardly a display of anger. You should witness my brothers when they explode. Especially Alex."

"Perhaps we should not talk about your family."

"Why were you so angry?"

He couldn't tell her it was because he had promised himself not to send for her. He'd sworn to himself the first time he'd see her again was on the road to Kenshire. But the control he'd spent years honing continued to abandon him where she was concerned.

"More importantly, why are you taking the news about Kenshire so well? I assumed you wouldn't want to leave Bristol."

She lifted her chin, a sure sign he was right. Although it didn't take a scholar to surmise she was up to something. Catrina schemed more than a falconer attempting to lure back his bird. And Lord help him, it was another thing he admired about her.

"Do with me as you will."

His cock instantly hardened. Of course she didn't mean it. In fact, she was clearly agitated by the turn of the conversation. He could appreciate her position...couldn't imagine feeling so powerless. But, by God, he wanted nothing more than to misinterpret her words, tear off her gown, and run his hands over every curve of her beautiful body.

When she finally understood the implications of her hastily uttered words, Catrina bit her lower lip. A plump lip he wanted to claim with his own.

Bryce forced himself to look away. He had brought her here

for a reason. He struggled to control his voice. His thoughts. "Pack a bag for an extended journey. And be ready to leave at sunrise."

"Fine. But you need to answer a question first."

"Need? Are you sure about that?"

He chose to ignore the fact that she rolled her eyes.

"What's your question?" This game of questions reminded him of the afternoon they'd spent stranded at Bristol Sprout.

"You told me not to scowl, but your smiles are so rare that I can count the times I've seen them."

"The nature of—"

"Yes, yes, you've made it quite clear that I'm your prisoner and you need not answer to me. No need to repeat that nonsense. I'll have the truth, please."

He owed her nothing. And much needed to be done before they left. But the stubborn chit would continue to ask...

"I told you once before. I've never been quite as jovial as my brothers. My mother called me the serious one."

"And?"

She was relentless.

"And smiling serves no purpose."

Catrina's look told him what she thought of that answer.

"Before I fostered at Huntington, it felt as if the whole world awaited me. As I told you, I was the first in our family to serve a great house. We enjoyed as much peace as could be expected along the border. I was to be knighted. Would someday marry. Serve my brother, perhaps, or find my own way in the world."

He paused, thinking.

"Tell me, Bryce. I need to know."

He didn't stop to think about her words. Something inside him wanted to tell her. *What the hell? What could it hurt?*

"For four years, I served my lord well. Learned much and benefited from training for endless tournaments. Huntington had built his own tiltyard for the purpose of holding as many such events as he fancied."

Bryce had participated in no less than thirty jousts and half as many tournaments at Huntington, first as a squire and later on his own.

"When his eldest daughter Elena returned—she'd been fostered by the Earl and Countess of Ramsey—I..."

Had he ever truly loved that scheming bitch?

"I fell for her. Lady Elena was beautiful. A blonde-haired, blue-eyed angel, they said. And it was true. Everyone was half in love with the lord's daughter."

Catrina frowned so deeply, he reconsidered the wisdom of finishing the story.

"And?" she pressed.

"Much to my surprise, she followed me around everywhere. Because she was the lord's daughter, I was properly hesitant. But Elena was persistent."

He had to be careful here.

"We..."

"You pleasured her?"

"Catrina!"

"You forget, I have three brothers."

He had indeed forgotten. But her bluntness was, at times, quite jarring. Endearing, but unexpected.

"Aye, I suppose you could say that. I fancied myself in love with her. Appealed to my father to ask for her hand in marriage. She assured me our stations were not so mismatched that her father would object. But I set out to prove myself to him."

"And that is why you're known as the Slayer. The champion of tournaments? The man who cannot lose? In the joust, hand-to-hand combat."

Bryce was unsure how to answer.

"Who told you that?"

"Evelyn. Before she was banned from seeing me—" another scowl, "—she took it upon herself to tout your finer qualities."

"Ahh, Evie. I suppose some of that is true."

"Some?"

"I'm not sure my reputation in tournaments is responsible for that particular name."

Her eyes widened.

He refused to say more. Why tell her this story? Only Thomas knew the tale. His brothers had surmised the truth since he hadn't, after all, come back from Huntington with a bride. But he'd always refused to talk about it.

Catrina raised her perfectly shaped eyebrows.

"Very well. One day, after giving me her ribbon in a tournament commissioned by her father as a show of peace for the lords of the north, she asked for it back. Because Geoffrey was in attendance."

He could tell she was confused.

"Elena realized I was not a first-born son. Somehow it was never discussed. When we talked of marriage, I assumed she knew of my family. And I guess *she* assumed a second-born son would not be so bold as to court a wealthy baron's daughter."

But her father had known the truth, and he'd still granted Bryce's request to formally court her. He loved Lord Huntington like a father. The man was strong, patient, and noble. Bryce had seen these same qualities in the daughter, but only because he'd wanted to see them. *Expected* to see them. The truth was a different beast.

"I'd just won the joust and dismounted. I assumed Elena wanted to congratulate me. Instead, in front of a half dozen knights and as many ladies, she asked for the ribbon back, angry that I had never told her about Geoffrey."

"That's terrible!"

Aye, it was.

"I kept them away from each other. Was mortified that I could have fallen for someone so shallow. Geoffrey would have—"

"Understood. And told you she didn't deserve you. Ungrateful bitch."

He did smile then. Even though it was years ago, his anger long since buried, it amused him to have Catrina so vigorously defend his honor.

"Perhaps. More importantly, what would Father Simon say about your choice of words for the Lady Elena?"

Catrina laughed, her eyes bright.

"He would have quite a bit to say, I suppose. But until he chastises men who speak thusly, saying 'I'm sorry' would be a lie."

She had the strangest ideas. "Your brothers?"

"Aye. They are much worse."

He no longer wanted to talk about Elena. And he was genuinely curious about Catrina's unusual upbringing. Much better to talk about her than to harp on the disappointments of the past. "When did your mother leave?"

She shifted in her seat, looking at the deep purple velvet cushion as if it were a fascinating curiosity. He shouldn't have asked.

"When Pa died."

He didn't say a word. Didn't move. The pained expression on her face forced him to shift in his seat. He wanted to comfort her but doubted it would be welcomed.

"I told you she was English. They met at the Tournament of the North. Father fell in love with her, and he nearly caused a war. As you can imagine, the daughter of a minor English baron was not who my grandfather had planned for his eldest son to marry. But he did so anyway."

Her tone was casual, but Bryce sensed the incident had been anything but. A chief's son did not marry whomever he pleased. Bryce knew better than anyone the importance of forging alliances.

"Luckily he wasn't alive to see her flee. Within a week of my father's death, she was gone."

She looked at him as she said it, too proud to look away, but perhaps for the first time, Bryce couldn't discern her feelings. Did it make her sad? Angry? He wasn't sure.

"We never heard from her again. As a child I begged Toren to find her, knowing in my heart she was still alive. But he refused, and I'm glad for it."

When he realized she wasn't going to elaborate, Bryce knew he had to say something.

"Ungrateful bitch."

He smiled.

Catrina's eyes widened and her lips curled into an answering smile. She laughed and laughed so hard tears began to stream down her face. He didn't hear Thomas's knock, and when the steward entered, they both laughed even harder.

Normally being caught in such a state would have mortified Bryce.

"What is it, Thomas?" He was impatient for his steward to leave. "Thomas?" he pressed when his friend stood there gawking.

"My apologies. Evelyn requests the presence of my lady. There seems to be a problem."

"What problem?"

What could be so urgent that Evelyn would go against his wishes to send for Catrina?

"If you will, Lady Catrina. I beg you to come with me."

13

Catrina was exhausted. Evelyn, it turned out, had summoned her to help with Elise's babe. She had spent the better part of the night trying to convince her maid's dense husband that it was just as natural to feed a babe with a cloth as it was a mother's teat. The ignorant priest had recently convinced him it would be blasphemy for the babe to get nourishment any other way even though the cloth was working.

When her reassurances didn't work, Bryce's intimidation did. He had insisted on coming with her, thank the saints, and he'd resolved the situation by threatening to throttle the man if he didn't comply. He looked to her first as if asking for permission to intervene. At her nod, he'd delivered the threat coolly, of course, which had done nothing to blunt its effectiveness.

Catrina stretched out on the bed. If only she could stay under the coverlet and not make the journey to Kenshire. The sun had not yet risen, but she knew Bryce would summon her any time. He had said they would leave at daybreak, and he was never late.

She smiled, remembering her favorite part of the evening. As soon as they left the maid's small house, Bryce had marched directly to the chapel at the center of the village. Unlike the diminutive homes that surrounded it, the chapel was a grand stone building. It even had small stained-glass windows. Curious, Catrina had followed Bryce into a room at the back of the building where the priest resided.

Catrina had never liked the man. Unlike Father Simon, who was educated and thoughtful, this priest had always seemed to relish more in the luxuries of his station than in administering service to the people of Bristol. After the incident with Elise, Bryce had ordered him to leave, immediately. Apparently he cared little about the repercussions. Who would offer service in his stead?

They had returned to the manor then, their intimate conversation in the solar apparently forgotten. Bryce had reminded her they would leave at sunrise and then promptly retired. She'd spent the remainder of the evening packing for their "extended" trip. How extended, she wasn't sure.

A knock announced Elise's arrival. After repeated requests for reassurance the babe was indeed fine, she helped Catrina prepare for the journey. Since her favorite riding dress had been ruined in the attack—she shuddered to think about the reivers and their fate at Bryce's hands—she wore an older one. The deep green gown was a bit snug around the chest, but it would have to do. The others were too impractical for travel.

By the time Catrina walked down the winding staircase into the hall, she was fully awake and ready, not only for the journey, but also to put her new plan into action.

There was only one issue with that. The man standing in front of her looked as if he wanted to kill her.

What did I do now?

"No," Bryce said, his eyes narrowing.

Every step toward him made her more aware of his scrutiny. "And a good day to you, my lord."

"You will not be wearing that dress, Lady Catrina."

She looked down at the fitted bodice and tight sleeves that

were perfect for riding. "I most certainly will. I'll thank you to remember, my other traveling dress was ruined."

What was wrong with him? Bryce looked like he would continue to disagree; a tic had developed in his cheek that reminded her of his brother.

Oh.

She'd almost missed the quick glance at her chest. Perhaps she'd grown in that area a bit since arriving at Bristol, but she'd seen ladies wear much more revealing gowns than this one, and it *was* her most appropriate. "I *will* wear this gown. You'll have to take it off me yourself if you mean for me to change."

Thomas, whose presence she'd only just noticed—had she really been that focused on Bryce?—chuckled. The alternate meaning to her words only then dawned on her. For Lord's sake, why couldn't she keep her mouth shut?

She couldn't look at either man, so instead Catrina concentrated on the woman who'd just slipped through the entrance to the hall. Walking toward Evelyn, she could feel Bryce's eyes on her back. The tingling his regard stirred deep within her was becoming a more familiar feeling as of late.

"Safe travels, my lady," said Evelyn.

As she hugged the older woman, it felt like goodbye forever. And they both knew it.

"Many thanks, Evelyn." She wanted to say so much more, but tears began to well in her eyes. Without her, Catrina would likely be dead. "For everything."

"Take care of him." Evelyn squeezed her hand and turned to walk away. What a strange thing to say…

She startled at the hand on her back. Bryce.

"It's time to go." His tone was gentler now. Did he understand this was the last time she'd walk through the great hall at Bristol Manor, this place that had become her home, too? She turned and looked up at him. His hand was still on her back, and the warm weight of it made Catrina shiver. Bryce wore the surcoat he so rarely took the effort of donning. And for the first time she realized he wore mail as well. How could she have missed that? He typically dressed so casually that she could almost forget what he was. A knight. The Lord of Bristol Manor, a powerful baron with the backing of one of the greatest houses in Northumbria.

Odd she never noticed how intimidating he could be.

"You look like a knight."

"I *am* a knight." His lips tipped up just a tiny bit.

"My lord? All is ready," Thomas said. Bryce dropped his hand from her back.

With one last hug for Evelyn and Elise, who had trailed down to the hall after them, Catrina followed Bryce and Thomas into the courtyard. A small retinue of men, five fully armored knights, waited atop their massive destriers.

A squire secured her bags to the packhorse and Bryce assisted her in mounting Davie.

As promised, they kept a steady pace. Bryce told her they should reach Kenshire Castle in three days, four at most, if they rode hard. She knew he wished to be on the road as little as possible.

By the time they camped for the night, Catrina's bravado began to wane. She prided herself on keeping up, not giving any of the men reason to doubt she was just as capable as them, but other than a brief respite for the horses, they traveled swiftly, breaking bread at a trot and not even stopping to relieve themselves, which was all Catrina could think about after a time. She watched the sun set, tried to concentrate on the beauty of the landscape—anything to distract herself. Fairly flat and verdantly green with rolling hills in the distance, Northumbria was indistinguishable from the Scottish lowlands.

Now traveling on old Roman roads, some no wider than the horses they rode, their small party finally encountered a thicket of trees. Catrina prayed Bryce was looking for shelter among the dense pine trees, and when he raised his hand to stop, she thought she might cry from relief. Dismounting on her own, she led Davie to the man who rode in front of her and held up the reins. Without question, he took them. She practically ran into the trees.

Leaving modesty behind and lifting her skirts, Catrina vowed never again to stay silent about her needs for so long. Damn stubbornness. Moments later, feeling much relieved, she was making her way back to the horses when a hand reached out and grabbed her.

"Bryce! I didn't hear you." How could a man so large make so little noise?

"What the hell are you doing?" he asked.

"If you must know..."

"Aye, I must."

Ah, he had taken her desperate dash into the woods for an escape attempt.

"We stopped twice all day, Bryce." If he made her say it out loud, she'd be mortified.

"What the devil does that have to do with...oh."

She pulled her arm back and lifted her chin. "Aye."

Bryce took off his helm. Despite the surcoat and mail, he wore no hauberk. His hair was damp with sweat. And were his cheeks actually tinged with pink?

"My apologies. I've seen you ride and knew you could keep pace."

Catrina glowed. She wasn't sure if he had meant it as a compliment, but it felt like one. And he'd apologized *twice* now. She liked that Bryce was not immune to admitting a mistake. It was a quality her eldest brother could learn to emulate.

They walked back to the small clearing where the men were already setting up camp. She knew two of the knights, but the other three were unfamiliar to her. Likely from Kenshire. They worked efficiently, starting a fire and erecting small tents. One escorted her to a nearby stream to wash. She didn't see Bryce again until after they ate a modest meal of roasted rabbit and bread. She was accustomed to being in the presence of men, and Catrina actually enjoyed herself. It was much preferable to being locked up in a small bedchamber. And though Bryce ignored her for most of the evening, the others did not. She was almost sorry when it was time to retire.

The third day of travel went much smoother than the first two thanks to more frequent stops. They slowed through a tricky incline, and she could tell the men were impressed with how she navigated Davie over the rocky slope. Now back on flat ground, they flew through the open fields, and Catrina felt wonderful. She was determined to speak to Bryce when they stopped that evening. He had retired early the previous two nights, but tonight he would not continue to elude her. There was no reason to wait for Kenshire to begin convincing him to let go of this feud with her family.

It would be a fine day indeed.

It was hell.

Bryce had started questioning his decision to accompany Catrina to Kenshire even before they left Bristol. He'd sworn under his breath upon his first sight of her in that dress, not caring if Thomas overheard him. By God, what had she been thinking? Her breasts nearly burst from the neckline of the otherwise fine-looking gown. While her explanation of the ruined dress made sense, he honestly didn't know how they would make it to Kenshire without incident.

He wanted her.

There was no use denying it. The small tastes, the blasted kisses, only left him wanting more. Bryce had finally resigned himself to that fact. Every time she entered the room, his pulse quickened. When he closed his eyes, he could feel the firm press of her chest again his own. How her buttocks felt as if they were made for his hands.

Accompanying her on this trip was an error in judgment.

But although he knew that, there was nothing to be done. He could not remain at Bristol wondering if she'd outsmarted her guards. The thought of her wandering toward the border again, prey to any reivers who crossed her path, was too much for him to bear. He would see her safe and secure at Kenshire before making his next move.

Clan Kerr was being watched. He would know if they remained at Brockburg or took the bait and followed them to Kenshire. And if Toren Kerr was stubborn enough to march on Bristol even though his sister was no longer in residence, he was prepared for that too.

Either way, the man would pay for his actions.

Just as Bryce himself was paying for his insistence on joining this trip to Kenshire.

The draw she had on him, stronger every day, convinced him that his best strategy was to stay away from her. Which is exactly what he tried to do. But as he lay awake in the small tent on the second night of their journey, he could hear her talking, laughing with his men. More than once, he considered putting a stop to their merriment—until he realized the source of his irritation was jealousy.

What did he care if she enjoyed the company of his knights? They would likely learn very quickly that she talked too much. Said the most outrageous things. Surely they would tire of her chatter and insistence upon swearing like a man.

Finally, he did put a stop to it, reminding the group of their early start. Other than an angry glare, he received no other indication from Catrina that she'd heard him. Instead, she continued to tell the group a story about the first rabbit she'd killed.

Of course the lady hunted. The woman could do just about everything.

The next day, he forced himself not to turn around. To ignore the itch that urged him to look back at her, just once. She was riding in the middle, keeping up with their grueling pace. Admittedly, he was impressed by her riding skills. Any other woman would have complained more than once about the harsh conditions of the journey.

But not Catrina.

Disgusted by the turn of his thoughts, Bryce called out an order and rode ahead. There were precious few inns this far north. Few had survived the ravages of being so close to the border. The Wild Boar was one of the lucky few that thrived in this in-between space.

Friendly to both English and Scottish, the owner was notoriously protective of its reputation. The inn was unique and somehow able to preserve its position as neutral dwelling.

Loyal men from both sides of the border helped guard the inn's peace. The Wild Boar was known for miles as being off-limits for settling disputes.

With any luck, there would be available rooms for the evening. Or at least one for Catrina. He and the men were accustomed to beds of leaves and sticks, but a hot meal and cold mug of ale would be welcome.

Spotting the stone structure ahead, he made his way toward the inn, anxious to put distance between himself and Catrina, who would—he assured himself—be safe with the men. After giving his horse to the groom and disarming with the help of a stable hand, Bryce walked under the wooden sign depicting a boar with a hunter's arrow piercing it.

The two-story timber-framed building was large for an inn. It boasted a great hall, both public and private accommodations, a kitchen, and stables large enough to house more horses than there were rooms. Making his way through the hall, Bryce spotted the innkeeper at the far end of the room.

She was an older, plump woman, but anyone who thought to

instigate trouble with the widow of the former owner was quickly dissuaded.

"My lovely Magge."

She turned swiftly, likely ready to box his ears. He knew what would be coming and braced for it.

"Sir Bryce. Or is it Lord Waryn now? Get over here and give ol' Magge a kiss." He attempted to kiss her ruddy cheek and was ready when she turned her head.

He managed to find his mark despite her best efforts.

"Ah, ye're wise to me, young lad." She reached behind him and slapped his backside.

"You forget I've been coming here since Father brought me as a child. You try that trick on every man looking for a warm bed."

She scowled at him, though he could tell she wasn't really angry.

"Not everyone, my young lord. Just the handsome ones." Turning from the table and giving the buxom maid who served him ale with a wink, he walked with Magge toward the hearth.

"Come, sit with this old lady," she said. "Tell me of Bristol. I hear you gave Clan Kerr the fight they deserved."

He sat in front of a roaring fire, letting the comforting and familiar sounds of men eating, drinking, and playing dice wash over him. If nothing else was familiar to him these days, Magge's hospitality was something he could count on.

"You already know."

Giving an overly rambunctious knight who nearly stumbled into them a whack on the leg, Magge nodded. "Your brother told me about it on his way from Bristol to Kenshire." Magge leaned in as if imparting an important secret. "He's smitten, that one. Is this Lady Sara so good in bed then?"

Bryce nearly smiled. "I wouldn't know, Magge. But she is a strong, kind woman. You'd like her."

Magge cackled. "The only girls I like can cook and clean and serve ale without managing to get a cock stuck in them while they're at it."

Which was precisely when Catrina cleared her throat from behind them. They both looked up. Bryce stood and introduced the women.

"Catrina, meet Magge, owner of this fine establishment. Magge, may I present Lady Catrina..." He stopped.

Catrina lifted her chin and finished the introductions. "Kerr," she said boldly.

Magge's eyes widened, as expected. She looked from Bryce to Catrina and back again, as if trying to understand their relationship. Although she was his hostage, for some reason, he didn't want Magge to know that.

"Lady Catrina is my guest. We make our way to Kenshire."

Catrina's eyes narrowed as she glared at him, but thankfully she remained silent.

"I see." But it was clear Magge did not, though she made no further comment. "And I suppose you'll be wanting rooms for the night, you big brute?"

Catrina eyed Magge curiously. "Aye, what do you have?" he asked.

"Only two rooms. One bed in each. Take 'em or leave 'em."

"I'll take both. Thank you." He gave the innkeeper a kiss on the cheek. "And we're not too late for a hot meal?"

Magge was already walking away, having spotted another traveler entering the hall. "Get yer men in here, Lord Waryn. And lock yer door this evenin' unless you want an extra visitor." She nodded to the maid filling mugs of ale, staring at him with moony eyes.

Bryce shook his head and guided Catrina to an empty table.

The hall was filled near to capacity. Candles stood on metal stands throughout the room. The only other light was from a fire, its smoke emptying into the night from an opening in the ceiling.

The inn smelled better than most, its rushes regularly cleaned with herbs.

Bryce had joked once after stopping at the inn for a night that he wanted to make it his permanent home. But although Magge loved his family, she loved money even more. Since her husband died, she and her son managed The Wild Boar, but all knew it was Magge who kept the inn thriving.

Bryce sat next to his men, keeping as far away from Catrina as possible. If she had noticed he was avoiding her, she hadn't made mention of it. Or seem to care.

Most women would be intimidated by the inn's patrons or the aggressive flirtations of the serving wench.

But not this one.

Catrina ate the hot porridge as if it were her favorite meal. She laughed among his men and even spoke at length to Magge, when she returned, about the quality of her ale.

He tried not to look at Catrina but failed miserably. His eyes kept returning to her, unbidden.

"More ale, my lord?"

The press of the maid's overly large bosom against his shoulder merely irritated him. And for a man who'd earned the nickname of 'the Slayer,' it was not a welcome revelation. She was more than passing fair, and though she flirted with all of the men throughout the meal, she paid him the most attention. But he was not interested.

"Aye." Trying his best to concentrate on anything other than Catrina's laugh, he turned to the girl despite his disinterest.

"What's your name?"

"Helen, my lord." She smiled, and he was surprised by her straight, white teeth.

"You're new." It was a statement, not a question. He'd been coming to The Wild Boar for years and had never seen her before.

"Aye, my lord. But not too new to know what I like."

Her invitation wasn't subtle. He had a room. There was no

reason not to accept. But the thought of a tumble with the attractive serving girl left him cold.

"Not tonight, love."

She filled his mug and lingered over his shoulder longer than necessary. He turned to dismiss her, but she abruptly winked and walked away.

He'd expected an argument and was glad to be left alone with his thoughts. Leaving the newly poured drink and his half-eaten meal, he stood and addressed Magge.

"Magge, dear—"

"My lord?"

"I wanted to thank you for a wonderful meal and bid you good eve." "And?" Her partly toothless grin told him the innkeeper was wise to him. "Can you see Lady Catrina settled for the evening?"

She followed his gaze to where the woman in question continued to hold court with his men. Magge looked as if she wanted to question him further but thankfully decided against it.

"Aye. And your men are welcome in the hall, of course."

"My thanks, Magge, but they've already set up camp nearby." With a short bow, he left, intending to take a cold swim in the stream that ran behind the inn.

14

It was scandalous.

Even by her relaxed standards, it was…not the best idea for an unmarried woman to visit a man in his bedchamber. But, Catrina rationalized, she wasn't exactly in a position to pick and choose her opportunities.

As much as she enjoyed the freedom of being outdoors—she had not realized how much she'd always taken freedom for granted until her confinement—the past few days had been extremely frustrating. After the torture of the first day's ride, her bottom had become more accustomed to spending a full day in the saddle. The men who accompanied them had accepted her and treated her as one of their own. Although they were English, the knights from Bristol and Kenshire were very much like the men of her clan: sometimes crude, always anxious to hone their battle skills, and quick to jest with one another.

She would actually be enjoying the journey if it weren't for one man in particular.

It had proven difficult to engage Bryce in conversation. They were always either riding or making camp. She'd approached him multiple times, and on each occasion, he'd made it clear he wanted nothing to do with her. Despite herself, Catrina's heart sank when he turned from her.

During the day, Bryce rode at the front of the pack. In the evening, he took his meal alone in his tent. Whenever she managed to catch his eye, he looked away immediately. She thought they had begun to form a bond. Apparently not. And tonight, he had made sure to leave dinner early.

How could she possibly convince him to give up his quest for revenge and let her go if she couldn't even get his attention?

Catrina knew she was running out of time. Her brother and his men would very likely be marching to Kenshire to get themselves killed

Washed and prepared for bed, it wasn't until Catrina lay on the lumpy straw mattress in her room that she decided to act. Pulling out her only cloak from the bag at the foot of the bed, she shook out the soft wool garment and draped it around her shoulders.

Scandalous or not, she would speak to Bryce this night.

She peeked into the hallway. Aside from the bellows of the men below them, there was no other noise. The hall was indeed empty.

Was that a sound coming from his room?

She knocked.

A moment later, Bryce swung the door open. The wide-eyed serving girl who'd practically draped herself on him at dinner was once again hanging onto his shoulders. Catrina hadn't considered that he might be with someone. The last thing she saw before she spun and ran back to her room was the grin on the beautiful girl's face.

How humiliating!

She slammed the door, ripped off her cloak, and threw it onto the bed. She began to pace, heat creeping from her neck to her face.

The door opened and closed with nary a knock, and a bare-chested Bryce stood before her. The bedchamber suddenly felt even more confining. Aside from a bed, it contained only a chest and small table with a pitcher and basin atop it, but he filled up the small space with his mere presence.

Catrina took a step back. "I apologize for—"

"What were you doing in my room?"

He didn't sound angry. Of course, she rarely knew what he was actually thinking or feeling.

"I…" How did she begin? There was so much to say, and the outcome of her life, her clan's future, depended on these words. But at that moment she could not think.

Bryce's hair was wet, his chest bare. He wore only thick woolen hose that outlined every muscle in his legs. She remembered how it felt to be pressed up against him.

"You're rarely at a loss for words, Catrina."

When he said her name, it felt like a soft caress. As if he'd just reached out and run a hand along her back the way he had done at the waterfall.

"This isn't a good time to talk."

What could she have been thinking?

He took a step toward her. "And it was a good time a moment ago in my room?"

"Clearly it was not. Had I known you were occupied—"

"I didn't solicit her presence. I was preparing for bed when she entered the room without solicitation."

She didn't care. "What does it matter to me?"

He took another step toward her. Catrina's breath came in pants—as if she'd just run from Bristol to its village.

"I think it does matters. I think that's why you're so nervous."

Damn him.

Another step. He was no more than an arm's length away. She would not retreat. Not for any man, and certainly not for this one.

Bryce wasn't as emotionless as he'd have everyone believe. His face was anything but neutral at the moment. It was filled with expression now.

With desire.

"What you do with the serving wench is none of my concern. For all I care, you can—" He closed the space between them in two strides and pulled her toward him in a crushing

embrace, melding his lips to her own.

Catrina couldn't form another thought. She wrapped her arms around him, felt the taut muscles of his back, and marveled as they danced beneath her fingertips. His lips moved over hers expertly. Maybe too expertly.

His tongue slipped into her mouth, and she gave him what he sought. His hands held her head firmly against his mouth, as if worried she would break free. But she had no desire to be anywhere but here.

She wanted this. *Him.*

His hands lowered, moving down her back. "I want to see you, Catrina."

She didn't hesitate. "Aye."

And in one fluid motion, he grabbed the hem of her chemise and lifted it above her head. She'd never felt so exposed in her life. Catrina had never imagined a man who was not her husband would see her in such a state. But she would not cover herself with her hands. This man she hated for wanting to destroy her family, for keeping her against her will…

He looked at her as no one ever had before.

And she quite liked it.

CATRINA WAS MAGNIFICENT. Undoubtedly, she'd never stood naked before any man, but she held her head high. Her eyes dared him to criticize.

Which he would never do. Hers was the most perfectly formed body he'd ever had the pleasure to look upon. It was madness to reach for her, to slide his hand down her arm, but her full breasts invited his touch. His palm grazed the curved mound of her breast as it made its way even lower.

He should not be here with this woman. Bryce knew he was taking advantage of the fact that she had no chaperone, something no gentleman should ever do. Their situation was beyond unconventional.

She was his captive, dammit.

But his body didn't seem to care that she was a Kerr. Every time Catrina walked into a room or rode close to him, he could think of nothing else. *That* was why he'd kept his distance from her.

It had been a torturous day watching her sweet bottom bounce up and down on Davie—listening to her laugh with the men when he wanted to be the one to make her smile so sweetly.

He moved closer, continuing to revere the soft flesh beneath his hand while reclaiming her lips. This time, his movements were slow. Deliberate.

His mouth moved over hers instructively. He wasn't sure when he'd made the decision to please her, but that's exactly what he was determined to do. Bryce wasn't so naive as to believe he could lie with Catrina, no matter how much they desired each other. He'd not dishonor the lady by spoiling her chance at a good marriage. Not when he knew it was something she wanted desperately.

But to fight the desire that sparked between them? When the serving wench had brazenly entered his room—he'd forgotten Magge's warning to lock his door—Bryce couldn't have been less interested. She was beautiful, aye. But her hair wasn't a shade between red and brown. Her eyes didn't sparkle with mischief and intelligence.

She wasn't Catrina.

And then, before he could send the girl away, *she* had knocked at his door. Come to him. He didn't know why. And at the moment, he didn't care. Bryce only knew he wanted her, or at least wanted a taste of her.

His hands caressed Catrina's backside as his tongue continued its slow assault. He wanted—needed—to make her cry out in pleasure.

Her soft moans encouraged him. Bryce lifted her onto his hips, her strong legs straddling him without any prompting. He carried her to the bed and lowered her without quite letting go. She was poised beneath him now, and he lowered himself onto her to reclaim her full lips. He brushed away a stray strand of her long hair and ran his tongue along her bottom lip.

"I'm going to pleasure you," he murmured against her neck. She answered with a sigh.

He sat up, still straddling her, and looked down. The core of her womanhood was on full display. Rock hard and close to losing himself, Bryce found it hard to believe the position he found himself in this night. The same woman he had fantasized about for the past two evenings, longer, now lay beneath him. Naked. She was even more beautiful than he'd imagined.

He didn't care who she was.

Sliding his hand down her neck, he caressed her soft flesh and made a slow, winding path down to her breasts. He wanted to stop there—take a full mound in his hand, tease its taut nipple—but instead he moved lower and ran his fingers over the smooth flesh of her stomach.

Her eyes widened even more as she realized where his fingers were venturing next, but she didn't flinch. This woman was fearless.

His hand found its mark. Every instinct told him to thrust inside, but she was an untried maid. So he kept his hand there, not moving, and listened instead to Catrina's uneven breathing. He closed his eyes, afraid to disgrace himself. Not since Huntington, where he'd first learned how to please a woman, had he felt so little control.

He slowed his racing heart the same way he would before battle. Taking slow, even breaths, he forced his body to obey. Finally, he opened his eyes and slipped a finger inside her. Catrina's gasp told him what he'd already known.

He would make her first sensual experience a memorable one.

She stared into his eyes, not saying a word. She bit her bottom lip, and Bryce tried not to look down at her body splayed beneath his own. He was having a hard time maintaining control. At first she clenched tight against his finger, but he could finally feel her relaxing against him. So he started to move, slipping a second finger inside. Catrina closed her eyes then, and Bryce was sure he'd never seen a more beautiful sight in his life.

The bed was small and uncomfortable, but he did not care. Catrina tilted her head back, her moans making him impatient to show her more. To pleasure her fully. He quickened his pace, pressing with his palm and willing her release.

His cock throbbed, his hose the only barrier that would keep him from taking what wasn't his. Bryce concentrated instead on giving Catrina a powerful climax, and when he felt her wetness beneath his hand, he leaned down to capture her moans. He kissed her deeply, his fingers still within her. He could feel her hardened nipples beneath his chest and didn't know how much more sweet torture he could take.

But he wasn't done yet.

WHAT THE HELL WAS THAT?

Catrina knew she played a dangerous game. But from the moment Bryce opened her door, all thoughts of revenge and persuasion had fled her mind. Because she had known…down to the inner recesses of her being…something wonderful was about to happen.

She didn't know what exactly. She didn't care. Though the

thought of Graeme, who'd so patiently waited for her all these years, flitted through her mind, she wasn't actually betrothed to him. Was it still a betrayal? Would she have even considered such a thing if she were a man?

Catrina had watched her brothers' antics, listened to their talk, for enough years to know about the pleasure that awaited her. Bryce's kisses confirmed as much. And though it was wrong—very wrong—for Bryce to be the man she desired, Catrina was no longer willing to fight it.

She would make him see reason…but not now. Now, she wanted to concentrate on how he made her feel. On the muscles in his chest and arms. On his fingers inside the most intimate part of her body.

She had never thought a man could make her feel this good.

Better than good.

She knew he was watching her closely, but Catrina couldn't look at him. She could hardly concentrate on anything other than the building feeling of…something. Arching her back, she pushed him even deeper inside her, driven by the hunger for more, more, more. She felt the wetness as his fingers glided in and out.

And then he kissed her, his tongue mimicking the thrust of his fingers. She was undone. The pressure forced her hands to clench, to grasp him tightly. She throbbed against his fingers. The feeling was…indescribable. Her whole body pulsed, wild and uncontrolled.

She didn't want it to end.

Bryce pulled away and looked at her. Still stoic, but not as cold as usual. His bright eyes didn't flinch. He was waiting for something. What?

"How do you feel, Catrina?"

"I…that's not what I came to your room for."

His lips turned up into the most beautiful smile she'd ever seen. His smiles were so rare. And impossible to resist.

"But I'm not sorry for it."

"I don't expect you to be, my Scottish lass."

"I can see why they call you the Slayer."

His smile faltered. His hand moved to her breast, cupped it, and stilled.

"And if it doesn't please me?" His thumb ran across her nipple. He teased the hardened nub, squeezing gently. And by God if she wasn't already getting that same feeling again. A tingling between her legs that begged for his touch.

"Since nothing seems to please you, my lord, I'm not sure it matters."

He leaned down to her ear, his lips so close she could feel the feather-light touch of them. "That's where you're wrong, Catrina."

He left the rest unsaid. She couldn't help but smile. *She* pleased him.

"I don't want you to move." Where the hell would she move to?

Bryce moved to the foot of the small bed and looked down at her. His expression was one she'd never forget. His intent regard was so intense she thought he'd never look away.

When he finally moved, he surprised her by kneeling and pulling her ankles gently. "Come toward me." What was he about?

"But you told me not to move."

He didn't answer. She had no idea what he planned but did as he instructed. Moving toward him, straw poking out of the mattress to scratch her back, Catrina slid down, bending her knees and—

No, he was not!

Bryce lowered his head and she instinctively tried to pull back. "I told you not to move. Trust me."

Trust me. The man who wanted to destroy her family was asking for her trust. She was too curious to do anything other than comply.

At the first touch of his fingers, Catrina still didn't understand. But when he used them to position her for his mouth, she was appalled. Did people really do this?

Then his tongue touched the most intimate part of her, and Catrina thought she might expire. Or at least it felt that way. Slow at first, he circled and teased, increasing the pressure. Her embarrassment fluttered away, leaving her with a wonderful, building feeling of pure bliss.

With increasing speed, Bryce licked and kissed her, his hands holding her in place. She grasped the coverlet as if holding onto something would keep her from being completely swept away. She began to move with him, a rhythmic back and forth that creaked the bed beneath them.

And before she could fully comprehend what was happening, the same explosion, this time somehow more intense, burst forth without warning. Her flesh throbbed against his mouth. She wanted to scream but had the sense not to. Her heart beat so fast she feared it would hurt her.

What...was that?

She opened her eyes to see Bryce, still kneeling at the foot of the bed, watching her. He was staring at her with such open admiration, she forgot to feel self-conscious. Catrina closed her eyes and lay back down.

She opened her eyes when she felt the mattress buckle under Bryce's weight. The bed was hardly fit for two people. She looked frantically for her chemise and spotted it on the floor. Bryce reached out and ran his hand down her arm.

"Now you're shy?"

She was grateful when he stood up and fetched the garment. Now, after everything they'd done, she felt exposed. She slipped it on awkwardly as she sat up on the bed. Bryce helped her with one of the arms. It seemed like the most natural thing in the world for him to help her dress. But she couldn't let herself think that way. She couldn't get used to having him around.

"Why did you come to me, Catrina?"

His hair, wet when he'd walked through her door, was now

dry but tousled, making him look younger than normal. And unkempt. And immensely adorable.

Adorable? Bryce?

"I needed to speak with you. And you've been avoiding me."

His gaze traveled down the length of her body, making her tingle again in that most unlikely of places.

"And now you know why," he said.

"But you hate me." At least, she thought he did, but this was not their first encounter. Bryce swallowed and looked around the room. "I'm sorry for the accommodations." So, he wasn't going to deny it. She pulled her legs under her and wrapped her arms around them.

"You have to let me go."

She could tell it was the last thing he had expected to hear. "Pardon me?"

"Bryce—" She had sought him out for a reason, and what had happened between them, however wonderful, didn't change the fact that she needed to protect her brothers. "—I can convince Toren that Bristol is yours. To leave you alone. What's done is done. It's Bristol you want. Aye?"

He looked at her for so long, Catrina thought at first that he must not have heard her. "Please, consider it. Let me go to—"

"No."

She startled. No?

"You need to listen to me. I—"

"I need to do no such thing." Bryce continued to look at her but said nothing, the intimacy they had shared just moments ago already forgotten. This was the unflinching warrior. The one who cared about nothing. No one. Nothing except vengeance.

What could she possibly say to change his mind?

"This changes everything," she said it quietly. It was obvious he desired her despite her surname. Wasn't that a start?

"This changes nothing." He stood and made his way toward the door.

He stopped before leaving and turned back to her.

Catrina could not discern his glance. The man who had just given her such pleasure stared back at her. He opened his mouth, his expression softening. Just as she thought he would return to her, Bryce turned and walked out of the room. The sound of the closing door rang in her ears.

How could he say such a thing? Do such a thing and then walk out as if they had discussed ordering provisions for a dinner party? What was wrong with him?

What was wrong with her?

She gave herself freely to a man who was not her husband. What would Graeme think of her actions? How could she have allowed that to happen?

Even worse, she wasn't sure that it would never happen again. Though he was a brute, a stubborn, mule-headed Englishman, Bryce had showed her selflessness that night. She wasn't so ignorant to understand he'd left without taking his own pleasure.

She'd once overheard a conversation between her brothers Alex and Reid that still made her blush. She was well aware how men sometimes pleased themselves. Of course, she had no idea it had felt like *that*. She would be sure to tease her brothers about it.

If she ever saw them again.

Somehow she had to convince Bryce to leave her family alone. To set her free. But it now seemed unlikely it would happen before they arrived at Kenshire. What did he intend to do when they arrived? Stay until her brother's army moved south? Would he leave her at Kenshire? God forbid, that would be disastrous.

She needed help and had an idea where to find it.

15

As Kenshire Castle came into view, Bryce rode ahead to the gatehouse. They'd been riding all morning, though they'd stopped once for Catrina's sake. It was nearly evening, but since the sun failed to make an appearance, it was difficult to tell the exact hour. The weather was as dreary as his mood.

Last eve had been yet another mistake. He was reminded of that as he dressed this morn and his sister's ribbon fell from his pocket. How could he have even begun to think otherwise?

That was exactly the problem. He *didn't* think around her.

Even now, part of him wanted to relive every moment they shared. Bryce had never witnessed a more delectable sight in his life than watching Catrina reach her peak. A midnight dunk in the river hardly did the job. Even now, thinking of it, he began to harden.

Damn the woman. Nay, it was *his* fault entirely.

There was no doubt that if he'd lain with her, it would have led to an all-out war with the entire clan and their allies. He played a dangerous game, and Bristol's future hung in the balance. It was wrong, and Bryce knew it.

He should have stayed behind. He had convinced himself

seeing Catrina safely installed at Kenshire was good for his people. Good for Bristol. He now realized his actions were rash. He could have easily sent her with trustworthy men who would have kept her safe. Instead, he'd allowed his feelings for her to blind him.

Anxious to see his brothers, Bryce spoke to the guards and left the remainder of his party behind with a quick glance back to look for Catrina. Kenshire Castle, an earldom once the seat of Northumbrian kings, was as impressive a structure as any in England. Built on a rocky plateau high above the coastline, the castle made for a spectacular sight from every angle. Inhaling deeply, allowing the salt air to fill his lungs, Bryce waved to familiar faces as he rode through the outer bailey and finally the inner gate.

Bryce and his siblings had moved to Kenshire after Geoffrey and Lady Sara were married. It was here they planned the attack against Clan Kerr. It was here he'd learned Geoffrey planned to grant him the feudal barony of Bristol.

The courtyard was at least five times the size of Bristol's. Servants scurried back and forth and wagons transported goods. Children chased each other, and the chickens played unwilling participants in their game. Livelier than Bristol, Kenshire befitted the lady whose family had ruled for generations. One who had fought to keep the earldom—and won—after her father's death. Who had married his brother for love.

That very same lady approached as Bryce dismounted. He handed his horse's reins to a squire.

Sara embraced him. "Bryce, good den! I've missed you."

"Good den, my lady."

She pulled back to scowl at him. "'Tis Sara, never 'my lady' to you." Grabbing his hands, she looked over his shoulder. "Where is she?"

She. Catrina. Where, indeed?

"She should be coming anytime with the rest of the men."

Sara slapped him on the arm. "You brute. Why isn't she with you?"

His brother appeared just as he was being scolded. "Geoffrey, can you control your wife? Her greeting has been quite improper." Aside from his sister, Sara was the only woman with whom he felt completely relaxed.

With the exception of Catrina. Although she also unnerved him more than anyone else as well.

His brother laughed. "What would you have me do, Bryce? Shall I chastise the woman? Perhaps show her how to be more respectful?" Geoffrey grabbed his wife and pulled her toward him. Sara slapped his hands away playfully.

"You may try, husband. But see that you sleep in the hall with your men afterward." Though she chastised him, Sara was smiling. Geoffrey kissed her in an open display of affection. This, *this* was the very reason Bryce had vowed never to marry. Though he loved Sara like a sister, there was no doubt Geoffrey was softer because of her.

"I could use a training partner, Geoffrey. Or have you taken up the loom these days instead?"

Geoffrey looked behind him. "What about our guests? Where is the Kerr woman?"

Bryce frowned. As if he needed a reminder she was sister to the devil himself. He waved a hand dismissively. "I rode ahead."

His brother and Sara exchanged a glance. He didn't care what they thought of him. Distancing himself from Catrina was for the best. For everyone.

"You must have ridden hard to make such good time. Do you want to rest? It's late in the day," Geoffrey reminded him.

"Nay."

His brother, thankfully, stopped asking questions. He turned to Sara. "You'll see to the girl?"

"Aye, husband."

Then she turned to look at him. Clearly, Sara didn't approve of his treatment of Catrina. *She's a goddamn captive!*

Perhaps if he reminded himself often enough, he'd start believing it.

Bryce turned as Geoffrey followed him to the training yard. He tried to ignore the stares that were common enough when he and his brother were together.

"How is Bristol faring?"

Normally they would hear the sounds of clanging swords and men's shouts. But at this hour, most prepared for the evening meal. The yard was likely empty.

"The manor is fully staffed, the wall repaired. We've routed out sympathizers to the Kerrs and re-established old trading partners. Thomas had some ideas on how to make the wool trade more lucrative, and I think I know ways to expand it. But building an outer defense remains my top priority."

"And the men from Kenshire?"

Geoffrey stopped at the entrance and turned to face him. Bryce knew that look.

"What is it you really want to ask, Geoffrey?" His older brother was never good at hiding his moods. Something troubled him.

"You know I stand with you, Bryce—"

"But?"

"The war that brews with Clan Kerr. We both knew they would put up a fight. And I didn't disagree with keeping the girl hostage at first. It seemed like the right move."

Bryce could guess, easily enough, where his brother was headed. "I won't let her go."

After a moment, Bryce broke Geoffrey's stare and looked off into the distance. From this vantage point, only the curtain wall was visible in the distance. But beyond it lay the North Sea. He couldn't see or hear it from this distance, but it was there. The salty, briny smell carried on the breeze.

Geoffrey was a lucky man to call this home. Bryce could understand why he was reluctant to engage in a fight he thought they had already won. But that didn't mean he was content to let Toren Kerr's crimes against his family go unanswered.

That didn't mean he was ready to let Catrina go.

Bryce looked back into blue eyes nearly identical to his own. Right now, there was more than a spark of anger in them.

"Goddammit Bryce, why do you have to be so stubborn? Let it go. We have Bristol. By all accounts, they ran it well in our absence. We have the trade. Isn't that enough?"

They walked into the empty training yard, Bryce already mentally preparing for the sparring match.

"No. It's not. The chief of Clan Kerr will answer for the murder of our parents. And Catrina will help make that happen."

Bryce could tell his brother wanted to continue the argument, but he was done talking. "You gave Bristol to me. Now let me rule it."

And yet…when they squared off, Bryce's thoughts didn't drift to revenge or Bristol, but to a certain lady whose soft moans were forever etched into his memory. Thank God Kenshire was large enough that he could easily avoid her for a few days.

APPREHENSION NEARLY MADE Catrina ill as they rode through the massive gates of the castle. Bryce had told her at the inn that she would not be confined at Kenshire, but how much freedom would she be given? In his typical surly manner, he'd informed her that there was simply nowhere to go. Kenshire's guards would not allow her to pass without an approved escort. *Him*. Which meant everyone knew she was a captive. Worse, Bryce was nowhere to be found. Perhaps, after last night, he would stay lost.

And that meant she had to ride into this new prison without her escort.

It was an impressive structure. The guardhouse alone was nearly as big as the main keep of Brockburg or Bristol. Her heart sank when she realized the hundreds of men milling about would likely be at Bryce's disposal. Kenshire must have as many men as the king! If he fought her brother on the battlefield, even with deSowlis as an ally, her clan would lose.

Davie danced nervously beneath her as she dismounted. She knew how her horse felt. But Lady Sara greeted her, and she was the embodiment of grace. She was easily the most beautiful woman Catrina had ever met. Lady Sara's long, dark hair was unbound even though she was a married woman, but that didn't surprise Catrina. From what she knew about the countess, she was not a lady overly concerned with convention.

What did surprise her was that the countess engulfed her in the kind of embrace one would give a long-lost sister. Didn't the countess know she was a hostage? The sister of her enemy?

Of course she did. And apparently Lady Sara wasn't a bit shy with her words.

"I'd apologize for my brother-in-law's shameful treatment of you, but you must know by now he is an absolute brute." With that, Lady Sara took her hand and led Catrina into the keep as she called back orders to the men.

What could I possibly say to that?

"Let's get you cleaned up. Mayhap a hot bath?"

Catrina nearly fainted from relief. "That would be most welcome, Lady—"

"Sara. Please call me Sara."

"Sara. Thank you."

The lady of the manor flashed her a brilliant smile and stopped, sweeping her arms out with pride. "I give you the great hall of Kenshire Castle."

Holy Saint Thomas, it was immense! Warm and welcoming, the hall reminded Catrina of Brockburg, though it was, of course, much grander. Many grand families kept their most decorative and opulent tapestries for the lord and lady's solar. But like Brockburg, Kenshire's great hall boasted thick walls covered with colorful, thickly woven wall hangings, each telling intricate tales. The tartans, of course, that also hung in Brockburg were missing. Although the scenes were a bit different, the effect was the same.

"So you like it?"

"Aye, it's beautiful." And she meant it. Lavender-scented rushes and clean trestle tables were being set for supper, servants bustled about contentedly, and candles glowed in every crevice.

"As are you, Lady Catrina."

She wasn't used to such compliments. Catrina felt her cheeks getting warm. "Thank you. And it's Catrina, if you please." The countess was so poised. And perfect really. It was no wonder Sir Geoffrey had fallen in love with her.

Evelyn had told her the romantic tale of Lady Sara and Sir Geoffrey. Apparently, Hugh Waryn, Geoffrey and Bryce's uncle, had been a close friend of the now-deceased earl. The earl had sent for Hugh before his death, hoping that he could help protect Sara from an enterprising cousin who wished to rob her of her inheritance. Geoffrey had accompanied Hugh to Kenshire, and the rest was history. Only Lady Sara had been engaged at the time, to a man who was supposed to help her protect her title. Evelyn hadn't known the full story there, and Catrina would love to hear the rest.

"Thank you. And a bath would be most appreciated."

Sara showed her to a bedchamber and ordered a bath. Catrina could only compare the feeling of the hot water after so many days traveling to…

She closed her eyes and attempted to think of something else.

Anything else.

But her mind refused to obey. As it had so many times that day, her thoughts returned to

the previous evening. She should be embarrassed, ashamed. But Catrina was neither. Father Simon would have her in church for a week—a month—begging forgiveness. But what was there to forgive? Could something that had felt so perfect, so achingly wonderful, truly be a sin? Just thinking about Bryce's lips on hers...the things he'd done to her with his mouth...

And then there was Graeme.

She cared about him. Had loved him since they were children. But she could never imagine him doing that to her. The mere thought was mortifying.

Scrubbing herself with lemon-scented soap—Catrina had asked for the attendant to leave because she was perfectly capable of washing herself—she forced her thoughts back to the present. A short knock at the door undoubtedly signaled the return of the displaced attendant.

"Come in," she called.

But as she got out of the tub and began to dry herself, the countess—Sara, she corrected herself—walked into the room with a swath of lavender material draped across her arms.

"I trust your bath was satisfactory?"

Sara laid the material on the bed. Walking toward the garment, Catrina could see the lavender cloth was actually a rich surcoat. A cream-colored kirtle lay underneath.

"I know you brought your own, but they'll take at least a day to air. You're welcome to wear this to dinner. You'll be dining in the hall with us, of course."

When Catrina told her it was unnecessary and asked to dine alone in her chamber, using the weariness of travel as an excuse, Lady Sara would not consider it.

So it was by her hostess's gentle coercion that she now stood on a balcony overlooking the great hall, feeling every inch like a princess. Sara had even sent a lady's maid to assist with her hair. Normally it hung loose, but she'd allowed the maid to pull it back. The pearl caul, also borrowed from the countess, held her tresses in place behind her.

Unaccountably nervous, Catrina scanned the hall below. She

had sent her escort, the kindly lady's maid, ahead, needing a moment alone. Well, not quite alone—the hall was filled with knights, ladies, and more servants than she'd ever seen in one place in her life. So much activity. And music. She scanned the room until her gaze rested on the lutist, whose song made her think of home. Of Scotland. The man was either from the north or traveled extensively since the tune was familiar to her.

He reminded her of a troubadour who passed through Brockburg every so often. His tale of "The Buik of Alexander" was always her favorite, but not likely to be played here in England.

Bryce.

Catrina hadn't even realized she was looking for him. But *of course* she had been. He had just entered the hall with his brother and a woman who bore a striking resemblance to him. That could only be his sister Emma.

Not wanting to be found gaping, Catrina began to make her way down the spiraling staircase. Was it her imagination, or did the noise in the hall quiet as she walked toward the dais? There were plenty of other women in the hall. Why would they stare at her?

Because she was Scottish.

The Kerr girl.

Catrina wanted to turn and run back to her room, but Sara intercepted her at the foot of the steps.

"Where is Faye? I specifically asked her to—"

"I asked her for some privacy, my lady." She may be Sara in private, but they were most certainly not alone here.

"Sara," the countess chastised gently. Catrina drew her eyebrows together in confusion. Sara linked arms with her and led her to the dais as she attempted to explain. "We are slightly, how shall I say it, *unconventional* here at Kenshire."

"Barbaric," said the younger woman who'd arrived in the hall with Bryce.

"May I present Miss Emma Waryn?" Sara said.

So, she had guessed correctly. This was Geoffrey and Bryce's sister. The girl looked a bit younger than her brothers, but Catrina couldn't tell her exact age. She had the Waryn's pitch-black hair and blue eyes; the girl was undoubtedly going to be a beauty. Her smile made her look even lovelier. My, they were a good-looking family.

"Of course, I speak only of my brothers, Lady Sara," said Emma, looking behind her.

Catrina had avoided looking at Bryce all day. She had not spoken to him either. It would be necessary for them to communicate for her plan to work, but it was just too soon after...after what had happened between them. She was not giving up even though he was anything but receptive, but she wasn't quite ready to speak to him just yet.

She looked now. He was apparently being seated next to her. How could she possibly endure it? Dressed for dinner in a strikingly black surcoat with a bright white linen underneath, Bryce looked every bit as noble as the rest of his family.

Though it was warm in the hall, she shivered. He held out her chair, his lips pressed in a tight line.

Catrina sat, aware of every movement next to her. No need to be nervous. So she was surrounded by strangers. Seated next to the man who had given her sensual pleasure the evening before.

She swallowed. "I trust your day was pleasant, Sir Bryce?"

Catrina broke a piece of bread and dipped it into the sauce of the first course, which had already been placed in front of them.

"Exceedingly so, Lady Catrina. I see you found a new dress?"

She nearly choked on the bread. The lout.

"Your sister-in-law was gracious enough to lend me one while mine are being hung. How kind of you to notice."

Bryce looked at Sara and then back at her.

"I trust you're getting along with the countess?" His tone was neutral, his face inscrutable.

Lady Sara had been stealing glances at both of them. But she had evidently assured herself that Bryce was minding his manners, because she turned to speak to her husband.

"Exceedingly well. She is very kind."

A servant attempted to fill her wine goblet. Bryce held up his hand to stop her. "Ale for the lady. And for me as well."

The servant moved away to fill Lady Sara's cup and returned a moment later with two mugs of ale.

Catrina watched as the ale was poured. "I shouldn't bring attention to myself." She knew that although she did indeed prefer ale, it was unusual for a lady to favor it. It would be best not to stand out more in a room full of English men and women who already despised her.

"Too late."

She glared at him, assuming he'd meant it as an insult.

Bryce leaned closer to her and whispered, "I didn't mean it that way."

"Then how did you mean it?" As soon as the words left her mouth, she wanted to take them back. As usual.

Bryce sat back, took a bite of mince pie, and cleared his throat. Maybe he hadn't heard her question. Good!

Catrina had just lifted the mug to her lips when he leaned back toward her once again, lowered his voice, and said, "I meant that the minute you walked into this hall, not surprisingly, every male in the room was made aware of your presence."

She drew her eyebrows together.

"You're strikingly beautiful, Catrina."

And with that unlikely declaration, Bryce turned to Lady Sara and spoke to her as if nothing had happened. Catrina gently set her mug back onto the table without drinking from it. Her hand was shaking, and she feared she'd spill its contents.

He thought she was beautiful? He was usually too busy insulting her family to deliver compliments, though he had called her remarkable. And now this.

Some time later, after the meal was cleared and the lutist

began to play once again, Catrina finally had a chance to speak to Bryce in earnest. Couples paired in the space between the trestle tables and the dais as the music wafted through the hall like a soft, lilting lullaby.

This was her chance to convince Bryce of the folly of his actions. He was clearly avoiding her, and she didn't know when she might see him again.

Besides, he couldn't walk away from her if they were dancing.

Tamping down her embarrassment, she forced herself to ask, "Do you dance, my lord?"

His look told her he most certainly did not, but Sara answered for him before he could refuse. "He loves to dance! My brother-in-law would be delighted to dance with you, Lady Catrina."

When they both leveled her with skeptical looks, Sara admitted, "Well, perhaps *loves* is not quite the right word. But he will dance, won't you, dear brother?"

The man in question looked like he was liable to kill someone, but she would not allow him to back out. She needed to speak to him. Soon.

"Wonderful," Catrina said. "Then it's settled. It's been too long since I've had the opportunity."

With one final glower at Sara, Bryce stood up, trapped. He held out his arm, and they stepped off the dais to join the other dancers.

After a quick bow, she laid her hands in his as they lined up behind the other dancers, waiting their turn. Though she'd known this dance would require they touch hands, Catrina was still unprepared for the jolt it sent through her.

She took a deep breath, attempting to slow her breathing.

"Bryce, we need to talk."

As they moved forward in line, Catrina looked straight ahead, not wanting to see his reaction.

"Is that why you asked me to dance?"

His perceptiveness was one of the qualities she admired. "Aye.

Please. I beg you—" she didn't have time to waste words, "—please reconsider what you're doing."

In front of the line now, they marched forward and back, kicking up one foot to the front and then to the side. He didn't answer her. Didn't even acknowledge that she'd spoken.

They repeated the movements, the lutist playing faster with each step. Soon their hands were joined again and Catrina was circling around him. She would not look down as she moved around his perfectly sculpted backside. But she was tempted.

"This isn't the time or place, Catrina."

And then he mimicked her steps. As he circled her, Catrina could feel his eyes on her the entire time. She glanced at the dais and noticed every person there was watching them. It didn't matter. This was too important.

"It's never a good time or place to talk about my family, Bryce." They finished the movement and, hand in hand, moved to the back of the line. "Tell me," she finally looked straight at him, "Are you really going to battle with my brothers? Someone will get killed."

He didn't flinch, but there was something in his eyes…sympathy?

She was a fool to think her words mattered to him. "You don't care what I think. Do you?"

She looked away, regretting the decision to dance. When it came to her family, Bryce was as hard and unflinching now as he'd been the day they met. This was not the man who'd given her pleasure. This was the warlord, the hardened knight who'd never lost a tournament in his life. Who'd trained for the past five years for something he refused to give up.

Vengeance against the Kerrs.

She stopped talking, finished the dance, and begged pardon to be excused.

Bryce glared at her as if *she* had done something wrong. Geoffrey and Emma looked as if they wanted to say something to her, but neither of them spoke. She wanted to be alone. To think. To plan. Because *this* would not work. Bryce could never be convinced her brothers were not the enemy.

Maybe he was right. Maybe they were.

Which meant he was her enemy too.

16

After returning to her bedchamber, Catrina was, blessedly, left alone. As much as she adored Lady Sara, she didn't want to talk to her, or anyone, about her predicament. Because there was simply nothing to talk about. She couldn't escape. She couldn't convince Bryce to change course. First, she'd worried about Toren attempting to find a way into Bristol and getting himself killed. Now her entire clan was preparing for a battle they would not win.

The might of Kenshire's retinue was unmistakable. Not that she had extensive experience in that area, but she'd traveled a bit throughout her own country and seen enough holdings to know Kenshire and its retainers commanded an awe-worthy force. She couldn't imagine being responsible for it all—a duty Lady Sara had taken on after losing her father.

She respected the woman immensely.

Perhaps I should speak with her? After all, she was out of ideas but desperate to do *something*. They were on opposite sides, of course, but she had a feeling the countess would listen nonetheless. It was as good a plan as any.

She asked for privacy the next morning and received it.

Which meant she could only wear the loose yellow surcoat without ties. She searched her trunk for a belt and, finding it, tied it around her waist. A quick brush of her hair—there was even a small mirror in her chamber—and she was prepared to find Lady Sara.

"Pardon, my lady. Where are ye off to so early?"

It just occurred to Catrina that Faye was Hugh's wife. She didn't know him well, but Bryce spoke highly of his uncle. She was glad he could find happiness after losing his first wife.

"Good morning, Faye. I'm looking for Lady Sara, mayhap you've seen her?"

The plump woman, who looked to be in her late forties, cocked her head and gave Catrina a curious glance. "I have, but can it wait till you break your fast?"

She felt her cheeks warming. "I suppose. But I assumed after mass—"

"You'll not find her in morning mass, my lady." Faye waved a dismissive hand. "God rest her soul."

Catrina missed morning mass so often at Brockburg that Father Simon joked he would have to change the time because of her. It made her smile to learn she wasn't the only lady to do so.

"There ya go, Lady Catrina. Ye've been with Bryce far too long, taken on his sour disposition, I fear. A smile is much prettier."

She almost said, "Being a captive will do that," but thought better of it. This woman had done nothing deserving of her sharp tongue.

"Thank you, Mistress Faye, for the kind compliment."

Faye beamed and took her by the arm. "If you want ta speak with mi'lady, I'll show you the way. But try not ta be too shocked, if you please. She really is a lovely woman."

Well of course she was. Why would Faye say such a thing?

She found out a short time later.

They exited the castle through a back, ground-floor entrance after making their way through more than one pentice. Catrina had never seen so many external passageways in one place. If left to her own resources, she would never find her way back.

Outside now, Faye pointed to a concealed entrance. "The sea gate will take you below the curtain wall and straight out to the, well, you'll see."

And with that cryptic comment, Faye left her staring at what she assumed was a secret entranceway. Did she not realize Catrina was a captive? Why would she tell her such a thing? Was she testing her?

Hesitant at first, she wound her way through the dark tunnel, moving down and then up stairs, and finally exited through a postern gate. Blinking, the sunlight bright against vibrant blue sky, Catrina emerged in tall grass. She looked below her soft leather shoes to see sand mixed with small rocks. As she walked, the sound of crashing waves clearly marked her location. Faye had led her to the shore. Sure enough, as the tall grass gave way to pure sand, Catrina found herself standing in front of the most magnificent sight.

Her first glimpse of the North Sea.

She walked toward the water and abruptly stopped. The landscape was beautiful, the lady in front of her equally so. Propped on a large rock, legs bent underneath her, the countess of Kenshire, the most elegant woman she'd ever met, wore...a highly unusual garment.

A pair of breeches, specially designed to fit her small frame, outlined Sara's legs as well as any man's. They were paired with a loose white shirt. She'd never seen such a thing. As if sensing her presence, or maybe her shock, Lady Sara turned and waved. Catrina lifted her hand in greeting and made her way toward the rock outcropping. The strange calls of white-bellied birds signaled her arrival, as if they thought to protect their lady from the intruder.

"Good morn, Lady Catrina."

Catrina could not find her tongue to answer. Which, in itself, was exceedingly rare.

Sara smiled. "You haven't seen the sea before, have you?"

She shook her head.

"Isn't it lovely? Come." Taking Catrina's hand, she led her toward the shoreline. "Wait." She stopped and pointed to her own feet. They were bare. "You simply must take those off," she said, referring to Catrina's shoes.

Catrina lifted the hem of her dress to do as she was told.

"Here, let me help you."

Sara steadied her as she took off each shoe.

Barefoot, Catrina nearly squealed in delight. "It feels so...odd." She wiggled her toes and watched in fascination as they made imprints in the sand. As she walked closer to the water, the sand became harder and it was easier to walk. She was looking out toward the horizon in fascination when a wave crashed over her feet. She ran backward and straight into Lady Sara.

"My apologies. It's just so cold."

"I can't imagine what it must be like to see this for the first time," said Sara.

"I completely failed to consider that Kenshire Castle is on the coast. I may not have dreaded—"

Dammit.

"I mean to say—"

"Nay, tell me." Sara seemed genuinely interested, which reminded Catrina of why she'd sought her out in the first place.

She wanted someone to talk to so badly. But she had to know something first.

"Forgive me for asking such an impertinent question, but why are you being so kind to me? After all, I—"

"Am the sister of my husband's enemy. I know it well," said Sara.

Which didn't answer her question.

The extraordinarily beautiful woman crossed her arms and stared out to the sea. She didn't answer for a moment, and Catrina certainly didn't want to repeat her question. It had been an impertinent question to ask, and to repeat it would be to double the injury.

Finally, Sara answered. "After the raid, Geoffrey remained at Bristol long enough to learn that you apparently have somewhat of a reputation there."

That would depend on who was relaying the information.

"My husband had a difficult time reconciling what he learned about you, and your brothers, with the family he has hated for so long."

Catrina wasn't sure she understood. "What do you mean?"

Sara sighed, the corners of her mouth lifting in a wry smile. "Many of the people of Bristol have lived there for generations. They've become accustomed to unrest so close to the Border. But when your clan took it five years ago, even the most jaded among them were surprised. The Waryn family has claimed that barony for three generations. But despite the razed fields and burned and abandoned homes fresh in their memories, even the most skeptical villagers appreciated your brother. His reputation as a strong and fair leader did not go unnoticed."

Catrina wasn't sure what to say.

"Geoffrey said you are beloved there. The woman 'who learns in a day,' they call you. They say you're good at just about everything."

She knew the people of Bristol had warmed to her these past years, but this felt...bigger. More accepting. Catrina had just tried to eke out some semblance of normalcy while she mounted her campaign to convince Toren to allow her to marry Graeme.

"I'm not suggesting Geoffrey doesn't want the same revenge Bryce seeks."

Catrina's shoulders sank. She must look as broken as she felt because Sara immediately grabbed her hands.

"But he has me to temper that desire. I know better than

anyone the destructiveness a few seeds of hate can grow." Sara smiled, her gaze steady and sincere. "And now that I've met you, now that I've seen you together, I'm even more convinced my plan will suit us all."

"I don't understand?"

"Nay," Sara replied, "I don't suppose you would. So let me be direct."

Catrina was almost afraid of what Sara would say. She could hardly follow the conversation. From a woman dressed in breeches, one who treated her admitted enemy so kindly...'direct' could mean just about anything.

"Catrina...I want you to marry Bryce."

17

Catrina's eyes widened. She stood there for what seemed like an eternity, staring into the smiling face of one of the most unconventional women she'd ever met.

Marry?

She glanced up at Kenshire Castle. Catrina had been so mesmerized by the sea and the sensation of walking on sand for the first time that she hadn't taken the time to look back at the castle. It was even more impressive from this angle. Towering above them, it seemed to almost float in the sky.

She felt dizzy. She blinked, attempting to clear her mind. Catrina tried to focus on Lady Sara, who clearly expected a response.

"You're shocked," Sara spoke quickly, "I know it seems crazy. But listen to me." The countess squeezed her hands. "I've heard nothing but good things about you, which is surprising since, well, you are a Kerr after all."

She had the good grace to look embarrassed about that particular proclamation.

"Then the rumors started swirling—" Sara continued.

"Rumors?" Catrina finally found her voice. "What rumors?"

Sara released her hands and began to make lines in the sand with her shoeless feet.

"About you…and Bryce?" She looked up.

Catrina's heart began to race. Had he told someone about their encounters? How humiliating! She would *kill* him.

"I'm not sure what you mean," she answered, her voice hesitant.

"Just that, well, there's been a bit of talk about…how shall I say it. An 'interest' between the two of you."

"An interest?" Catrina was sure she sounded like an utter idiot.

"It's not important. What matters is the way Bryce looks at you. And you him. I must admit to being slightly excited about the possibility of a new sister-in-law. I mean, Emma is a wonderful girl, but she is still a girl, after all. When Bryce refused to eat dinner in the hall, I didn't understand why at first, but then—"

"A new sister-in-law?" she interrupted.

"But then last eve it became clear. He cares for you. Doesn't want to, of course. Probably hates himself for it. But that hardly matters because the rumors were accurate. You are meant for each other!"

Marry Bryce?

"Lady Sara—"

"Sara, please. We'll be related, after all."

Catrina doubted that very much. "I don't believe Bryce cares for me at all. Actually, I think the exact opposite is true. I sought you out this morning for advice. He refuses to reconsider letting me go free. He's intent on revenge. Understandably so, perhaps, but my brother *did not* kill his parents. Toren didn't want Bristol, but he was ordered to extend his holdings south. The king may publicly recognize the newly established border, but privately he does not. And neither does my clan." Catrina was speaking so fast, she could hardly get the words out. "But I think I can convince them that Bristol Manor is lost. Unfortunately, Bryce won't listen to reason. So he most certainly does *not* care for me. Otherwise he wouldn't be intent on killing the people I love."

By this point Catrina had worked herself into a state. She paced back and forth.

"Bryce doesn't know my brothers. They'll demand retribution for keeping me hostage. I've tried to talk reason to him, but it's no use. By God's bones and St. Mary's too, I refuse to sit by idly while the men I care for slaughter one another!"

She realized immediately what she'd said. And judging from Sara's face, the countess had heard it too.

"I knew it! Bryce has never hidden from a woman in his life, or not as long as I've known him. Just the opposite actually." Sara covered her mouth with her hands. "I mean, not to say—"

"The Slayer. I know. His reputation precedes him."

Sara shrugged her shoulders as if to apologize for the slip. "Then it's settled. Don't you see, it's a perfect solution. He's been downright pleasant since he arrived. And now I know why. It's perfect!"

Catrina had to disagree. "Pleasant? You're serious, aren't you?"

"Oh aye. Normally his disposition leaves much to be desired."

Catrina wouldn't argue that point. "That much is true. But even so..."

"I knew it!"

Sara smiled so broadly, Catrina almost hated to point out the flaw in her plan. "But it doesn't matter. I'm to be married already."

As much as she didn't want to talk about Graeme—her feelings for him over the last few weeks had felt anything but secure—Catrina felt compelled to tell Sara of him.

"Who?" Sara narrowed her eyes. Her expression looked quite familiar. She'd obviously acquired the Waryn scowl since marrying the family's eldest son. Sara began walking toward the castle. Catrina followed.

"His name is Graeme deSowlis. A neighbor and enemy to my clan. Until recently, that is. Rumor has it, Toren allied with him for my benefit. Which is exceedingly odd since I've spent the better part of three years trying to convince Toren to allow our marriage."

"So you're not betrothed?"

"Nay, not formally. But a marriage between Graeme and I, one that would unite our clans again, seemed very…natural."

Picking up her shoes, Sara shook out the grains of sand clinging to them.

"Natural? I'm afraid that doesn't sound very convincing."

Catrina picked up her own leather shoes and imitated Sara.

"Graeme is wonderful. A true gentleman. Now chieftain of his clan. He's a respected warrior. Any woman would be lucky to call him husband."

They walked through the grass toward the entrance of the hidden sea gate.

"Do you love him?"

Catrina stopped in her tracks. Sara looked at her expectantly. What could she say? Of course she loved him. She'd always loved him. Graeme was going to be her savior. The man who would give her the thing she'd always wanted.

A real family.

But Sara deserved the truth. As her feelings for Bryce grew, despite her best efforts to squish them, it had become clear to her that she did not love Graeme *that* way.

"Like a brother."

Catrina had not expected a response, and she didn't get one. She looked away from the looming castle above them. The sun rose high above the water, marking a new day. One she expected to be similar to the last. Stuck between wanting to protect her brothers and denying what she felt for her captor.

Must it be so? She had railed against her brothers so often about her lack of freedom that she'd convinced herself it was the only way. That the men in her life would, whether she liked it or not, decide for her. But somehow this conversation with

Lady Sara Caiser, Countess of Kenshire, had changed everything.

There *was* another way. Today would not be the same as the last. Or the same as every day she'd spent at Bristol, allowing Toren to control her fate.

This day would be different.

She looked at Sara, who nodded encouragingly.

Yes, today she would control her own fate.

18

It was just as he'd expected.

A force of over one hundred men marched south from Brockburg. The Kerr chief's motives were now clear. He came for his sister. The small army was headed toward Kenshire.

Kerr didn't hide the fact that he was gathering an army. If the scouts' report was accurate, representatives from no less than three clans—Kerr, deSowlis, and Moffat—were headed this way. That Kerr could have easily brought more men told Bryce this was nothing more than a show of force. Kenshire's walls could not be breached, and the chief knew that.

Bryce's new plan was a simple one, even though Geoffrey vehemently disagreed with it. He would insist on trial by combat for the crimes committed against his family. Hugh had ridden out to meet with the contingent from Brockburg to negotiate with the chief of Clan Kerr. The terms were simple. They would solve the issue of Bristol's lordship in a trial by combat, but they would champion themselves. The lord and the chief.

The winner would claim Bristol Manor, and the loser would relinquish all claims to Bristol, the lordship as well as its manor and village. Its people would be assured safe passage to leave or, if they preferred, to stay and serve the lord, whether he be English or Scottish.

Catrina would be returned to her clan either way.

He would not allow the people of Bristol to live with the threat of Clan Kerr constantly looming. The border was dangerous territory, aye. But he would never allow what happened at his home five years ago to repeat itself.

In a strange way, he had Catrina to thank for his plan.

Bryce had spent five years hating the name Kerr. Five years planning vengeance on those who had killed his parents. At first, Bryce had hated Catrina too—simply for who she was. But he eventually realized his hate for her was unwarranted.

He knew that now. He shuddered to think of how he had treated her at Bristol. She'd won the hearts of Bristol's people—from Evelyn to the maid, Elise, and Thomas and the men who guarded her. Every one of them had immediately seen what it had taken Bryce too long to notice. She was a kind and capable woman who said the most outrageous things.

Yet she was a Kerr.

Hatred had blinded him. The men who fought for Toren Kerr may be Scottish, but they spoke like his men, bled like his men. Why should they be casualties to this unending war over the border?

But there was one man he could not, would not, forgive. The one that gave the orders to destroy his home. Whose men had killed both his father and mother.

Toren Kerr had to die.

Of course, if Toren Kerr agreed with the arrangement, it was still possible their individual sovereigns might overrule the agreement. Luckily Lady Sara's connections at court ensured the English monarch, at least, would not interfere. And there was talk that Toren Kerr had more sway now than he had five years earlier.

Such a trial would put a legal end to their feud. It would end it for everyone.

Bryce made his way to the stable. Intent on an early morning ride to clear his head, he'd skipped the meal and asked the cook instead for bread. The saucy servant who was always free with her opinions had said he acted too much like Lady Sara. He wasn't sure what that meant, but she'd given him two slices of freshly baked bread, still warm.

Setting aside a niggling feeling of guilt, he ordered his horse ready for a ride. Bristol's entire stable, even though it was large for a modest manor, could fit inside a few stalls of Kenshire's massive structure. Only one stable hand appeared. The others and the marshal, Eddard, broke their fast in the keep. Sara's insistence that all the servants sup together with the lord and lady was not unusual at Kenshire.

Bryce had advised Geoffrey not to tell his wife of his plan. He had no desire to be followed for days as she attempted to talk him out of it, which was exactly what Sara would do if she knew. And then there was Catrina. Bryce tried to force his mind elsewhere. He hated thinking about how she would react.

It will kill her. The niggling feeling of guilt became an iron weight in his chest.

As he waited, a beautiful chestnut seemed to be looking at him. Of course, Davie was no more aware of what he had planned than his lady, but as Bryce moved closer to Catrina's beloved horse, he couldn't help but feel…sorry for her, for himself, for this whole sordid situation.

The inn had been a mistake. And when Sara had insisted he dine in the hall, he'd known nothing good would come of it. Then she'd entered the hall dressed as fine as the countess, her hair held back like a queen's, and Bryce had worried he would embarrass himself. Which was absurd since he'd stopped caring about others' opinions long ago.

He had to remind himself every day that her brother had caused his parents' deaths. It was the only thing that could allay the spell she seemed to have cast on him. Lust for a beautiful woman had gotten him into trouble only once before in his life. Since Lady Elena, he had kept himself at a distance. Women sated his desires, nothing more.

But Catrina got to him in a way that, frankly, scared him. It was entirely different than his boyhood fascination with Elena. The closer he and Catrina became, the more he thought of her. Now, he found himself banishing the woman from his thoughts every waking hour.

He could sense a presence behind him and turned to find the object of his thoughts—and his desires—leaning casually against the entranceway. He'd seen the strange garment before on his sister-in-law. Although it had jarred him the first time he spied Lady Sara in such a state, Bryce had spent quite a bit of time at Kenshire since the wedding.

So he was used to seeing the countess dressed that way. But Catrina was an entirely different matter. He was jolted back to the evening they'd spent together. He imagined his hands caressing her long legs, every curve so much softer than his own.

Those very legs were now clearly outlined for all to see. And if the stable hand's expression was any indication, Bryce was not alone in his admiration.

"Get out," he snapped at the boy.

The lad jumped and led Bryce's horse out of the stable.

"That wasn't very nice," Catrina said.

He stared at her as fixedly as a squire who was seeing a naked girl for the first time. Her reddish-brown hair was pulled back in a long braid. Her full lips pursed together in an expression of displeasure. How he longed to soften them with his tongue. Taste her as he'd done at the inn. Watch her expression change from alarm to pure, unbridled pleasure. Bryce shifted his weight, suddenly uncomfortable, and glared at her.

"What are you wearing?"

She walked toward him, and by God, he knew this was some sort of test. A test he could not help but fail.

"What does it look like I'm wearing?" Catrina moved past him, her arm briefly grazing his own as she reached for Davie.

"It looks like you're wearing a pair of Sara's breeches. The question is, why?"

Davie clearly loved the attention, neighing softly.

"I accepted her very kind offer. When I mentioned giving Davie some exercise this fine morn—"

"You're not permitted to leave the castle grounds."

His tone was harsh. Necessarily so.

"Aye, which is why I'm going with you."

Oh no, she isn't.

"No."

She turned and laid a hand on his arm. Bryce was not strong enough for this. She looked at him expectantly, eyes wide. Her dark lashes fluttered as she blinked. Innocent was never a word that came to mind when he thought of Catrina. And neither was 'seductress,' but unless he was mistaken, that was a fairly accurate description of her at this moment.

"It won't work, Catrina."

Her eyebrows drew together in mock surprise. "Whatever do you mean?"

He nearly laughed. Catrina had many assets, but subtlety wasn't one of them.

Unlike her, Bryce did have experience in the art of seduction. She wouldn't change his mind, but he could have some fun showing her how this particular game was played.

"I mean—" He took a step closer, so they were near touching, and reached out to stroke Davie's sleek flank. He watched the horse's muscles flex under his fingers. "—that if you intend to seduce someone—" he covered her hand with his own, stroking the horse with one joined movement, "—then do it correctly."

Bryce intertwined his fingers with Catrina's and lifted her hand from the horse. Turning it over, he rubbed her palm with his thumb in slow, circular movements. When her mouth opened to speak, he cut her off.

"Nay, don't. I know Sara well. And I'm beginning to understand the Scottish lass that is my reluctant hostage." He slid his thumb through the opening of her odd garment—something between a thick chemise and surcoat with sides—and exposed the wrist below. Lifting it to his mouth, he kissed her softly, allowing his tongue to graze the sensitive skin there.

The hunter had become the hunted. Bryce watched her swallow hard and knew he'd accomplished his task.

But he wasn't finished.

"Would you like to know how to seduce someone, Lady Catrina?"

Waiting for her nod, he did the one thing he knew she loved. The thing everyone said was rare for him, but which seemed to happen so naturally in Catrina's presence.

HE SMILED. A slow, sensual smile that reached his eyes.

Catrina had lost this battle.

When Sara had first suggested she marry Bryce, she'd thought the woman was mad. But if Catrina was being honest…she was in love with Bryce. It made no sense—the man was her captor and wanted to kill her brother. He was as stern as any man she'd ever met, slow to smile and even more unlikely to laugh. The exact opposite of Graeme, the man she had always *thought* she loved. And she did love him. But not in the way a woman should love her husband.

After the night at the inn, the truth had become clear to her. He was like another one of her brothers. Kind, at least to her, and safe. With him, Catrina had always imagined a "normal" life. A mother, father, children…the things she'd never had. But truly, what *was* normal? While her mother had abandoned her and her brothers, they'd never really wanted for anything. She'd grown up with love, security—and until she'd insisted on venturing to Bristol—the kind of freedom most women in her station didn't have.

But Bryce was another matter altogether.

There was nothing brotherly about the way she felt for him. She had admitted as much to the countess, and Sara had whisked her away to her own bedchamber—Catrina was sure it was the size of the entirety of both Bristol and Brockburg's upper chambers put together—to lay out their plan.

Getting Bryce to admit his feelings was the first step.

Once he did that, Sara insisted, he would reconsider his need for revenge against her family. But they were running out of time. According to Sara, her clan marched toward Kenshire even now. Drastic action was necessary.

Hence the attempt at seduction.

She would hate to tell Sara how miserably she'd failed. Bryce knew exactly what she was doing—even if he didn't know the real reason for it.

Now, as his lips touched her wrist, she shifted her weight to support her legs, which would surely give out at any moment.

"Well?"

He waited for an answer, but she couldn't remember the question.

"Would you like to know how to seduce someone properly?"

Oh, aye. What possible answer could she give to that outrageous question?

"First, you must not be so obvious."

He didn't move. Didn't even touch her. But his eyes made it very clear what he intended.

There it was again. That feeling deep in her core, the fluttering she'd felt when he lay beneath her. She remembered the precise moment he had poised himself to wickedly touch his mouth to the most intimate part of her body.

She had that feeling again.

They stood so close she could hear his intake of breath. She breathed deeply, and the smell of hay mixed with the increasingly familiar musky scent that was Bryce made her lightheaded.

"Kiss me."

Was he serious? She would do no such thing.

"I will not move, Catrina. If you want to turn around and walk away, do it. If you want to stay, then kiss me."

She disliked being ordered about and would not do it.

True to his word, Bryce simply stood there, staring at her. "Every time we've been intimate, I've made the first move. How am I to know you want me as badly as I do you?"

He wanted her? Well, of course he did. Isn't that exactly what Sara said? That, by the way he looked at her, there was no denying Bryce desired her. Their encounters told her as much. And she must use that desire to "bring him to his senses."

He opened his mouth slightly, as if inviting her toward him. Catrina was strong, but not that strong. She leaned toward him and hesitantly lifted her lips to his.

Bryce didn't move. He didn't wrap his arms around her or move his lips over hers. Instead, he stood as still as a statue, looking down at her as if to say, "that was not much of a kiss." It wasn't, of course, but she didn't have much experience in this area. Still, she knew what he had taught her, at least. She leaned in, closed her eyes, and put her lips to his again. But this time she slipped her tongue inside and forced him to part his lips. He gave his own tongue in surrender, and she took advantage of that small movement.

Forcing his mouth to open wider, she swept her tongue over his, willing him to respond.

And he did.

Bryce picked her up, and she wrapped her legs around his waist on some nameless instinct. She reached around his neck for support, and after carrying her deep within the stable, he backed her up against a stone wall and gave her full access to every inch of his mouth. He kissed her hungrily, every movement making her more and more sure of her decision.

She couldn't get enough of him.

Catrina knew there was more. And she wanted that. Wanted Bryce to make her his in every way. Unfortunately, he didn't know it yet, and his honor would not allow him to take her virginity.

Or would it? *How far can he be pushed?*

Catrina had seen the sex act before—inadvertently, of course. But in a small castle that afforded little privacy save the lord and his family's private bedchambers, she'd seen things her brothers wished she had not.

But she didn't know how to tempt a man enough to make such a thing happen.

It seemed like a good start when Bryce lifted her shirt and slid his hand underneath. Still propped against the wall, Catrina marveled at the ease with which he held her in place with one hand. The other scorched a path from her stomach toward her breast before it finally found its mark. His hand splayed across her breast and squeezed gently. When his thumb circled and teased her nipple, Catrina instinctively pressed herself closer to him.

Kissing her harder, more deeply, Bryce groaned against her mouth. Or was that her? She couldn't tell. Couldn't think. The wave of passion, the feeling of his large hand caressing her...

Catrina had never felt anything like it before. Well, maybe once or twice—with *him*.

But she wanted more.

"Make love to me, Bryce."

The words escaped her lips on their own accord, but she didn't regret them.

His hand stilled. It reached around her back and moved to its original destination underneath her buttocks. Supporting her with his hands, he pulled back to look at her. For a moment, she thought he would take her advice. Instead, he lifted her up, the mask of indifference firmly back in place, and set her down.

"Consider yourself schooled in the art of seduction, my lady."

With that, he walked away.

She stood there for a moment, trying to understand what had just happened.

She should be embarrassed. Mortified, actually, that he'd rebuked her offer. Instead, she took a deep breath, lifted her chin, marched out into the bright sunlight, and watched as Bryce rode through the courtyard.

When he disappeared through the gatehouse entrance, she walked determinedly toward the main keep. The meal was apparently at an end, and the courtyard sprang to life.

Catrina navigated her way through the crowd to find Lady Sara.

"My lady, may I help you find someone?"

She recognized the steward from the previous evening. He was weighed down by three sacks balanced in his arms. "Good day, Peter."

Catrina managed to surprise him. She rarely forgot a name, and although they hadn't been formally introduced, she was sure her memory served her well.

He bowed, an odd gesture given the fact that she was technically a captive. But aside from the fact that she was not permitted to leave the castle grounds without an approved companion, Catrina was starting to feel more like a guest even after just one day. And she was surprised by the kind reception she'd received from Kenshire's staff.

"Good day, Lady Catrina. Are you looking for my lady, perhaps?"

"Aye, do you know where I may find her?" Catrina looked over his shoulder into the arched entranceway that marked the final passage into Kenshire's main keep.

"I do, but she asked not to be disturbed as she looks over the accounts. Of course, she may make an exception—"

"Nay, please don't trouble her."

Peter shifted his weight to accommodate the sacks he carried.

"Here, let me help you."

Before he could protest, Catrina reached for one of the sacks and positioned it easily in her arms.

"My, lady, I insist—"

"As do I. Now, where do these belong?"

He looked at her strangely, but for St. Peter's sake, she would not let an aging gentleman burden himself unnecessarily. She was perfectly capable of carrying a sack of...

"What's in here?" she asked.

With a final glance her way, Peter walked off in the direction of the kitchens. "Wool for the chandler. To make wicks. The poor man's apprentice up and died, God rest his soul. So until he finds another...."

He never finished, but Catrina understood. In a castle of this size, the chandler must keep busy. She couldn't imagine the number of candles needed to light so many rooms.

"The poor apprentice. Was he young, then?"

Peter shook his head and opened a door to the same building that housed the kitchens.

Catrina had expected a stench from the animal fat used to make tallow, but the large room—with candles hanging from every available space—was a pleasant one. An old man was bent over a large cauldron, and he didn't even hear them enter.

Catrina put her sack on a wooden table and moved closer to see what the chandler was doing. She'd assisted the chandler at Brockburg before, so she knew a little about his craft. He dipped wicks into the melted wax repeatedly, forming a tall candle. The shade was slightly different than she was used to...

And then she realized. "You're using beeswax!"

The old man jumped back, as if only then realizing he wasn't alone.

"My apologies. I didn't mean to startle you-"

"Alfred, may I introduce Lady Catrina Kerr of Clan Kerr," Peter nearly shouted.

She understood why immediately. "Lady Catrina Kerr," she repeated even louder.

In nondescript brown robes tied at the waist with a rope, the man looked more like a monk than a merchant.

"A pleasure," Alfred answered before turning back to his work.

"May I?" She picked up a wick and held it over the cauldron, waiting for the man's approval before getting to work.

Although the chandler nodded and worked silently beside her, Peter had a harder time accepting her assistance.

"Lady Catrina, I must ask you return with me. You are a guest at Kenshire Castle. There's no reason for you—"

She dipped the wick up and down, not bothering to look up. "I'm not a guest, Peter. I'm a captive." Alfred either didn't hear or chose to ignore that bit of information. "And Alfred could clearly use my help. Besides, I have nothing better to occupy my time. But thank you for your concern."

After a few moments, the sound of Peter's footfalls told her she was alone with the chandler. Catrina didn't mind the repetitive work. It was only the smell she'd hated while assisting the chandler in Brockburg. She belatedly realized she wore Lady Sara's clothing. It was a good thing they used beeswax here. She'd only heard of beeswax being used in monasteries and churches. Kenshire must be very wealthy indeed.

And although Alfred didn't speak, she could tell he appreciated her help. From time to time, he looked at her and smiled. His kindly, wrinkled face made her think of Father Simon. She wasn't sure why. Alfred was much older and looked nothing like the priest. Maybe it was his smile. It reached the corner of his eyes, which crinkled when he grinned.

She had no idea how much time went by. Thinking of home, her brothers, and her decision to marry Bryce, Catrina couldn't help but wonder what Toren would do when she told him. If he was reluctant to agree to a betrothal with the chieftain of a neighboring clan, how would he feel about her wedding an Englishman? One who wanted to kill him?

She wasn't overly concerned. After all, he wouldn't have a choice. If she could convince Bryce, she and Sara had agreed the wedding would have to take place with or without her brother's permission. He might be angry...well, he would be furious...but at least he would remain alive. As would her future husband.

Bryce, a husband. Was that really what she wanted?

Yes, it was.

Falling in love with Bryce, she decided, was quite like being a woolen wick on its way to becoming a candle. One moment the hot vat of wax threatened to burn you alive. The next you were yanked back out, allowed to cool, and eventually you became a thing of beauty.

Now how to get Bryce to realize he felt the same way? At least, Sara was convinced he did. Catrina wasn't so sure. He may desire her. But love?

"What in God's name do you think you're doing?

There was no mistaking that voice, and he did not sound like a man in love. Quite the opposite.

Not for the first time, Bryce was furious with her.

19

After he left Catrina in the stables, Bryce couldn't seem to accomplish any task. He was even knocked to the ground during his workout. A rarity unless Geoffrey or Thomas served as his sparring partner. Visions of his "lesson" with Lady Catrina had forced their way into his thoughts, distracting him.

When the field roared at his mistake, he congratulated the elated knight who'd knocked him down. Abandoning his workout, he'd headed back to the hall for a meeting with Geoffrey and his captain of the guard.

Make love to me. The words kept repeating themselves in his mind.

Setting her down and walking away was excruciatingly difficult. But she was clever enough to understand the consequences of such an act, and Catrina had made it clear how much she wanted to marry her Scot and have a family. He would not jeopardize that.

Though he couldn't imagine why she was so smitten with the man. If he truly wanted to marry her, then he should have brought Toren Kerr to heel. Or to hell with his permission.

Bryce pushed the thought of Catrina with another man out of

his mind, but somewhere on his way to the hall, he changed his destination. The meeting could be delayed. Catrina deserved an apology.

Bryce had assumed residing at Kenshire would make his job of avoiding Lady Catrina easier, but he found himself seeking her out at nearly every turn.

Only he couldn't find her anywhere.

After his search turned up nothing, he looked in Lady Sara's solar. Sara, Faye, and Emma all claimed not to have seen her. He finally learned Catrina had walked through the courtyard hours earlier, but no one could tell him where she'd gone.

His strides became longer and more deliberate after he left the hall. He spoke with men at the guardhouse and even those in the east tower since Catrina obviously knew of the sea gate. He'd heard about her pre-dawn visit with Lady Sara, and one could only imagine what the two women had discussed given Catrina's seduction attempt in the stables.

Anger and anxiety and, little though he wished to acknowledge it, fear thrummed through him. Could she be hiding somewhere on the grounds?

"My lord?" Peter laid a hand on his shoulder from behind. "I've been told you're looking for Lady Catrina?"

Bryce turned. "Aye, do you know where she is?"

Bryce could tell by his expression he did. "Where is Catrina?"

"The lady is with Alfred," Peter's greying eyebrows drew together. "Are you quite all right, my lord?"

No. "Fine, Peter, my thanks. What is she doing with the chandler?" But he was already walking toward the building where the candlemaker worked, too impatient to wait for an answer. "Never mind. I have a feeling I already know."

He'd never met a woman in his life, or man for that matter, who knew so many things. A lady of her stature had no business brewing ale or, if his suspicions were correct, assisting the chandler. Most would never know how to do such things. At first he'd assumed Brockburg had a small staff and utilized its lady out of necessity. But he had come to realize Catrina was not just an extraordinarily quick learner. She also enjoyed working with her hands. Staying busy.

Her confinement must have nearly killed her.

He had mistreated her in so many ways. And though she looked like an angel stooped over the pot of wax, her cheeks reddened from the heat, he found himself raising his voice at her. "What in God's name do you think you're doing?"

He regretted his tone, but she'd worried him, dammit. He'd begun to think something had happened to her. Or that she'd somehow managed to escape.

Catrina turned, calm and untroubled by his question.

"One would think that was obvious, my lord. I'm making candles. You know, the sticks of wax used to—"

"I am well aware of the purpose of a candle, Lady Catrina. But Alfred is a more than capable chandler, are you not, sir?"

Belatedly he remembered the man couldn't hear two broadswords clanging in battle.

"He is quite capable," Catrina cut in, "but lacking a staff. Were you aware his apprentice was killed in a wagon accident? And that the man's replacement ran off with the blacksmith's daughter?"

It didn't surprise him that Catrina would know such things. She was incredibly intelligent, yes, but she was also kind. Although she was undeniably a Kerr, she was a good person. A wonderful one.

"Nay, I was not. May I speak to you, Lady Catrina? In private?"

She looked startled. Had he been that harsh with her? Enough for any semblance of kindness to be met with apprehension?

She hung the perfectly formed candle to dry and brushed past him to step outside. Before he could follow her, a frail voice beckoned him.

"My lord?"

He moved closer to the man Catrina had spent the afternoon assisting.

"Yes, Alfred?"

"I am capable. I've been supplyin' candles for Kenshire my whole life, and Lady Sara is findin' a replacement to assist me. But it was mighty kind of Lady Catrina to help an old man this afternoon."

"Aye, and I'm not angry for it." He didn't want the man to think Catrina was in trouble.

"I know it. You were worried for her. Did you know I've been married three times, my lord?"

Lord help the man. One wife was too many.

"Nay, I did not." But he did know the chandler had no wife now. "I'm sorry for your losses."

"Three wives, but only one I loved."

Bryce watched Alfred's automatic movements. Did he even realize he was still working as he talked to him?

"I may be a chandler and not a great lord. I can't read or write or even climb stairs any longer. But I do know some things."

The old man's quiet tone and subdued demeanor didn't lessen the impact of his words. Quite the opposite.

But he wasn't finished.

"Lady Catrina...the angel that was sent to me today. She's in love with you, my lord.

And you're a mighty lucky man for it."

Catrina. In love with him?

Nay. She hated him. With good reason. He thanked the chandler for his words and quickly exited the building.

HIS MIND still reeling from Alfred's revelation, Bryce followed Lady Catrina as she wandered through the courtyard, letting her choose their destination. The day grew late, and Kenshire's people began to prepare for the evening meal. Wagons were unloaded and children ushered home. The air, cooler now that it did not have the sun to recommend it, somehow felt lighter this close to the coast.

He thought of the first time he had seen Lady Sara in her breeches, the only way he could describe such a garment though they were thicker and designed for a woman's legs. At the time, he'd wondered why she would want to dress like a man. But over the last months, as he and his brother and their uncle had prepared to take back Bristol, he'd came to know, and admire, the woman who so ably ruled an earldom.

Geoffrey told him the garment was more than just a replacement for her typical attire. The explanation had confused him at the time, but as he watched Catrina pace back and forth, her hands twisting and turning the long braid at her side, Bryce thought he might finally understand what his brother had tried to explain to him. Catrina was similar to Sara in many ways. He shouldn't be surprised the women got along so splendidly.

Could Alfred be right?

"Lord Waryn!" A boy no older than ten and two came running toward them. "Master Peter told me I could find you here. Come quickly."

"Who sent you?"

"Sir Geoffrey, my lord. He needs to see you immediately. They're coming."

Bryce looked from the boy to Catrina, whose eyes widened. Her face drained of color.

Without waiting for a response, the boy ran away, likely to tell his brother he'd been found. That the scouts had returned so soon could only mean one thing. The Scots were closer than they'd assumed. They moved fast for such a large party.

"My lady." He nodded to Catrina and walked away. There was nothing to say. The apology he'd intended for his treatment in the stables would no longer be welcome. Certainly not when she learned what he had planned for the days ahead.

"Bryce, wait. I must speak to you."

He would not turn back.

"Bryce?"

Her pleading tone was like a knife in his gut. An enemy's knife, twisting and turning. Except the blessed numbness that came with such a wound was absent. With every step he took, the wound continued to tear at him until it reached down to his soul. He wanted to turn back. To heal the pain in her voice.

But he wanted one thing more. He walked into the hall and was guided to the solar, where Geoffrey sat with the captain of his guard and Kenshire's constable. He could tell from their expressions the thing he desired most would come to pass soon.

"Clan Kerr is no more than two days from here," said Gerard de Winters, the constable.

He turned to his brother.

"Geoffrey, do not say it." When his brother opened his mouth to speak, Bryce cut him off. "I've spent my life as your little brother. I've admired you, tried to be you, for as long as I can remember. We took Bristol back together, and I still looked to you for advice. Every man in this room knows without Kenshire's support, Bristol Manor and its village would still be in the hands of the clan that marches here to destroy us."

He turned to Gerard. "I thank you for your support. Then and now."

Sitting across from his brother, he finished what he came here to say. "You gave Bristol to me. And as its lord and commander, I will do what is necessary to protect it. Clan Kerr will never again take what is ours. I leave at dawn."

"Bryce, you can't—"

He raised his voice. "Hugh has just sent word that Kerr is in agreement. I can, and I will. Send your men, if you'd like. Though I did not come here to put Kenshire at risk."

"Kenshire is not at risk, my lord," Gerard said.

Bryce ignored him.

"Send for the sheriff."

No one talked. Or even moved. He didn't intend to be swayed on this, although he knew Geoffrey would try. He would settle this matter once and for all. Either Toren Kerr would be killed and Bristol freed from his clan's threat, or Bristol and the feudal barony that accompanied it would be lost. Either way, the people would remain safe. They would not live in fear of another raid every day.

"You gave me your word, brother, and I'll have it again."

"Bryce, I never imagined you'd go through with this—"

"Your word."

Geoffrey's jaw locked the way it did when he was extremely unhappy, but there was nothing he could do. He would not go back on a promise, and they both knew it.

"The sheriff will be here at dawn to accompany you. As will I. Nay, do not argue with me. If you're intent on this trial, I'll be there to deal with the outcome. Either way."

There would be only one outcome.

For the first time in Bryce's life, he felt like a coward. But the thought of telling Catrina…

He couldn't do it. She'd find out soon enough. In the meantime, he meant to avoid her. The next time they met, if there was a next time, her brother would be dead, and she would hate him. With good reason.

So be it.

20

The last few hours had been a whirlwind. After Bryce was called into a council meeting, Catrina attended an extremely subdued meal. The head table, at least, was subdued. The other fifty or so people who dined on manchet and spiced rabbit spent the evening blissfully unaware that anything was wrong.

Lady Sara claimed not to know what was happening, and Catrina believed her. All of them furious at being left out of the discussion, Sara, Catrina, and Emma huddled together, speculating about the meeting. Sara only knew as much as Catrina, that her clan and their allies were marching toward Kenshire. Peter refused to talk, insisting it was Geoffrey's place, not his, to do so. According to Sara, they had argued—a rare occurrence. They normally made decisions together, but when she'd demanded to be brought into the discussions, Geoffrey had insisted it was Bristol's business and Bryce's story to tell.

"What do you think he has planned?" Sara asked Catrina.

"Damned if I know." Catrina clasped a hand over her mouth. She'd done so well lately, but the epithet simply slipped.

The other women broke into giggles, eliciting stares from those seated closest to them.

"You have to remember, I'm naught but his captive."

Sara waved a dismissive hand. "Poppycock, you're no such thing. You are my future sister-in-law, ours both," she motioned to Emma. Apparently the younger girl had been apprised of Sara's plans.

Emma smiled and laid a hand on Catrina's. "My mule-headed brother will need some convincing before he admits to falling in love with a Kerr—"

"He's not in love with me."

Both Sara and Emma stared at her and then began to laugh. *What was so amusing?*

"He isn't!" She couldn't tell them about their encounter in the stables. It was mortifying enough to think about.

"I've seen my brother with plenty of women. Pardon me, Lady Catrina, for saying such a thing. But they don't call him the Slayer without reason."

She stared at the younger girl, a female version of her brothers. "You mustn't say such things, Emma. You must be—"

"Ten and nine, my lady."

"Ten and...how can that be?"

"I've always looked younger than my age." Emma smiled, but she sensed a sadness behind it and wondered at the cause.

"As I was saying," Emma continued, "I know my brother well and agree with Sara. He's never acted this way around a woman. Since..."

Emma hesitated.

"Lady Elena?" Catrina ventured.

Emma cocked her head to the side. "You know about her?"

Sara looked at them both. "Who is Lady Elena?"

Neither woman answered. Catrina was surprised Emma knew of the woman who had scorned her brother. It was a topic he clearly avoided.

Emma answered, "A woman from Bryce's past. But it's his story to tell. Not that he will, mind you. I only got it by kicking him so hard he limped for two days, and he still hasn't told our brothers."

Sara laughed, apparently accustomed to such behavior. But Catrina was stunned. "Kicked him?" She'd been plenty angry with all three of her brothers, but couldn't remember ever actually hitting one of them. Well, at least not since she was a child.

"A long story," Emma said.

"Somehow I'm not surprised. That you kicked him, or that Bryce relented." Sara took a sip of wine. "A tale for another day. In the meantime, what are we to do about Bryce?"

The three women sat in silence. Catrina had no idea what Bryce was planning, but if her clan was making its way toward Kenshire and Bryce and Geoffrey were preparing to leave, it could only mean one thing. Trouble.

"I have to go with them."

Emma looked appalled. Sara, startled.

"Let me talk to him this evening," Sara said. "The men aren't leaving until dawn. I'll try again to—"

"Nay."

Both women looked at her as if she were mad.

"If Geoffrey is anything like his brother, he'll not yield. I must find a way to accompany Bryce."

Emma shook her head. "Bryce will never let you go with him. It's too dangerous—"

"Emma's right," said Sara. "Think about it. Bryce and my husband believe your clan to be the enemy. Are they planning to negotiate your release—" she took a deep breath, "—are they going to battle? Either way, it's much too dangerous for you."

Catrina would not be swayed. "They are my people. My family. They would never harm me. If anyone has the right to be there, it's me. And I'm the only one who can avoid bloodshed."

She held her breath, waiting. Her heart hammering, Catrina

silently prayed for Lady Sara's help. Without it, she feared the worst. Everything she dreaded was coming to pass. For there was no doubt, without her intervention, someone would get hurt. Possibly many people.

Sara looked from Emma to Catrina. She lifted her chin and nodded. "Very well. But you must go with the men—"

"They will never allow it."

Sara's eyes narrowed. "They will if they don't know you're there."

What was Sara planning? Even if she could travel with them undetected, they would turn around immediately if she were discovered.

"Come." Sara abandoned her meal and took Catrina's hand. "We've much to do before dawn."

Catrina and Emma both followed Sara out of the great hall. The countess of Kenshire was a woman to be reckoned with. And she thought Bryce was in love with her. So did his sister. Was it possible?

She would find out soon enough. In a few days' time, her fate would be decided. Nay, *she* would decide it. And she chose both Bryce *and* her family.

The fates be damned.

THE NEXT MORNING, before dawn, Catrina pulled on the long modified breeches and slipped out of her chamber into the hall below. Even though Sara had assured her that she was an early riser and would not allow her to miss the men's departure, Catrina had hardly slept.

Avoiding the hall, Catrina lifted the hood on her cloak as she navigated the corridors Sara had showed her the night before. She didn't dare carry a candle, so it took a considerable amount of time to find her way through the dark hallways to the door Sara had insisted she use.

Once outside, Catrina allowed her eyes to adjust to the moonlight. She could see just enough to make her way to the stable. It was so quiet. Eerily quiet.

"Catrina?" Although it was whispered, Sara's greeting made her jump.

Just as they'd planned, Sara led Davie and her own palfrey, Guinevere, around to the back of the stable.

"Did you have any trouble?" Catrina asked.

They walked toward the gatehouse, encountering only a handful of chickens and a few barrels of hay as they made their way through the courtyard.

"Eddard didn't much like my plan, but the marshal has known me since I was a babe. He gave his word not to tell Geoffrey. I've instructed him to tell the men we left just before they did for a morning ride."

Catrina let out the breath she held. Now for the most dangerous part of their plan...waiting until daybreak without being discovered. Eventually Sara would get Catrina past the guards under the guise of going for a morning ride. Catrina would slip away and wait, hidden, until the men rode past. She and Sara would follow, joining their group. If she were discovered too soon, they would send her back immediately. And since she had little chance of following for very long without being discovered, Catrina knew her first task would be to convince Bryce to allow her to accompany him north.

So they waited for a respectable time to "go for a morning ride." So far, they were in luck. They'd risen so early in the morn, no one, with the exception of Eddard, had seen them.

Yet.

If either Guinevere or Davie made too much noise, they risked discovery. But there was no hope for it. Though Sara was confident she could trust Eddard, she wasn't as confident about the stable hands or guards who may see them.

"What is this building?" Catrina asked.

The women sat behind a small stone structure at the far north of the courtyard adjacent to the inner curtain wall. Their horses were tied and, for the moment at least, quiet.

"A storeroom. It was once the dovecote, but they moved there —" she pointed to another structure not far from them, "—a few years ago."

"I've never seen a castle this large." Catrina was still in awe at the sheer magnitude of the place.

"What is Brockburg like?"

Though certainly not as grand as Kenshire, it was every bit as clean and comfortable, thanks to her efforts. "Tis lovely, though the entirety of the castle would fit inside Kenshire's main keep."

"Is it much different in Scotland, then?"

Though she asked the question casually, Catrina could tell it was an important one. Sara had already admitted she'd never crossed the border.

Wherever that was.

"Nay, it's not. The Highlands, however..." She'd been north of Brockburg a few times, and the people and customs were as foreign to her, maybe more so than those of the English. "When I came to Bristol, that's what surprised me most. How similar our people were. Being English and all." She stopped, not wishing to insult Lady Sara.

They talked for what seemed like hours. About England. And Scotland. About the dangers at the border and, eventually, about the men they loved. Catrina finally heard the full, unfettered story of Sara and Geoffrey's courtship, which made her relationship with Bryce seem positively uncomplicated.

"So you were formally betrothed when you met Geoffrey?"

"Aye. A betrothal sanctioned by the king. Luckily the earl was just as content to take Caiser's southern holdings as he was to take a bride. But there was a time—" She stopped and reached for Catrina's hand. "There was a time I thought we would never be together."

A feeling Catrina knew well. The obstacles between her and Bryce seemed insurmountable. But she didn't care. She loved him and was determined to help him understand what everyone else around them already seemed to have realized.

They were meant to be together.

"I don't know what will be more difficult, getting Bryce to listen to reason or convincing my brother not to kill him on the spot."

Sara released her hand, looking around the corner of the building. Catrina had also heard the noise, and her heart was thumping in her chest. When a pig came flying past them a moment later, she nearly laughed aloud. Sara held her hand to her mouth, and Catrina did the same. It took them both a moment to compose themselves.

Soon after, before the sun made an appearance, Kenshire slowly sprang to life. The women were well hidden behind the storeroom. Though she couldn't see much from their position, Catrina could hear a woman calling to her child and the wheels of a wagon creaking past them. When the sky finally lightened enough not to raise suspicions, they left their hiding place and walked around the building, leading their horses away from the keep.

As promised, Sara had no trouble at either gate. "Good morrow, Eddard."

"'Tis early for a ride, my lady," one young knight ventured.

"Indeed. This business with Clan Kerr has made Emma and I restless. Good day to you."

Catrina tucked her chin close to her neck, making the most of the concealment offered by the hood. It was imperative for the guards to believe the illusion.

Without giving him a chance to answer, they rode through the massive gates and made their way around the outer wall.

"Just up here," Sara called. Without trees to conceal them, they hid behind a corner of the wall. Sara dismounted and inspected Guinevere's hoof. "The closest watchtower is there." Sara pointed above them as if to explain her impromptu care of her palfrey.

And so they waited, again, until they heard the distinct sound of horses on the march.

Catrina looked at Sara, who smiled. She felt a rush of warmth for her new friend. This was something she could never have accomplished alone. Without Sara, she would not have gotten past the guards. She would be eternally grateful to her—something she was about to tell her when the thunder of hooves and clanging of metal caught her attention.

Before long, they could see the retinue of men riding north. There were so many. Fifty men? One hundred? They moved so fast Catrina couldn't tell. She couldn't see Bryce, but he and Geoffrey would be riding in the front.

She shivered, but not for lack of warmth.

I must not fail.

Waiting until the men were out of sight, Catrina and Sara finally followed. The wide-open moors to the north forced them to put a distance between themselves and the men. Catrina wished to lag even farther behind; she knew the men were trained to sense danger in every direction. And while she and Sara didn't pose any threat to them, the men would not know that. Sooner or later, they would be discovered. But Sara insisted on riding close enough from them to be heard at a shout.

Considering her close call on the failed escape attempt, maybe Sara was right. They couldn't see the men any longer, but could hear them in the distance.

It's working. It's really working.

There was a chance Bryce could still send her back with an

escort once she was discovered. But for now, they were free. For the first time since the raid, one of her plans was working.

Some time later, Catrina sensed, rather than saw, that they were being followed. But how was she to get Sara's attention without alerting the others to their presence? Her heart beating fast, Catrina thought of the reivers who'd grabbed her off Davie. Sara finally slowed, thank God, and Catrina pointed behind them. Sara nodded. She felt it too.

The potential danger behind them could not be ignored, so in silent accord, she and Sara urged their mounts to a full sprint. Luckily, the ground beneath them was flat and solid. Speeding past the lush green landscape, Catrina and Sara fled toward the very men they had spent their morning trying to avoid.

When the mounted knights came into view, Sara called out and waved one arm furiously. She wanted them to recognize her, and they did.

Slowing to a canter, Catrina finally looked behind them and smiled. They had outrun mounted knights! As the small party approached, it became clear they were Kenshire's men. And while the distance they'd closed was not a great one, it was still a fine accomplishment. . .

Even though it meant the ruse was at an end.

"What in God's name are you doing here, woman?"

Geoffrey.

Catrina spun around to see two very large, very angry men riding toward them. The only time she'd seen Bryce this angry was when he saved her from the reivers. Neither he nor Geoffrey wore a helm. If they needed to intimidate their enemies, a helm wasn't necessary. Both men appeared so...powerful. With the exception of the Waryn crest on their surcoats, they were dressed in black from head to foot.

"That's a fine greeting, husband," Sara replied.

"Greeting? That I should be greeting you *here*—"

He appeared too angry to continue.

Bryce had a more measured way of displaying his anger. Rather than raise his voice or bluster at her, he looked directly at her, gaze unwavering, and said, "You're going back."

"I will not." She lowered her hood, and though she could sense everyone looking at her, she refused to back down. "I will accompany you to my family. This will end, Sir Bryce Waryn. One way or another. I will not be held captive any longer. I have more of a right to be here than any of these men." She waved her arms in the direction of their…army? Aye, that's what it was. These men were going to battle.

She gripped the reins, attempting to calm her shaking hands.

"You lead men into battle against my brothers." She should not raise her voice in front of his men, but Catrina didn't care. "Without so much as a word in parting? If I mean so little to you, then send me back."

No one spoke. Bryce stared at her, his jaw set and eyes piercing, as if she had done something wrong.

She loved him.

Catrina wanted him to come to her, tell her he loved her too and that she meant more to him than vengeance against her clan.

But it appeared that was not to be. He only nodded.

Bryce turned to Sara and frowned. Before he could say a word, Geoffrey cut in. "You," he spoke to Sara, "*are* returning to Kenshire."

In response, Sara smiled. A brilliant smile that would surely melt the heart of any man. She really was quite lovely, and apparently her husband was not immune. He rode toward her, and they spoke a few words with their heads tipped together before Sara waved her hand in parting as she rode away accompanied by two men. Catrina had said her farewells to the countess earlier that morning. And when Sara had said with such conviction that they would meet again, Catrina had almost believed it.

Looking at Bryce right now, she wasn't so sure.

21

Before Bryce could continue, a commotion drew everyone's attention. The Waryn brothers rode ahead to speak with a man Catrina knew to be the captain of Bristol's guard. He pointed toward a ridge in the distance, and after a few moments, Geoffrey and Bryce sped away. Within minutes, the entire riding party was on the move. She could barely hear the captain, who shouted to her over the noise.

"Come with me, my lady."

He guided her outside the group, riding to her right, and another mounted knight rode along her left. *What just happened?* This was similar to how they'd ridden to Kenshire, one man on either side of her, but this time an entire army surrounded them. Whereas their earlier pace had been measured, steady, there was an urgency now. Watching the men's faces, Catrina became convinced something was amiss. She wanted to ask the captain what had happened, but his grim expression stopped her.

When they finally slowed, she found herself surrounded on every side. Was she being protected? Or guarded?

Hot, dirty, and annoyed, Catrina had a mind to urge Davie forward and find Bryce, but there was no need. The circle around her parted and there he was. He motioned for her to follow, and she did. They climbed a slope and rode toward a thicket of trees. Davie expertly navigated a small stream. A freshwater source and shelter meant they were likely at their journey's end for the day. Catrina was surprised they had stopped so soon, and this close to the border, but Bryce's demeanor didn't invite questions.

She'd seen him angry, passionate, and curious. But never like this. Determined was the best way to describe his current mood. And, as always, serious.

Bryce dismounted and helped her do the same. He led both horses to the stream without a word, and she found privacy behind a tree. Feeling a wee bit better, she approached her sullen Englishman—but she still didn't say a word. For some reason, she didn't want to be the first to speak. Instead, she knelt down to wash her hands and face. Catrina took out the braid at her back and shook her head.

"They injured one of my men," he finally said.

Who injured one of his men?

She stood. And waited.

"Your clan. Your brother. They're camped less than one day's ride from here. A small scouting party returned with the body of one of Bristol's fiercest warriors. According to the others, it was Toren himself who injured him."

Her shoulders slumped forward as she bent back down to the stream, her legs unable to support her weight. Catrina's cheeks tingled and her eyes filled with tears. She allowed them to flow down her cheeks. Covering her face with her hands, she didn't think about being strong. She cried, harder than when she'd learned she was an Englishman's captive. Harder than when her brother had refused to accept Graeme after she'd traveled all the way to England to beg for his approval. Harder than when her mother had left her just days after her father's death.

Catrina cried for the knight who was injured by her brother's hand and for the loss of the man who stood ominously above her.

She could not stop this fight. Not now. Maybe not ever. Bryce would avenge his men. His people. His parents.

He was lost to her.

AFTER THE SCOUTS returned and Robert reported his injury, Bryce had momentarily forgotten about Catrina's presence. He'd pushed the men hard, wanting to get closer to their destination, aching to come face to face with the man who had consumed his thoughts for five years. The man who continued to wreak havoc in his life.

Granted, he did hold the man's sister captive, but she had not been harmed. Just the opposite. But that hardly mattered now. Nothing mattered beyond the battle that was to come between the Clan Kerr's chief and the lord of Bristol Manor.

Nothing else *could* matter.

Bryce had brought Catrina here to tell her exactly what he thought of the man she held in such high esteem. To show her that her brother didn't deserve her pity. No matter the cause of the incursion, Toren had injured a man after agreeing to a temporary stay before their trial. But she didn't rail at him, excuse her brother or, surprisingly, curse any saints. Instead, he watched her dissolve into tears.

A woman who'd nearly died in a raid on her family's home and who was being held captive by her enemy. A woman who'd attempted to traverse dangerous territory in England, alone. Who had smiled through it all, helped when she was needed, and showed more passion than he'd thought possible from an untried maid. This wasn't the response he had expected from such a woman.

For some reason, it made him think of her body lying on a river bank, blood seeping from a scalp wound. She could have died that day. Would have, if he'd had his say at the time.

He shuddered and went to her, his anger melting away as

quickly as the current that took bits of rock and dirt with it toward the south of England. He felt like one of those bits.

Insignificant. Powerless. Tugged by currents that had become bigger than him. More powerful.

He didn't remember pulling her up against him and wrapping his hands around her. But now that she was in his arms, it felt right. Bryce squeezed as if to tell her what he couldn't say out loud. "Please," he begged. He didn't know what he asked for.

Eventually her sobs became sniffles. He smoothed the wild tresses of her hair beneath his fingers, the soft locks like silk beneath his calloused hands.

"I apologize." He should never have told her about Robert. Catrina was not at fault.

"Wh-what happens now?"

He pulled away and looked at her, beautiful though puffy and red. He attempted to measure his words. She would find out soon enough.

"We camp here tonight. Tomorrow, I meet your brother at Norham Castle, the seat of the Bishop of Norham. The constable there has agreed to designate it as neutral ground."

That much, at least, was true. Before she asked the inevitable next question, he took Catrina's hand and walked toward the horses.

"How did you leave Kenshire unnoticed?"

Luckily, Catrina allowed herself to be distracted. By the time they prepared to meet the others at camp, his lady even smiled as she described how she and Sara had conspired.

After learning of Sir Robert's injury, Bryce had nearly reconsidered his plan and marched straight toward Norham that day. But although their men were prepared for battle, they would not engage in one. This was his fight and his alone.

He had never intended to be the lord of Bristol Manor. But he was, and he would earn that title. Prove to Geoffrey he was worthy of it.

By the time they reached the others, night had begun to fall. Camp was nearly set. Tents were erected across an open field. Fires burned and the clanging of swords could be heard even before they could be seen.

He found his brother at the center of camp speaking to a group of young knights. Not wanting to interrupt them, Bryce led Catrina to a tent with his crest emblazoned on it.

His squire had served him well. The tent was erected behind all of the others on the eastern side of the camp near a patch of trees.

It was not overly large, but he hadn't known it would be used for two.

Bryce pointed toward the opening.

Catrina peered inside. The front flap was held open with two wooden poles. Its contents were sparse—a makeshift bed and his armor and weapons.

"But...this is your tent?"

Lord help him, he knew that. He considered all of their options. Traveling light to move quickly, each knight carried his own equipment. Driven by the need to move quickly, Bryce had allowed only two supply carts, which were filled with armor and weapons. There would be no extra accommodations. And while one of the men would undoubtedly sacrifice his tent for Bryce, the thought of Catrina sleeping alone less than one day's ride from her clan gave him pause. Would she somehow try to reach them?

In the end, he had settled on his own tent, not trusting anyone else to guard her properly. This was, after all, the same woman who'd attempted to cross the border, alone, and who'd snuck out of one of England's most fortified castles.

No, she would stay with him for the night. And Lord help him overcome the temptation he knew would consume him.

CATRINA'S HEART RACED.

This was her chance.

Earlier, after he told her about Robert, she'd lost all control over her emotions. It had seemed inevitable that her plan would fail, which meant it was likely either Bryce or Toren would not walk away from this fight. Maybe both. While she didn't know his exact plan, Catrina was no fool.

But then Bryce had wrapped his arms around her, and there was no denying the tenderness in his embrace. She knew, without question, that Sara and Emma were right. He loved her. But he didn't want to admit it—not when loving her meant giving up his dreams of revenge against her family.

By the time they arrived at camp, Catrina's mind had sped through all of the possibilities. He was allowing her to stay, but he'd said nothing of his plans for the morrow except that he would meet her brother at Norham. Which meant she had one night, one last chance to convince him to stop this madness.

Bryce left her at their tent, but a short time later a young knight, barely older than herself, handed her a lantern. He followed her as they made their way to a nearby stream. After splashing her face for the second time that day, she took out a sprig of mint from her pocket and chewed it. Braiding her hair, Catrina looked down at her dirty garment, wishing she'd thought to bring a gown.

As she followed the knight back to camp, Catrina marveled at the sight before her. Darkness enveloped them, but the landscape was dotted with light from multiple fires. A small army camped before her, and another waited just north of them. Tomorrow she would see her brothers...her clan. A few weeks ago, she would have already made plans to escape to them.

But not tonight.

They ate a modest meal of...rabbit? She hardly tasted it. Half-listening to the men around her, Catrina sat between Bryce and

Geoffrey, who watched her throughout the meal. Did they expect her to say something?

Though it was undeniable the brothers looked alike, their demeanors were quite different. Geoffrey's smile was quick to appear as he joked with the other men. But Bryce simply stared into the fire, glancing at her every so often. Not talking, just staring.

"Do you agree, my lady?" a knight asked.

Geoffrey and the others looked at her.

"Pardon?" She had not been following the conversation.

"John here—" he gestured to the young knight sitting next to him, "—plans to ask for his lady's hand in marriage. He already has approval from her father. I told him to wait for May Day."

John grinned.

"I think it's a lovely idea," Catrina replied.

John leaned forward and placed his elbows on his knees, a thinking posture, as if giving their advice serious consideration.

"I'll be bringing in the May, and something else besides," John finally said. He laughed at his own joke, and the others joined in.

"An engagement is not a wedding." She knew they were jesting, but felt it fair to point out that fact to the would-be bridegroom.

"Nor is a bedding an engagement." All eyes turned to Bryce, who had made that curious proclamation.

Catrina had a feeling she was being goaded, and yet she couldn't help but answer. "Whatever is that supposed to mean?"

Bryce took a swig of ale and looked at her. The hairs on her arm stood and the same fluttering feeling that had assaulted her at the inn returned in force. Bryce spoke to her alone and not the group.

"One has nothing to do with the other, my lady. Lovemaking, engagement, marriage..."

What was he trying to say? "Maybe so, Sir Bryce. But for some, they are intertwined." She almost pointed to Geoffrey and Sara as an example but thought better of it with the man seated beside her.

Bryce snickered. "I doubt it very much."

Sometimes she wanted to kick him. As undignified as that might be, it would give her immense satisfaction. "Well, ye'll likely never know, will you, Sir Bryce?"

She realized her comment had more bite than was appropriate to a playful conversation when the laughter died and everyone looked at Bryce for his response. She hadn't meant it that way.

"With any luck, I will not."

"Churl." Catrina looked away and was surprised to see Geoffrey grinning. "I apologize for my—"

"Nay, do not apologize, Lady Catrina," Geoffrey said. "I quite agree. My brother is a churl, and more besides."

The men laughed and watched Bryce stand. "Good evening, gentlemen." He bowed to Catrina. "My lady."

His mood darkened even further after her comment, and she was sorry for it.

Bryce walked away. The other men started up the conversation again as if it had never stopped, needling at John about his lady, discussing the wedding.

"Take heart—" Geoffrey leaned in toward her, "—you have the remainder of the evening to convince him otherwise."

Catrina's eyes widened. Geoffrey's grin confirmed it—Sara had spoken to him before about their plan.

He knew everything.

Embarrassed, she made to stand, but Geoffrey's hand on her shoulder stayed her. "You're the only one who can convince him, my lady."

"So you approve, Sir Geoffrey?"

"I do. I've never seen Bryce act this way before. He's sotted but refuses to admit it."

"Your wife said the same."

"Listen to her," he said with a grin. "Sara is as smart as she is beautiful."

Geoffrey was clearly in love with his wife.

"And I agree with you. One can have all three." He winked at her and turned back to the conversation.

She smiled. Catrina genuinely liked Geoffrey.

Why can't Bryce be more like him?

Because he wasn't Geoffrey. Bryce was serious—something that made his rare smiles all the sweeter. And he was also determined and loyal. If he hadn't been spurned by the Lady Elena for being a second son, he would likely not be so mistrustful. But his one near miss with marriage had convinced Bryce he didn't believe in love. Or that he wasn't worthy of it.

Well, he was wrong and Geoffrey was right. She needed to show him otherwise.

Tonight.

22

When she returned to the tent well after the sun had set, Bryce was not there. After awkwardly pulling off her breeches and makeshift tunic in the small space, Catrina placed her clothing and leather boots to the side. She extinguished her candle and lay down on the makeshift bed, which consisted of nothing more than heather and pine needles covered with two woolen blankets.

Every so often she could feel a prickle beneath her.

Slowly the camp began to quiet. Large fires became smoldering embers, or so she imagined. She couldn't see anything, not even her own hand, but Catrina knew the routine from their earlier travels. Although this time, there were more men present.

She refused to think about their purpose for being here and instead concentrated on her own plan. But as she lay in the darkness and the noises around camp began to quiet, her nervousness was replaced by hopelessness.

Because he wasn't coming.

He'd obviously found another place to sleep.

When the tent flap opened a moment later, Catrina immediately knew it was him. She couldn't see his face in the darkness, but that scent was uniquely Bryce. She lay on her side with her back turned to him, listening to the sound of him disrobing.

Did he purposefully attempt to avoid her? Is that why he had stayed away so late into the night? What should she do? Listening to Sara's advice was much different than acting on it. Her heart beat painfully in her chest.

Bryce eventually lay next to her, so close she could hear his even breathing.

She couldn't do it. It was too…bold.

But then, if she didn't, Bryce would never know how she felt.

She turned and propped her head on her hand.

"Do you truly believe it impossible for man and wife to be in love and to…you know?"

She couldn't see his face, but the shadow moved.

"I'm not sure I understand, Catrina."

Her name rolled off his tongue like a sensual embrace. Slow and deliberate.

"Never mind."

He was hopeless.

"I do mind. What exactly are we discussing?"

"Oh, for the sake of St. Thomas." She was glad it was too dark for him to see her face.

"You are intimately familiar with a large number of saints, Catrina. Although I don't believe your Father Simon would approve of the way you choose to honor them."

Honor them indeed. Using a saint's name in vain was the worst kind of epithet, but she blamed her brothers for her lack of restraint in that area.

"I don't suppose he would." As a matter of fact, he'd have quite a bit to say about the matter.

Better just to say it. "Lovemaking."

There, she'd said it. Aloud.

"Ahhh, I see."

"Are you deliberately trying to make me uncomfortable?"

"Yes."

"It's not working." Actually, she was pretty sure it was.

"Nay? In that case, I'll leave you to your sleep."

He turned away. Bryce was not making this easy. Though, come to think of it, when had he ever made anything easy? "I want you to kiss me again."

Catrina didn't move. And neither did Bryce.

"Catrina, it's not a good idea—"

"Aye, it is."

She wished there was more light. Without it, she couldn't see his expression. Had no idea what he was thinking. Before she thought better of it, Catrina reached out and tentatively touched her hand to his face. The stubble there fascinated her. He felt so…masculine.

Just when she was about to pull away, convinced it was a mistake, Bryce grasped her hand with his own.

She jumped when he placed her finger in his mouth. The smooth wetness of his tongue as he wrapped his lips around her sent chills down her back. And then he began to suckle, slowly moving her finger in and out, increasing pressure until she felt the slight grazing of his teeth.

There it was again. The same feeling she'd experienced at the inn before her release. She wanted that again. Catrina inched closer until her body was nearly pressed against him. She could feel his bare chest under her own thin chemise.

He released her finger and replaced it with his lips. Then, in one quick motion, Bryce shifted her body so it lay atop his. He devoured her mouth, and she allowed him full access, pressing her tongue against his own, frantically trying to show Bryce the depth of her feelings for him.

She wanted to touch and taste every part of him. She gave her tongue freely as he captured it with his own. His body, gloriously bare, pressed below her like a hard slab of rock turned to warm flesh. Catrina moved her hands along his broad shoulders and then down the length of his arms. Muscle, everywhere.

He groaned. Was she giving him as much pleasure as he gave her?

She wanted to give him more. Wanted to know all of him.

Catrina reluctantly pulled back.

"Make love to me, Bryce." He'd denied her once. Would he do so again?

HE NEVER SHOULD HAVE ALLOWED her to stay. And certainly should have found alternative sleeping arrangements. Bryce had convinced himself that he alone could ensure her safety and nothing more. He'd stayed away from their tent for as long as he could, thinking she would be asleep when he returned.

Obviously, he had been wrong.

He'd heard her breathing quicken as soon as he entered the tent. It had been a mistake to lie next to her, pressing closer than was needed, but by God, he couldn't regret it. It felt so good. *She* felt so good. Every time he was near her, Bryce could not stop thinking about the look on her face that night at the inn. When he'd tasted her. Made her climax. Thinking of it instantly hardened him.

Make love to me.

There was nothing he wanted more.

"If I could, Catrina, I would have done so a hundred times already."

He couldn't see her face, but he could smell her. The sensation of her two heavenly breasts pressed up against his bare chest made him itch to remove her chemise. But she wasn't his to take.

"Why not?" she asked.

Why not, indeed? He could hardly say 'because I plan to challenge your brother tomorrow and one of us will end up dead.'

"You know why, Catrina. You've kept your maidenhood for a reason. To give it to your husband." He had to grind out the words. The thought of her with another man—this deSowlis or anyone—made him want to break things.

"But I want to give it to you."

"Catrina, you don't want that."

She shook her head, her hair brushing against his chest, tantalizing him. Teasing him.

"I am a grown woman. Please don't tell me what I want. *This* is what I want."

He could not disgrace her in that way. "Catrina, tomorrow—"

She placed a hand on his mouth.

Saucy wench.

"Nay, that doesn't matter now. *This* matters."

She placed her lips on his, touching her tongue to his, and Bryce was undone.

It was simply too much. He groaned, grabbed her around the back, and rolled her under him. He felt for the hem of her chemise and pulled it over her head. Lying atop her, propped on his elbows, Bryce pressed their bodies together. No woman had ever fit him the way she did. No woman had ever felt this good against him.

Then she began to move. He still wore his hose, the garment the only remaining barrier between them. Without them, Catrina Kerr would no longer be a maid. He'd deflower a woman on the eve of the most devastating night of her life. He simply couldn't do it.

"Catrina, I can—"

"Bryce, please." Her normally light voice, now anything but, broke him. She was serious. "Please," she repeated.

He couldn't deny her any longer. Couldn't deny himself. He stood, tore off his hose, and positioned himself over her once again.

"How…where…"

"Shhhh..." He kissed her, gently at first. He teased her mouth with his lips, circling and nipping at them as he allowed her to become accustomed to the feel of him above her.

He reached his hand down and slipped a finger inside her.

She was wet, ready for him. He moved his hand against her mound, increasing the pressure until she pushed back against him. Bryce slipped a second finger inside and thrust. The sounds deep in Catrina's throat told him she was getting close.

Expertly moving his hand to bring Catrina to climax, he finally felt the spasms beneath his fingers. Although their tent was at a small distance from the others, Catrina must have realized they could still easily be overheard. As she came beneath his fingers, only her movements told him she was well pleased.

With any luck, he could remain as quiet.

Bryce positioned himself above her, prepared to make her his. "This can't be undone."

He reached up to cup a full breast. Using his thumb to harden its peak, he leaned down and took it into his mouth.

"Please, Bryce."

He continued to tease her with his tongue as he guided himself toward her. Should he warn her that it would hurt? Or would the anticipation of pain be worse? He wasn't in the habit of bedding virgins, but he decided to make it quick. Slipping himself inside and giving her a moment to adjust, Bryce found the barrier he had known would be there and stopped. She'd never taken a man inside her before. He knew that, even expected it, but for some reason, the evidence pleased him.

"Catrina—"

"I'm sure."

It was enough.

He thrust into her and covered his mouth with hers, capturing her scream. So much for silence.

He tried to distract her with his mouth, and it seemed to work. After what seemed like an eternity, she began to move under him.

Slowly at first, he moved in and out, the exquisite sensation unlike anything he'd ever experienced. She was tight, aye, exceedingly so. But there was something more to their joining. An unfamiliar emotion swelled within him—something that had nothing to do with lust.

He pushed it aside.

Bryce moved quickly, his cock throbbing, threatening to explode. He took a deep breath and attempted to calm his rapidly beating heart. He'd seen her naked before, but the feel of her soft body surging in movement against him, in concert with him, was nearly too much.

Nothing else existed but the two of them in this small tent on the edge of camp. He had imagined being inside her so many times, but never…never…had he imagined *this*. She met his every thrust, her hands splayed on his backside. She wanted more, and he gave it to her.

"Come, my sweet Catrina. Come with me."

He wasn't sure whether she understood what he meant, but she lifted her hips, forcing him to bury himself full hilt.

By all that is holy, what the hell is happening?

He reached down between them and found the sensitive flesh between her legs. Almost immediately, Catrina cried out and began to pulse under him. Her slickness allowed him to find his own release. One final thrust and he collapsed against her, taut nipples pressing into his chest.

What the hell did I just do?

HEARING about the act and having the man she loved inside her were two completely different things.

Now she understood.

Her brothers' preoccupation with the topic. Her lady's maid's secret smiles after she became a wife. She understood it all.

"Does it always feel as such?"

She hadn't meant to ask the question aloud.

Bryce pulled out of her and rolled to the side. She immediately felt the loss of his warmth, but he lay next to her, his leg touching her own.

"Nay."

What does that mean?

"Catrina, I apologize—"

"Don't. Please don't." She did not want him to regret it. *She* didn't regret it.

"We need to talk," Bryce said.

She yawned, "Aye. We do." She reached for him in the dark. He pulled her even closer, fitting her against his body. She laid her head on his chest and tentatively placed her hand on his stomach. Muscles tensed under her fingertips. She traced the ridges with her finger. Bryce pulled a blanket over them, and the last thing Catrina remembered before she fell asleep was how perfectly they fit together and how hard his chest was under her head.

When she woke up, he was gone.

23

Why is the bed so hard?

She remembered everything at once. Where was Bryce? How long had she slept? It was still dark, but he was gone. Could he have left already?

Please God, no.

She sat up and felt a new tightness between her legs. She looked down to see spots of blood on the woolen blanket. She was no longer a virgin.

She shuddered, thinking about how her brothers would react.

And Graeme. She'd thought for most of her life she would become his wife, but that was no longer possible. Nor did she want it to be.

She loved Bryce.

But unless she could find him and stop whatever he had planned, it may not matter. Dressing quickly, Catrina folded the blanket into the bedroll in case Bryce's squire came into the tent. Pulling open the flap, she saw soldiers beginning to stir around camp. Did any of them know what had happened? It was bad enough that she and Bryce had shared a tent. And while part of her didn't care, another part of her was embarrassed that she had given herself to a man who was not her husband—a man who had not even discussed the possibility of marriage with her.

She walked through camp and received only grunts and nods. Nothing extraordinary. No one seemed to know their lord's whereabouts. She considered seeking out Geoffrey when something suddenly occurred to her.

The men were not preparing for battle. Their leisurely pace was at odds with what she'd expect of an army readying to meet the enemy on the battlefield.

Bryce had said he was meeting Toren at Norham Castle today. Though she'd realized Bryce—and probably Toren—wouldn't be satisfied until one or the other was dead, she'd assumed their forces would meet on the battlefield.

What is he planning?

She found Bryce's captain warming his hands over the dying embers of a small fire.

"Good morrow." She couldn't remember the man's name.

"Good morrow, my lady." The man's full red beard reminded her of a Highlander who had once challenged Toren to a fight. Supposedly her brother had stolen the man's wife. For an evening, at least. Toren denied it, of course.

"I'm looking for Sir Bryce."

"He's already left."

The man's expression gave her chills. Something was amiss.

"Left for where?" Catrina had a feeling she wouldn't like the answer.

The captain looked over her shoulder as if assessing who was listening. Very few men moved through camp, and none were nearby.

Scratching his beard, he said, "If the lord didn't say, it may not be for me—"

She summoned her most authoritative tone, the one she used on her brothers when they refused to listen to her. "Where is your lord?"

"Lady Catrina—"

"If you don't tell me, I will go looking for him myself."

His self-assured smile implied he knew something she did not. He nodded toward the edge of camp near the tent she'd shared with Bryce. There was a man standing there, his arms crossed, looking at them.

"Your guard may have something to say about that," the captain replied.

"God's bones! What is going on?"

Her heart raced. Where was Bryce?

"He's gone off to meet your brother." The captain spat on the ground next to him and took a bite of a large chunk of bread.

"Meet?"

For a moment, she didn't think he would answer. Maybe he took pity on her, or maybe he just wanted her to go away. Either way, he finally offered useful information.

"My lord challenged your brother to a judicial combat. He accepted."

"And their champions?" Lord help her, she already knew the answer.

"They'll have none."

Catrina sank to the ground. She could feel the wetness seeping through her breeches and reaching her knees. Today, one of the men she loved would die. A trial by combat always began at sunrise. So that was the reason they'd brought so few men, only a small portion of Kenshire's army. They weren't here to fight.

Oddly, she didn't cry. Catrina simply stood and walked back to the tent. She heard Bryce's captain calling her name, but the sound was like a wind's whistle through the trees, distant and imperceptible.

She sat and stared at Bryce's bedroll and shoved it to the side. Catrina wanted to hide the evidence of their lovemaking. That bastard had actually spent the night with her knowing he was facing her brother this morn.

How could he do such a thing?

Perhaps he truly was the stoic, uncaring, heartless man everyone thought him to be. Glimpses of vulnerability? She must have imagined them. Only a monster could do such a thing.

But in the end, it didn't matter that she hated Bryce. Or that she also loved him. She couldn't bear for either him or her brother to die. She wasn't even sure if he or her brother had the advantage. Both men were equally braw. Bryce had dedicated his life to proving a second son was not worthless. To proving to his brother, and everyone who worshiped Geoffrey, that he was just as strong.

Toren had his own demons that had driven him to train beyond the endurance of any ordinary man. He was one of the only warriors she'd match fairly against Bryce.

This is madness.

Catrina ran out of the tent and into the arms of the man who guarded her. She tripped, and the poor fellow had to catch her from falling flat on her face.

"Please." She didn't need to sound desperate. She *was* desperate. "Take me to Sir Bryce."

He looked at her as if she were daft. And maybe she was. But she would not let them kill each other.

"I must get to Norham Castle. Immediately."

"My lady, I can't—"

She would not be refused.

"You will either escort me to Norham, or I'll find a way there myself. I escaped Bryce once before, and I'll find a way to do so again."

She wasn't finished.

"I have explicit orders from Lady Sara to relay a message that has not yet been received. Are you prepared to answer to your lady if you deny me?"

Although the young knight appeared slightly uncomfortable, Catrina could tell he would not disobey Bryce's order, which was apparently to ensure she did not attempt to follow him. But the stakes were too high for her to give up now.

"Taking me to Norham may save Sir Bryce's life." Which was the truth. "He challenged my brother Toren, the chief of Clan Kerr and the most formidable warrior in the Borderlands."

"No disrespect, my lady—"

"With the exception of Sir Bryce and his brother." That seemed to pacify him a bit. "I don't know what the outcome will be, but I do know this. One of them will die on this day."

His expression softened as he looked at her.

Catrina embraced the startled young man. "Please. I beg you, sir. I must get this message to him. Please." He coughed and stepped backward.

"I will regret this."

"Nay, nay you won't! I promise, you will not. Hurry."

She wasn't sure how long ago Bryce had left, but she knew from the talk around the fire last eve they were more than an hour's ride to Norham Castle. Leaving her belongings, Catrina ran to Davie and began to untie him. She watched as the young knight spoke to an older man. He pointed at her, and for a moment, her stomach lurched. Would the other man stop them?

When the older knight slapped her champion on his back, she let out a sigh of relief.

But would they already be too late?

"YOU'RE SURE ABOUT THIS?"

Bryce gave his brother a hard look. He didn't like having to explain himself. Again.

"We've discussed this all morning. How many times do you plan to ask the same question?"

"As many times as it takes. I agreed to this before I realized you and Catrina were—"

"Stop," he bellowed. Bryce rarely raised his voice, and even fewer times at his brother. But the suggestion that he should marry Catrina—marry, for God's sake—and allow her brother to simply ride back across the border was just not possible.

They waited with a small retinue of men who had accompanied them to Norham Castle. The bishop was not in residence, but the constable met them just inside the castle's inner courtyard. Bryce couldn't concentrate as the elderly man read the terms of their trial. He looked toward the gatehouse. They all awaited the arrival of the man who was responsible for arranging this judicial combat. Hugh would be arriving with Clan Kerr.

As if on cue, the piercing blow of a horn heralded the arrival of three men, the agreed-upon number, plus his uncle. He spotted Hugh at the rear, looking no worse for his travels. Bryce assumed the man in the lead was the chief, Catrina's brother.

Catrina.

Bryce could not, would not, think of her. He had considered waking her before he left, but there was nothing to say. The events of this day would devastate her. She would either hate him or he would be dead.

Catrina deserved more.

The constable, who had not yet spoken, looked decidedly worried, and it was undeniable the men made quite a sight. Without armor, their only markings a crest on each of their tunics, they could have hailed from Southampton rather than the Scottish lowlands. As the group approached them, their faces became clearer. Bryce recognized the chief of Clan Kerr from the scouting mission he and his brother had conducted years earlier. The man to his left bore a strong resemblance to him, so it had to be another of her brothers. The third man he did not know.

Hugh made his way toward the brothers and slapped them on the back in greeting. Bryce couldn't take his eyes off the Kerr leader. Although his hair was a different color, more brown than anything, his look reminded him very much of Catrina. It was the eyes, he realized, as Toren came to a stop just opposite him. Hazel with flecks of gold. And his expression too. Though he wasn't smiling, there was a buried mirth behind the eyes that was very much reminiscent of Catrina.

He had to stop thinking of her. If he didn't stop, he *would* lose, and the Waryns would have to forfeit their claim to Bristol *forever*. Bryce was determined not to let that happen.

Norham's constable spoke. "Bryce Waryn, Lord of Bristol, and Toren Kerr, Chief of Clan Kerr, enter into an agreement decided by judicial combat for sake and soke of Bristol Manor, the caput, the village of Bristol, and all lands pertaining to it. Villein tenants and all present banalities including the demesne of Gouldsboro will relegate to the winner of the aforementioned trial. Lady Catrina Kerr shall be returned forthwith at the conclusion of the battle, surrendered no later than ten days from this date. The winner shall be declared—" he hesitated, looked up, and then back at his scroll, "—as the man not deceased at the conclusion of this trial. You've chosen to settle the dispute without armor, without shield. The weapon shall be a sword of your choosing. And this I do decree on the twenty fourth of May in the year of our lord twelve hundred and seventy one."

Bryce nodded and Kerr did the same.

"Any man who interferes is subject to the charge of treason. You may offer last words and assume positions when you are prepared."

He stood back, rolled the scroll in his hand, and handed it to the sheriff.

Bryce turned toward his uncle and brother.

"If I lose—"

"Toren—" Geoffrey started.

"Nay, Geoffrey. You entrusted me with your inheritance. This is my decision. If I lose, bring Catrina to her family straightaway. Ride immediately with my men to Bristol and apprise Thomas of the situation. Remember you promised to take in any man or woman who wished to leave, and I hold you to that promise, brother."

Geoffrey, his face no longer neutral, nodded. Bryce could not stand to look into his eyes a moment longer, so he broke his gaze.

"Uncle, please speak to Geoffrey about his appalling lack of faith in his brother's fighting skills."

Hugh smiled. "Aye, my lord." He grasped his arm. "You will be victorious."

"No one wins this day," Bryce said blackly. Turning back to face his enemy, he thought of Lord Huntington, who admonished his knights never to taunt an opponent. There was so much he wanted to say to the man whose eyes bore into him. He expected to have more hatred and bile in his heart, but he did not. Yet that did not make him any less determined for Toren Kerr to pay for his parents' deaths.

"Positions ready," yelled the sheriff.

Bryce had eyes only for Toren Kerr, who stared back at him intently. He had never been more ready for a battle.

"Begin!"

THE GUARDS WOULD NOT ALLOW them entry. Catrina had a feeling she knew why. *God, please don't let them start fighting yet.* Father Simon always told her the time to pray was before the time of need, not during. But she didn't care. She was out of ideas.

She begged, pleaded. Invoked the name of every saint she could name, and there were many. All to no avail.

It was her companion, bless him, who finally got through to the mule-headed guards.

"There has been a mistake. We know a trial is taking place, but we have information that may sway the outcome. You say the terms were set, only three men from each side allowed entry. She

—" he pointed at her, "—is not a man. Give her escort. Surely you don't fear one woman will overtake anyone?"

It worked. Catrina was surrounded by three of Norham's guards—she should be pleased they thought so highly of her fighting skills—and admitted into the gates. And the sound that greeted her as they made their way through the second set of gates nearly made her heart stop.

Metal on metal. The fight had indeed begun.

"Quickly!" She tried to run ahead but was stopped by one of the guards.

"You stay with us."

Was he daft? They knew she was there to stop the fight, and Bryce or Toren could be killed at any moment.

As they approached, Catrina forcing the guards to keep up with her frantic pace, her heart beat faster and faster. The clanging became louder and she could see the outline of men standing to either side of…

Holy St. Stephen, they were going to kill each other! She began to run, not caring about the guards. Or her own safety. Or anything other than saving the lives of these two men she loved.

"Stop! Stop!" she screamed…yet no one seemed to hear her or heed her. Toren swung his sword to kill. Tears began to stream down her face as she watched Bryce evade the thrust.

"Stop!" One of the men watching the fight noticed her. And then another. Everyone but the two whose attention she needed most. Then the witnesses began running toward her. She couldn't see what was happening. She screamed again and continued to run. Catrina didn't register who'd grabbed her, but suddenly she was being held by one man. And then another. She clawed at them and continued to scream.

"What in bloody Christ do you think you're doing? Let go of me!"

She kicked blindly, and then a voice penetrated the haze of her blind fear. "Catrina, stop. You're going to hurt yourself. Stop it."

Hugh? It was Bryce's uncle.

"Sir Hugh, make them stop. Please, I beg you. Let me go. Make them stop. Please."

Tears had blinded her. The blurry vision of her brother kneeling in front of her made her cry even more. Alex. Oh God, and her other brother was going to be killed.

It was Geoffrey who held her. He was so strong. But she would be stronger. She hoped he'd forgive her later, but she'd do what she needed to stop this fight. She'd do anything. Catrina went limp as if she were defeated, but as soon as Geoffrey loosened his hold, she used her knee as hard as she could the way Toren had taught her. She took advantage of his surprise—and his pain—to spring up and away from him. Then she ran as fast as her legs would carry her.

It was only when she reached the combatants that she realized there was no longer a fight to stop. Both Toren and Bryce stood with their swords at their sides. Their blood and sweat was a testament to the fight they'd already weathered. She had the urge to grab one of their swords and kill them both for being fools.

Knowing the fight was ended, at least for the moment, Catrina sank to the ground and buried her head in her hands, her sobs loud and uncontrollable.

It was all too much.

She heard voices but didn't know what the men were saying. She didn't care, so long as they weren't fighting. They had nearly killed her. Catrina had thought she would die when she'd heard the first sounds of clanging metal.

Bloody hell!

She stood and wiped her face. On the ride to Norham, she had thought about nothing else but what she would say to make them stop. But now that the moment had arrived, every word she'd prepared was forgotten.

"How dare you." She turned to Bryce. "How *dare* you."

"Catrina—"

"Nay, do not speak my name. Do not *ever* speak my name again. You will turn around, get back on your horse, and ride back to Bristol. You will never look at me or speak to me again."

She wasn't finished.

"And you." Catrina turned on her brother. On Toren. God, how she had missed him. As tall and muscled as Bryce, he was every bit as intimidating, but neither man would sway her resolve. She simply would not allow them to murder each other.

"It is done. Bristol is theirs. I will speak to the king myself and tell him as much. But you will not ever..." She walked toward her brother and stood so close she could smell the stench of battle on him. "Ever attempt to raid their land again."

"Catrina, I didn't—"

"Nay." She was done listening.

"You will not kill each other. Do you hear me? I will not bloody allow it."

"Sister." He reached for her, but she backed away.

Toren looked at Bryce, his eyes narrowing. "This bastard stole you. Refused to return you to us."

Damn stubborn men.

"Stole?" As usual, Bryce kept his composure, even though she knew he wanted to take his sword and run it through her brother's gut. "You mean rescued? Brought me back from the brink of death after you *lost* me."

Toren had the good grace to look embarrassed. "You refused to ride with anyone and took the closest mount yourself to ride. When we saw your horse unmounted, we feared the worst but were unable to find you." Toren turned to Bryce and raised his voice. "Her rescue is not at issue. You tried to ransom her. Trade her like a piece of livestock."

Well, that was true. But Catrina had no desire to stand here all day and negotiate.

"Enough, both of you." She was proud of how strong her voice sounded. Truly, all she wanted to do was dig a hole and crawl into it until this entire ordeal was over.

"Toren, let's go." She took his hand. "We're going home."

Although she tugged as hard as she could, he didn't move. Instead, he continued to stare at Bryce, whom she refused to look at.

"I am willing to negotiate according to Catrina's terms," Toren finally said.

Catrina wrapped her arms around her brother. "Thank you, Toren. Thank you." Her eyes began to water again, but she had cried plenty these past two days. She'd had enough of it. Catrina willed the tears back and managed to remain strong.

No one said a word. Finally, she looked at Bryce. She shuddered. His pained look almost made her run to him and throw herself into his arms. She knew he still blamed Toren for the death of his parents. But his eyes weren't guarded as they usually were. They were filled with an emotion she couldn't identify. Almost as if…

Nay. If he cared for her, they wouldn't be standing here now. This day could have been avoided all together.

"Go."

That was all he said. He didn't try to fight for her. Didn't profess his undying love or ask for her to stay with him. Just 'go.'

But she would take it. Both men were still alive.

It would have to be enough.

Catrina ran back to Alex, embracing her brother.

"What in the devil's name are you wearing, Catrina?"

She looked down at Sara's breeches. With a pang, she realized she would never again see the woman who had given them to her. "Excuse me, Alex."

Catrina turned to Geoffrey. "Please thank your wife for me… for everything. And if I ever have an opportunity, I will return these." She gestured toward the unusual garment.

Geoffrey leaned down to whisper in her ear. "Tell her yourself. Don't give up on him, Catrina."

She threw her arms around him. "Thank you. For everything. And please tell Lady Sara the same. I…will miss her. And my apologies for the. . . injury." Before she could break down again, Catrina walked back toward her brother. Only then did she notice that her brother's second witness was someone she knew well.

"Graeme? What are you doing here?"

The man she'd once wished to marry took a step toward her. Still handsome, always smiling. "It's good to see you, Catrina. We've all been worried."

"*That* is Graeme?" She heard Bryce's voice behind her but refused to turn around.

"Your stubborn brother finally admitted he needed me. When it looked like there would be a battle, he agreed to an alliance."

She looked at Toren. So it was true? She honestly hadn't believed it possible.

"We're finally to be married, Catrina."

Her head snapped back toward Graeme.

"The chief agreed to honor our betrothal as a show of good faith between our clans."

He looked so pleased. Of course he would. They had wanted this for so long. At least, she had thought it was what she wanted. How could she marry him now?

What did Bryce think?

Did it matter? He had made love to her and then ridden off, without even saying goodbye, to do battle with her brother. Whereas Bryce had never, not once, fought for her, Graeme had never stopped seeking her hand, even when it had seemed hopeless. She allowed him to take her arm.

"Graeme…please take me home," she said.

She walked away with him and didn't once look back.

24

Catrina's hands were shaking.

She sat on her bed at Brockburg, staring down at the letter in her hands. It had been delivered to her earlier that day, and she'd nearly dropped it at the sight of the seal. The contents had not changed. Nor had her indecision.

Her homecoming had gone exactly as expected. Not much had changed in Brockburg. Alex and Reid continued to wage war on neighboring clans—at times for amusement and other times in earnest. Father Simon continued to chastise her for her swearing. It wasn't her fault she'd been so excited to greet him she'd nearly fallen flat on her face while running toward him. The epithet that had accidentally escaped her lips had caused Father to exclaim she was the "very same Catrina who left us."

Growing up without a mother or father, she had always dreamed of raising children who knew the love of both parents. Being away from her brothers, not knowing if she'd ever see them again…Catrina had realized how much she valued them. Though their parenting had not been conventional, they were all the family she needed.

Which was why she had decided not to marry Graeme.

Catrina knew Toren, Alex, and Reid would never hurt her, but that hadn't made it any easier to convey the news to her eldest brother.

"You're telling me you spent all that time at Bristol insisting a match between you and Graeme was ideal. That I should forgive my enemies for the sake of the clan. I should forge an alliance 'that only your stubborn arse is preventing,' I believe you said."

After Toren finished shouting—God, she missed Bryce's even temperament even when he was angry—Catrina had decided to confess everything. He couldn't possibly be more angry, she'd reasoned.

"I can't marry Graeme because I don't love him. And I'm no longer a virgin."

Though she certainly had not been grinning at the time, Toren's reaction made her smile now.

Although all three of her brothers were pleasing to look at, Toren's size and strength singled him out as a leader the moment he walked into a room. He was a big man and, to his enemies, an intimidating one. When she told him about her relationship with Bryce, he looked as ominous as she'd ever seen him.

Toren threatened to break his agreement and ride immediately to Bristol to "slay that bastard's throat." But when she reminded him of his promise, both on that day and since in private, he reconsidered. Catrina also explained her role—which, though it was clearly difficult for her brother to understand, was not insubstantial. She had wanted it as much as Bryce, mayhap even more.

Toren didn't speak to her for days, which was just as well. Catrina didn't much feel like talking. To anyone. She took meals in her bedchamber. Refused the alewife's pleas for assistance. After all, the woman had gotten along just fine without her these past years. When her brothers tried to coax her to participate in her favorite activities, Catrina feigned a headache, but she never lost sight of the true source of her pain.

A certain man who nearly always refused to smile. One who thought mirth was a weakness and had a stubborn streak as strong as Toren's. A man who lived in his brother's shadow but was learning, as the lord of Bristol, to be a leader in his own right.

Bryce was also kind, though he refused to admit it.

And handsome, of course.

Every night before passing into the darkness that relieved her from the dull ache in her chest, Catrina fell asleep thinking of his touch. She dreamed of the night they'd spent together on the hard ground of that small tent so close to the border that stood between them.

It was the best night of her life. Followed by one of the worst.

Each day, she heard Bryce's voice ask, "Graeme?" In her mind, he sounded almost pained. As if he *cared* the man she was supposed to love stood beside her. But clearly he did not, otherwise he would have stopped her. Or come to Brockburg. For all Bryce knew, she was already married.

Yesterday, all three of her brothers had come to her bedchamber and forced her to supper. They'd hired her favorite musician to entertain a small gathering in the hall. Alex had told her more about the events leading up to the near catastrophe in Norham. About all the preparations and alliances, and how worried everyone had been about her safety. When Toren grabbed and squeezed her hand under the table, Catrina knew she had finally been forgiven. Later that night, he assured her that they would find a good husband for her when she was ready. When she reminded him she was the youngest of the four siblings, and none of *them* were yet married, he pinched her nose as he had so many times when they were children.

For the first time since her arrival, Catrina had actually smiled.

And now this.

"Lady Catrina," the note signed by the Countess of Kenshire started, "Please come immediately. I'm in need of an extra set of breeches."

That was it.

She read the words over and over, trying to understand what they meant. Lady Sara wished for her to visit Kenshire. *Why?* Didn't she know how painful it would be for her? Did Bryce know she had sent the missive? Would he be there?

She doubted it. He would have been more direct. If Bryce wanted to see her, he would have done so already. The lord was likely back at Bristol, fortifying it against future attacks. Though none would come from Clan Kerr, the Borderlands were still dangerous territory.

Toren already knew of the message, and his reticence had come as no surprise. But if she did choose to visit Kenshire, all three of her brothers would accompany her. They'd promised, nay, insisted. What a sight that would be!

Perhaps it would be better to allow Lady Sara to remain a memory.

Like Bryce.

"BRYCE, sit down. You're making everyone nervous," said Lady Sara.

"I don't give a shite about my brother's tender sensibilities," Bryce replied.

He looked at Geoffrey, whose glare could freeze a blacksmith's fire. "My apologies," he directed his words at Sara, "I did not intend to—"

"Enough. Sit." Bryce didn't willingly take commands from many people, but his sister-in-law was one of the ones he heeded.

He sat and looked out of the small stained-glass window. The same scene continued to greet him. There was nothing out of the ordinary in Kenshire's courtyard save the commotion of children running from an errant hen. From his vantage point in the lady's solar on the second floor of the castle, he could see as far as the gatehouse that separated the curtain wall from another courtyard beyond it.

Construction had begun this week on Bristol's second wall. It would take nearly a year to complete according to the master builder. Thomas was overseeing the first stones being laid as he sat here, waiting.

"Looking out the window won't magically make them appear," said Sara.

He didn't answer. This nervousness was something he hadn't experienced before. Not when Lord Huntington had called on him to discuss Bryce's feelings for his daughter. Not even when he had stood across from Toren Kerr, prepared to fight for his life.

But waiting to learn if Catrina was traveling to Kenshire with her brother? He simply could not sit. Weeks of uncertainty weighed on him. "I was an idiot. An utter arse."

"I won't disagree with you, brother." Geoffrey crossed his legs and smiled. Bryce wished his brother would make more of an effort to hide his obvious pleasure.

Bryce had been a mess of emotions after the conclusion of the fight at Castle Norham. On the one hand, he was furious Toren had escaped with his life. His parents would not be avenged. Worse, Catrina would marry Graeme—and *he* was the reason her brother had finally agreed to their engagement.

Geoffrey had immediately told him he'd made a mistake by letting her go. But what was he to do? Chase her home to Brockburg? She was engaged, for Christ's sake. And he'd nearly killed her brother.

He knew she wouldn't have him.

Instead, he made his way back to Bristol. By the time he arrived, Bryce knew he'd made the biggest mistake of his life. Vengeance had blinded him. He didn't need Evelyn or Elise to look at him as if he were the enemy to realize how stupid he had been.

But Thomas did more than just glare at him. He told him the unvarnished truth.

"You deserve to be alone. It's what you've wanted since Lady Elena spurned you. Well, you got what you wished for."

He wanted to lash out at his friend, but Thomas was right. After Lady Elena, he had set out to prove himself. Instead, he had only proved that he was an idiot.

"Catrina is betrothed to a man she loves. And…she hates me."

Thomas spat on the ground and stroked his beard. "If you're that blind, man, then do what you will. Let her marry Graeme deSowlis."

He wasn't entirely blind. He'd thought of their night in the tent enough times by then to realize what everyone had told him was true.

She loved him. She would not have given herself to him otherwise.

And he had repaid that love by doing the one thing that would ensure she'd never forgive him. If it was too late to get her back, he deserved it. But Geoffrey and Thomas were right. He had to find out if there was any chance she would forgive him.

He sent Fergus to Brockburg on his behalf. He hadn't made the connection the day Catrina had visited the alewife on their trip to the village. But later, knowing she looked for an ally to help her escape, he had realized the true purpose of her visit. The man's loyalties were questionable. But the fact that he'd stayed behind to watch over Catrina told him he cared for her happiness. After a lengthy discussion, Fergus agreed to travel to Brockburg to ensure Catrina's impending marriage didn't happen until he could speak to her.

Next, Bryce wrote to Sara asking that she request Catrina's presence at Kenshire. He knew the ladies had formed a bond and suspected Catrina would be more inclined to answer her call than his. Bryce did consider a trip to Brockburg, but he worried she'd refuse to see him and that her brothers would be less than inclined to intervene on his behalf. Besides, depending on what Catrina had shared with them, he may be lucky to leave Scotland alive.

And now here he was, waiting. Pacing. Uncomfortable in his own skin. Sara had received word that her "garment would be returned," but there'd been no mention of who would be traveling to Kenshire.

"Bryce, look," said Sara.

His heart leapt into his throat.

A knock at the door confirmed what he could now see for himself.

"Pardon, my lady. My lord. Your guests have arrived," Faye called from the door.

"Thank you, Faye," Sara said as she joined him near the small window, which allowed for a very limited view of the courtyard. Bryce held his breath and waited.

Bryce was surprised by the number of riders. He counted at least ten. He couldn't tell if Catrina was among them, but none looked like a woman.

She wasn't coming.

Sara looked at him, her eyes filled with pity. "I must go meet our guests."

Bryce stared at the men who began to dismount. One by one, their horses were led away. He recognized Alex Kerr, his height unmistakable.

And then he saw her. Of course...she wore Sara's breeches. As she moved closer, Bryce knew it by the way she carried herself. A moment later, Catrina reached for her hood and pulled it down to reveal her unbound reddish-brown locks. His chest constricted at the sight of her, and a flood of longing and fear threatened to unman him.

She was here, but would she forgive him? Did her betrothed accompany the group?

He vowed, not for the first time, to do everything in his power to win her back.

And he would start with the most difficult task of all.

25

He was here.

Catrina didn't see Bryce anywhere, but something told her he was at Kenshire. Perhaps it was that Lady Sara seemed to be looking for someone. Or maybe she could simply sense his presence.

It no longer mattered.

When they couldn't dissuade her from answering Lady Sara's request, Alex and Reid insisted on accompanying her. Toren would have joined them, but he'd had to deal with an uprising that threatened an ally. Ushered into the hall by Lady Sara and her husband, Catrina and her brothers were offered rooms above stairs to refresh themselves before the meal. Unfortunately, her well-meaning brothers refused to leave her side.

Apparently, they preferred to stare at Geoffrey and his steward than act like normal visitors. Though they'd recovered from their initial shock after learning she'd lost her virginity to Bryce, she knew they hadn't fully overcome their resentment. They were worried for her future, but oddly enough, for the first time in her life, Catrina didn't care to consider marriage. Mayhap she would avoid it altogether. Although Alex and Reid would not reside at

Brockburg forever, Toren would remain chief. Which meant she'd always have a home there. Would it be so awful? Then again, Toren would eventually marry.

Sara's greeting pulled her back to the present.

"Look at you! A proper English lady." Sara enveloped her in a hug that nearly broke the bones in her back.

"A proper Scottish lass," Catrina replied, fully aware neither was true as she wore her own set of breeches to match the ones Sara lent her. Brockburg's seamstress may have been appalled by her request, but no more so than her brothers. Alex, for some reason, was especially put out, and had tried to convince her to change into more proper attire.

"When you don a gown for a long ride, I'll do so myself. In the meantime, I'll thank you to allow me a bit of comfort." It wasn't as if they'd stayed in a public place on their journey.

He had finally relented.

She'd known Sara for such a short period of time, but there was something about her that made Catrina feel as if they'd known each other for years. An openness that was rare, especially from someone in her station. Of course, Catrina did not know any other countesses, but she didn't imagine very many of them were like Sara.

Sara turned toward Alex and Reid. "Allow Faye to show you to your rooms. I promise to take good care of your sister."

Her brothers both looked to her for approval. She nodded, eager to be alone with her friend. Besides, while Geoffrey seemed to be in good spirits despite the fact that his sworn enemies stood a few feet from him, Catrina knew the mood could change at any moment.

There was still obvious tension between the men.

And then Bryce appeared.

While this was not entirely unexpected, Catrina was nonetheless unprepared for his arrival. He was dressed casually, as was his custom, and looked incredibly relaxed as he descended the stairs at the opposite end of the hall. He didn't take his eyes from her for a moment.

She moved closer to Alex, grateful he hadn't yet left. Catrina didn't trust her voice. Her hands began to tremble, and she balled them into fists to make them stop. No one spoke, not even the servants. Catrina could hear the crackling of the great fire that warmed Kenshire's hall as the sun set outside. Actually, she was feeling quite hot, which was unusual for a hall of this size.

"My lady." Bryce's voice was calm, smooth.

She wanted so very much to rail at him. She had imagined these last weeks what she would say if they ever met again. She left her belongings—and her heart—at Kenshire Castle. If only he had come for her that day. Stopped her from leaving Kenshire

But he hadn't.

"Damn you to hell, Bryce Waryn."

She grabbed Lady Sara's hand and began walking out of the stifling hall. This entire venture had been a horrible mistake. Why had she come?

"Lady Catrina, may I have a word?"

She must have imagined the waver she heard in his voice. Bryce was like the precious curtain wall he planned to erect at Bristol. Always strong. Unbending.

She spun toward him, prepared to unleash the blistering he deserved. What she saw made her stop and stare.

The lord of Bristol Manor was bent on one knee in front of her brothers. Head bowed, he spoke clearly for all to hear.

"My apologies to you both. I've acted dishonorably toward your sister. And when I entered into an agreement with your brother, I did so reluctantly. You have every reason to hate me, and I would not presume to ask for your forgiveness. But I do ask for you to uphold our agreement with the full confidence I shall do the same."

Catrina could not move. What was he doing? What was he even apologizing for? Taking her virginity? Her brothers both turned to her. Catrina told them with her eyes, in no uncertain terms, that they would *not* refuse the man who knelt before him. Despite her personal feelings toward Bryce, their truce must stand.

They apparently understood her silent plea.

Alex put his hand over the hilt of his sword. She knew he would never use the weapon as an invited guest of Kenshire, but it was a habit, not a show of force. His words confirmed as much.

"We're in need of allies, not enemies." Alex reached down to lay a hand on Bryce's shoulder. "The countess mentioned a room?"

Bryce stood. But before she could see what happened next, Sara pulled her away.

"The sea gate," she said.

Sara smiled. "Aye."

They practically ran down the path. The sea was beautiful when they emerged on the other side, and the cool breeze felt heavenly on her face, but Catrina could not stop thinking about Bryce and her brothers.

Apparently, Sara felt the same way. "Did they just make peace? Again?"

Catrina took off her boots and closed her eyes, enjoying the breeze. The sound of the crashing waves. "It appears so."

"Why am I here, Sara?" Catrina opened her eyes. She wanted to see the expression on the other woman's face.

"Bryce asked me to do it," she spoke quickly. "I am happy to see you, of course. And pleased to know I've had an influence on you." Sara looked pointedly down at Catrina's garment.

"Mayhap you should bring them to London," Catrina suggested. "I'm sure they would be all the rage at court."

Sara made a distinctly unladylike noise. "They may get us thrown out of court, I'm afraid." Her smile faltered.

"I apologize, Catrina. He begged me to do it."

"Why?"

"Isn't it obvious? Bryce realizes he made a mistake. He wants—"

"Stop." She didn't want to hear this. She wasn't sure she could bear to hear it. "Sara, you have no idea what it was like to watch the man I loved attempt to kill my own brother. I will never forgive him."

"Catrina, listen to me—"

"Nay. Sara, I owe you so much. You were kind to me, tried to help me. I will forever be in your debt and hope we can be friends." Catrina hated the look of sorrow in Sara's eyes. She was hurting her, but it couldn't be helped.

"But I can never forgive what he did. How he left. I could be a married woman by now."

Every bit of color drained from Sara's face.

"Are you?"

Mayhap she should be. Marrying for love seemed a ridiculous notion at the moment. Every one of her brothers seemed to think it such.

"Nay. But don't look so relieved. It doesn't matter."

Sara didn't say a word, but Catrina could tell she didn't quite believe her.

SHE WAS LOST TO HIM.

Kneeling to men he would have slayed on sight a month earlier was as difficult for Bryce as anything he'd ever done in his life.

With the exception of losing Catrina. That loss made every other one he'd endured shrink in comparison.

He walked the ramparts for most of the evening. Bryce had no desire to join in the evening meal. It would be too painful, though no less than he deserved.

"May I join you?'

The deep voice was one he didn't recognize. Bryce turned, his hand at his side.

"Will you challenge every member of Clan Kerr then?"

It was Catrina's brother Alex. After speaking with him earlier, Bryce had understood Catrina a bit more. Her adventurous spirit. Her quick wit. And her propensity for cussing. Alex Kerr may not look like his younger sister, but his behavior was eerily similar.

"Nay, no longer. I just didn't expect anyone up here."

They stood side by side, watching flickers of light as people holding lanterns made their way through the courtyard.

"Who killed my parents?"

"Your father, I know not. Your mother, a man by the name of Rurark. Toren had no wish to attack Bristol, and even less to slaughter innocent women. To hear the story told, your mother came at Rurark with a pickaxe."

That sounded like his mother. She wasn't one to hide meekly in her bedchamber with a battle unfolding in her home.

So it was not Toren.

"He would have been dead had your mother had her way. We would all be dead if your king had his."

Bryce couldn't argue that. And it was likely to get worse.

"Catrina told me once the raid was ordered by your king." He had not believed her at the time, but Bryce knew now it was true.

"Tis true. Toren was none too pleased about the prospect."

Bryce felt as if he'd been punched in the gut. "Why are you here?" he asked Catrina's brother.

Alex cleared his throat but didn't answer.

"You know about Catrina and me." Bryce said. It was a statement, not a question. The fact that Alex had sought him out meant she'd told them the full truth. He was surprised they hadn't tried to run him through as soon as he stepped into the hall earlier that evening.

"Aye, she told us. It's the reason I'm here. And also because she loves you."

Loves. If only it were true. "She may have once. But your sister feels nothing but hate for me now." As much as he wished it were otherwise. He'd seen the look in her eyes earlier.

"She does," Alex conceded. "But she doesn't want to. She nearly fell off her horse more than once watching for you the day we returned to Brockburg."

That only made him feel worse.

"Catrina doesn't hide her emotions very well," said Alex.

Bryce frowned. "I noticed."

"She wanted you to come for her. Even after what happened."

He said it with such confidence, Bryce could almost believe it was true.

"I know why you sent Fergus. He asked too many questions for his return to be a coincidence." Alex moved toward him. "Listen to me. Do you think this is easy? Appealing to the man who held my sister captive? Who took her virginity the night before he nearly killed my brother?"

Bryce took a deep breath. What the hell was the blasted man trying to say?

"Fix it," said Alex.

"I'm trying, damn it."

Neither man moved. For a moment, Bryce thought Catrina's brother had changed his mind about their tentative truce.

Fists clenched, Alex abruptly turned and walked away.

If there was any chance…if Alex was correct about her feelings…Bryce was sure as hell going to find out.

But he needed help.

26

Was someone calling her name?

Opening her eyes, Catrina was startled to find Sara's lady's maid, Faye, standing next to the bed.

"Good morn, my lady."

Catrina blinked away the fogginess of her fitful sleep.

"Is it so late, Faye?"

The maid stood to the side as Catrina reluctantly left the comfort of her temporary bed.

"Nay, but I've a message from Lady Sara."

Sara knew she and her brothers were planning to leave immediately. It was just too painful to be here with Bryce.

"She requests you join her on the beach before leaving for Brockburg."

Catrina inwardly groaned. She wanted to leave as soon as possible, but her gratitude for all that Sara had done for her left only one possible response.

"Of course, Mistress Faye. Please tell Lady Sara I would be delighted."

"Very good, my lady. I shall send someone to assist you straight away."

"No need. Thank you, Faye."

The maid left, promising to relay her message to Sara and inform Catrina's brothers of their delayed departure. She also bade her to prepare quickly.

What was the hurry? What did Sara have planned?

Once dressed in her new breeches paired with a soft blue tunic that stopped at her waist, Catrina braided her hair and tied the end with a ribbon. Faye told her Sara would bring a light repast with them, which was just as well. Catrina was hungry after spending the evening meal pushing food from one corner of her trencher to another.

After she arrived at their prearranged meeting spot, Catrina took a deep, salt-tinged breath. Why hadn't Sara walked with her from the keep?

Her answer emerged on the same path she herself had taken moments earlier.

When she sensed a presence behind her, Catrina turned to see the very man she hoped to avoid. She looked in every direction for an escape, but found none. He had chosen the location wisely.

With each step he took toward her, Catrina felt more and more trapped. Her chest tightened as the man who had stolen her heart made his way down the rocky decline. She watched him get closer until he stood just a few feet away.

"I have nothing to say to you."

"Catrina, please—"

He grabbed her arm, and she yanked it away from him, ignoring the heat even that brief touch shot through her.

"Nay, do not touch me."

"I was wrong," he said.

She stared straight into his eyes. "You made love to me knowing you planned to murder my brother." Saying it aloud strengthened her resolve.

"Not murder. And that was a mistake."

"Why are you doing this? Why now?" She wanted to turn away.

Her stomach lurched, but something held her back. What was she expecting from him? Nothing he said could make this right.

"I love you."

Before she could regain control of herself, her eyes welled with tears. She loved him too. But that wasn't enough. Not now. Not anymore.

"It's too late." The words nearly stuck in her throat. She concentrated on staying calm, the way Bryce seemed to do even when he was anything but. "If you had really loved me, Bryce, you wouldn't have tried to kill Toren."

He reached for her again, more slowly this time. She just wasn't strong enough to resist. His touch felt as it always had.

Assured. Comforting.

His large hand engulfed her own. He took her other hand, and Lord help her, she was lost.

"That isn't true. It can't be true. Because I do love you." He released one of her hands and reached into a pocket in his tunic. His hand emerged with Emma's tattered yellow ribbon. For the second time in two days, she watched as he got down on his knees. He dug a small hole in the sand, placed the ribbon inside, and smoothed the sand over it.

Standing, he wiped away the single tear that had escaped despite her best efforts to remain unmoved. Bryce took her hands once again. "I held on to that for too long. I couldn't see what my own brother tried to tell me. What you tried to show me."

She wanted to ask but couldn't get the words out.

"You weren't responsible for my parents' deaths. Your brother wasn't responsible. I wasn't responsible. You told me once we weren't all that different, with the exception of the place of our birth. But it wasn't until I lost you that I realized...a woman like you could only have been raised by someone equally as honorable. And loyal. It just so happens you're loyal to a different king than I am."

"Bryce I—"

"Nay, I'm not finished. I owe you an apology. For mistreating you as my prisoner, for taking your innocence. It wasn't mine to take. In my need to secure Bristol, I failed to remember why it was such an important task."

She immediately understood. It was to protect the people who lived there.

Standing before her was the man she'd vowed to hate for the remainder of her days.

The man she loved.

Catrina sighed.

AS HE WAITED for her response, Bryce thought of his last tournament. Lord Huntington had insisted his "champion" participate in the Tournament of the King even though he'd left his service two years earlier. Held once a year on the first day of spring, the tournament celebrated the people's loyalty to their sovereign—a play by Huntington to enlist the king's attendance and solicit his approval. Bryce was living with his Uncle Simon and Aunt Lettie at the time. He, Geoffrey, and Hugh were attempting to gather men to retake Bristol and agreed it was an opportunity to enlist mercenaries to their cause.

The lord's only daughter, Lady Elena, now a married woman, presided over the opening festivities. Bryce watched her from the field and felt nothing for the woman he had thought he'd loved. He'd assumed that utter lack of emotion would be with him always. Indeed, he had worked hard to ensure that feeling of emptiness would protect him from another Lady Elena.

Until Catrina.

It seemed like he waited forever for her response. The sound of the waves was near deafening.

"I thought I lost you," she whispered.

"You nearly did."

Bryce reached for her and, in one quick motion, lifted her off the ground.

"Where are we going?"

Rather than answer, because there were no words for what he felt, Bryce took long strides until he reached the spot he looked for. Unlike the open space near the sea gate, this was a secluded spot surrounded by tall grass.

He set her down and reached for the bag over his shoulder. His sister-in-law had prepared him well.

Spreading out the blanket Sara had provided, Bryce pulled Catrina to him. With her body pressed against his own, he let her feel the need that threatened to explode.

He opened her mouth with his own, willing her to feel his desire. His love. She met his tongue with her own, but Bryce willed himself to slow down.

Not yet. This time he would do it right.

He had held back that first time knowing what the next day would bring. But not today. It didn't take long to relieve Catrina of the strange tunic and shortened chemise that accommodated the belted hose she wore. He tore off his own shirt, wanting to feel her against him, and groaned when the tips of her breasts touched his bare flesh. He reached for them.

Catrina's breathing quickened.

He softened the pressure of his lips and ran his thumbs over the peaked nubs. Coaxing. Teasing. He cupped both breasts and squeezed gently. His cock throbbed, demanding attention.

It would have to wait.

Bryce reluctantly released her firm, heavy breasts and bent down on his knees. He planned to worship her with his hands… and his mouth.

He started by trailing kisses down her body. He unbelted her hose, removed the strange breeches, and pulled both of them down in one swift motion. After freeing her from every last stitch of clothing, Bryce kissed her thighs and splayed his hands across her buttocks, pulling her closer. He kissed her hip, ignoring the gentle tug on his hair as she tried to pull him back to her. Every inch of her required his worship. He ran his tongue across her smooth flesh but avoided the siren's call of her womanhood. That would come later.

She didn't say a word. Instead, the woman he had nearly lost forever watched him warily. Waiting for his next move.

God, she was beautiful.

His throat thickened. Was she truly his? He wanted to ask, but the words would not come out. He cupped her face, wanting to tell her what he was feeling. But how could he put *this* into words?

He leaned into her instead and ran his tongue between her closed lips. They opened for him. Slowly, softly, he touched the tip of his tongue to hers and cupped her down below. Pressing his palm to her, Bryce slipped a finger inside. So wet.

But it wasn't enough.

His tongue and his finger moved as one until Catrina moved against him. He increased his speed then, pulling down gently on the back of her head to give him greater access to her mouth. She thrust into his hand.

She was close.

He continued until she screamed. It was a beautiful, sensual sound that he would never forget. He stilled his hand. Then, unable to wait a moment longer, he tore off his own boots and hose. Bryce scooped her up and clenched his jaw. Her soft thighs against his hard cock…he couldn't wait much longer.

He tugged Catrina to the ground with him and looked around. Nothing but sand and tufts of grass. The sound of the sea not far from where they lay caught his attention. He knelt on either side of Catrina's luscious thighs. The air was warming, but it was the sight below him that had every hair on his body standing at attention.

The same full lips that had enticed him from the very first day they met were swollen from his kisses. Red-brown hair spilled everywhere. Catrina's gold-speckled eyes lit with a promise that made his already hard cock throb in pain.

Suddenly she moved her hand toward him. *She wouldn't?*

She did.

She touched the tip with her fingers, exploring.

Blood pounded in his ears at the gentle caress. "Wrap your hand around me."

She did. Though he'd been touched that way many times before, never, not once, had he nearly spilled his seed over such a tentative touch. Bryce opened his eyes and guided her hand away.

Bryce positioned himself above her and entered slowly.

"By God's bones, Bryce, what are you waiting for?"

He smiled. "Your tongue is as sharp as ever." The urge to thrust was so powerful, his legs shook with the restraint it took to hold back.

"And will be sharper still if you continue to torment me," she bandied back.

"I can't," he said.

Her eyes widened.

"I have to know, Catrina."

She squirmed beneath him. His hands, which held him above her, began to shake.

"Bryce." Her voice, low and thick, begged for him to continue.

"I love you, Catrina Kerr." Oh God, he had never loved anyone more. "I need to know, do you forgive me? Will you be my wife?"

He watched her expression turn from shock to…something else. A barely detectable lift of the sides of her mouth allowed him to breathe for the first time since asking the question.

"Aye. I do, and I will."

He thrust into her, the sound of her agreement ringing in his ears.

"Oh my…" Catrina's fingers dug into his back.

He pulled out and thrust once again.

"Kiss me," she said.

He would do that and more. Bryce pressed his body to hers, careful not to crush her. But he wanted to be as close as possible. His tongue matched the movement of his cock deep within her. He thrust and pulled back, slowly at first and then with increasing speed. He wouldn't be happy until she cried out. Murmurs of pleasure weren't enough.

Bryce wanted everything.

SHE WAS GOING TO DIE.

It was a shame because, for the first time since she'd come to in the middle of nowhere, half immersed in a stream, Catrina was truly happy. Maybe happier than she'd ever been in her life.

And now she would die.

Because there was no way one could survive such delicious torture.

Bryce's muscles strained under her fingertips as he held himself above her. The feel of his mouth moving from her lips to her neck. And damn. The fullness of him. She pushed herself up, wanting to be closer still.

If the entirety of Kenshire's army rode by them now, Catrina would not know it. Nothing existed except the man making love to her. She wanted so badly to feel that release again.

"Please Bryce." She knew he could make it happen. "I beg you."

His tongue touched the sensitive flesh of her ear. "Anything, my love." His deep voice penetrated her soul. *My love.* It tore through her as he thrust deep inside, forcing her to scream. Or was that Bryce who had called out?

Throbs of pleasure made her dizzy. Eventually Catrina became aware of his back, slick with sweat, the muscles dancing under her fingertips. She could hear her own heartbeat in her ears. Slowly, she started to notice their surroundings again. Catrina closed her eyes, her body covered by the man she had just agreed to marry.

The man who was once her enemy. "Holy hell."

Bryce laughed. It was such a rare sound that it startled her. She pushed against him, and he rolled onto his side. Propping himself up with one elbow, he watched her. His eyes lowered from her face and settled on her breasts. She drew her brows together, confused by the stirring deep within her. When Bryce shifted inside, her eyes widened.

"Is something wrong, my foul-mouthed lass?"

He didn't seem disturbed but rather amused by her unfortunate affliction for using words deemed improper by polite society.

"Already?" she asked.

He ran his hand over her breast and across her stomach. It ventured lower still until it came to rest down below.

"Aye, already. Though it may be too soon. You're likely quite tender." He brought his hand back to rest on her stomach. "You are *mine,* Catrina."

She smiled and was pleased to see his answering smile. This time, all it had taken was one look at her.

"Just as you are mine, my lord."

And though a part of her wanted to forget everything other than the blessedly peaceful feeling of lying next to her English knight, she had to be sure.

"You realize that marrying me means aligning yourself with Clan Kerr?"

Did she imagine it or did his normally harsh features look softer than before, even now, after she'd just mentioned her family?

"I do."

"And I am extremely close to my brothers. They will be visiting often."

"I understand."

He actually smiled.

"And I will want to visit Brockburg as well. With my husband."

His eyes held hers. "I look forward to speaking to the esteemed

Father Simon and taking him to task for the wretched job he did of curbing your blasphemous tongue."

She opened her mouth to chastise him, but nothing came out. He was actually teasing her.

"At least you don't deny it, my lady."

That he continued to smile told Catrina everything she needed to know.

"My tongue may be blasphemous, but my future husband seems to enjoy capturing it well enough."

"Aye, I do." He reached out and pulled her on top of him.

His hands explored her body, making it difficult to think. "Bryce! You said it's too soon."

"I've changed my mind." He stopped caressing her and cupped her face in his hand. "About many things."

And she was glad for it. But she liked this playful side of Bryce too much for him to stop. Her smile broadened, the cool morning air barely noticeable in the warmth of his embrace.

"Well then, there is one thing I'm curious about."

"I suppose I'm your prisoner now. Do your worst, my lady."

And though she was just learning, Catrina intended to do just that.

EPILOGUE

She missed Bryce horribly.

Catrina and Sara sat on the countess's overly large bed poring over details of the upcoming nuptials. Although she was thrilled with the idea of a wedding at Kenshire Castle, it entailed a temporary separation from Bryce.

The banns had been posted. And both Bryce and her brothers had wanted to return to their respective holdings before returning for the wedding. Her future husband had been none too pleased with Sara's insistence that Catrina remain at Kenshire to assist with the preparations. The countess's counter-argument was that the bride shouldn't be without an escort before they were married.

Catrina thought it a rather weak argument since they had not been escorted for some time, not to mention the fact that it was Sara who'd insisted she seduce her husband-to-be. Still, it was great fun to plan with Sara and Emma. Catrina had thrown herself into the preparations, meeting with the tailor and others who would assist with the wedding. This was about more than two people coming together as husband and wife. Her marriage to

Bryce also meant the official end of a decades-long feud between Waryn and Kerr.

Though she was thrilled her brothers would be returning, Catrina was sorry some of her friends at Brockburg would not be in attendance. Most of all, she was disappointed that Alex and Reid had denied her request that Father Simon be allowed to accompany them. They'd told her it was too dangerous. The border was becoming more and more dangerous, and there were too many raids of late.

"Catrina?"

She looked up at the expectant face of her future sister-in-law, who was even more beautiful, if such a thing were possible, when she smiled.

"I wondered your opinion on—"

A knock at the door was promptly followed by Faye's entrance. "He's back," was all she managed to say before Catrina sprang off the bed and ran down the corridor. She slowed her pace at the top of the winding staircase that led to the hall. Darkness had already fallen, so she'd assumed the earliest Bryce would return was tomorrow.

Lifting the hem of her deep green gown, Catrina hurried down the narrow stairs.

Once she reached the bottom, she froze.

Bryce stood before her as proud and stoic as the day they had met. It wasn't his demeanor that gave her pause, however. It was the cloaked man behind him that made her smile.

How is this possible?

She ran to Father Simon and threw her arms around the priest who had been like a father to her. She had her brothers, of course, but even they took advice from this wise man.

"Good eve, my sweet lass. I've missed you."

She pulled back to look at the priest, who was much older than Toren but so wise they'd always said Father Simon must have lived another life. His deep brown hair fell to his shoulders. He smelled distinctly like…Father Simon.

"Where are my brothers?" She assumed they must have changed their minds and brought the priest with them. But where were they?

"All three are on their way, but they are at least two days behind," said Father Simon.

"Then how—" Catrina looked at Bryce, who stood to the side watching their exchange.

He hadn't gone back to Bristol.

"You brought him here." It wasn't a question. Bryce knew how much Father Simon meant to her.

"But Alex and Reid said—"

"They changed their minds," Bryce said. And she had an idea of who'd changed them.

If Catrina had once thought her brothers stubborn, it was only because she had not yet met Bryce.

When Father Simon cleared his throat, Catrina realized Sara and Geoffrey stood just behind her. Sara must have followed her down to the hall, and Geoffrey had likely heard all of the fuss. She wanted to run to Bryce and throw her arms around him, but it wasn't the time or place. It was her duty to make the introductions.

"Father Simon, let me introduce you to Lady Sara, the Countess of Kenshire and her husband, Sir Geoffrey Waryn, Bryce's brother."

Father Simon inclined his head first to Sara and then to her husband.

It was all rather polite until Catrina remembered something. In her haste to reunite with Bryce, she had forgotten about her promise to Emma. The girl was the best chess player Catrina had ever encountered, and she was determined to beat her just once. She was supposed to have met her in her chamber after the meal.

"Goddamn it." She placed a hand over her mouth.

Father Simon looked at Bryce. "Mayhap you can do better than I, my lord, in curbing the lady's habit of taking the Lord's name in vain."

Though his words were scolding, Father Simon's eyes twinkled as he allowed Sara to lead him from the hall. Without waiting for an answer, they disappeared up the stairs with Geoffrey following close behind. Catrina was left with Bryce, who reached her in two strides and pulled her to him.

"Bryce...Father Simon will see us!"

He kissed her in response, his mouth moving over hers in a way that was sure to drive her mad. When he finally released her, Catrina looked over her shoulder, relieved to see no one other than a few servants milling about.

"If he does, I'll tell him I'm working on containing that errant tongue of yours."

Catrina smiled as she imagined the priest's response to that particular impertinence. "You wouldn't."

He kissed her nose, her cheek. Her lips. And whispered into her ear, "I would never lie to a priest."

"In that case, you should begin immediately, my lord. I can be quite stubborn."

"I'm sure I don't know what you're talking about, my lady."

She returned his kiss.

He may have taken her captive, but it was she who had stolen the English lord's heart.

ALSO BY CECELIA MECCA

The Ward's Bride: Prequel Novella

English knight Sir Adam Dayne, to keep peace along the border, must accept a betrothal to the Scottish Marcher warden's beautiful daughter. Lady Cora Maxwell hates everything English. When Adam proposes a unique challenge, Cora is forced to face her greatest fears and the burgeoning desire he has awakened.

The Thief's Countess : Book 1

The son of a baron, Sir Geoffrey has been reduced to stealing the resources he needs to reclaim his family legacy. Lady Sara is distraction he resents. With her betrothed coming to claim her hand in marriage and a distant cousin intent on usurping her earldom, the countess feels beset by controlling, unwanted men including the reiver sent to protect her. As the threats continue to mount, Sara must decide what's more important—her duty or her heart.

The Chief's Maiden: Book 3

The Scottish king gives Toren Kerr a dangerous but important mission—kill the English Warden. But when he travels to England to participate in the Tournament of the North, he's immediately drawn to Lady Juliette Hallington. The English noblewoman longs to escape her sheltered life, but learns the very thing she wants most might consume everything she holds dear.

BECOME A CM INSIDER

The absolute best part of writing is building a relationship with readers. The CM Insider is filled with new release information including exclusive cover reveals and giveaways. Insiders also receive 'Border Bonuses' with behind the scenes chapter upgrades, extended previews of all Border Series books and a copy of *Historical Heartbeats: A Collection of Historical Romance Excerpts* from various authors.

CeceliaMecca.com/Insider

ABOUT THE AUTHOR

Cecelia Mecca is the author of medieval romance, including the Border Series, and sometimes wishes she could be transported back in time to the days of knights and castles. Although her actual home is in Northeast Pennsylvania where she lives with her husband and two children, her online home can be found at CeceliaMecca.com. She would love to hear from you.

Stay in touch:

info@ceceliamecca.com

ACKNOWLEDGMENTS

I have a lot of crazy ideas. From starting a cosmetics company with an education background and no retail experience, to spending every spare moment of my free time writing medieval romance, some of these have worked and others . . . not so much. Thank you to my husband Mike for supporting all of them including the Border Series which is so dear to my heart.

Thank you to my father, Mont, for showing me what a real knight in shining armor looks like.

There are three people I intend to thank profusely in every book. Without Angela, Kim and Wendy, The Lord's Captive would never have reached its full potential. I'd also like to thank those I've learned so much from in the past year including Marie Force and Mark Dawson. Their willingness to share has likely saved me from more missteps than I can possibly count.

And to all those who have lent support and continue to do so including my family and friends who have endured years of listening to me talk of medieval romance . . . thank you.

Finally, I'd like to thank the early readers who joined my Border Ambassador group and spread the word about the Border Series. I have so many more stories to tell, and thanks to these super fans, I now have an audience to listen.

ISBN: 978-1-946510-04-4